EXPIRE

EXPIRE

DANIELLE GIRARD

THOMAS & MERCER

Published by Thomas & Mercer, Seattle

www.apub.com

Amazon, the Amazon logo, and Thomas & Mercer are trademarks of Amazon.com, Inc., or its affiliates.

ISBN-13: 9781542040259
ISBN-10: 1542040256

Cover design by Kirk DouPonce, DogEared Design

Printed in the United States of America

For Jessica—for your brilliant guidance in Anna's journey and for always finding the best damn eatery wherever we are!

1

One week earlier

Spencer tucked the cell phone jammer behind the pot on the front porch and took another look at the street. All quiet. Mistress Keres would have chosen this area of town for exactly that reason. The houses were small, the yards well kept. These were not wealthy people who could afford to sit around and watch out their windows. People in this area worked, and at 10:30 a.m. on a Monday, there wasn't another body in sight. He looked up at the front door and let himself relish what was about to happen, holding the excitement in his chest.

The plan was in motion. It was earlier than he'd anticipated by at least a few weeks. But Bryce Scala had made that happen. Anger burned in his nose at the thought of Scala—a man who had been unknown to him until a week ago. A few more weeks, and Spencer might never have known him.

Had Spencer been successful in convincing Scala that he'd had nothing to do with his own mother's death? Hopefully, the conversation had allayed some of Scala's suspicions. Only time would tell. While Spencer had someone keeping an eye on Scala, he was not willing to risk everything to wait around and see.

And when Scala discovered Spencer had disappeared . . . What then?

Would Scala turn over to the police the letters from Spencer's mother when Spencer was gone? Would the police bother to look into her death now? Spencer had weighed the option of making Scala and the letters disappear rather than expediting his plan, but how could he be certain that Scala didn't have copies somewhere? That the letters wouldn't still make their way to the hands of the police?

He drew a long, deep breath and filled his mind with images of the pleasure the next hour would bring. He would be gone, and it wouldn't be his problem, he thought, using his knuckle to ring the doorbell. Gloves would have been too obvious. Above all else, Mistress Keres was a student of human nature. The electricity of warning ran up his spine. He shouldn't have been here. This was an unnecessary risk.

But if he didn't have this outlet, he'd blow.

She was the one safe venue for his rage. How many times had he come here for her beatings? Mistress Keres. After the Greek goddess of violent death. Perhaps this final meeting of theirs was predestined.

A tingling spread through his groin. He'd always felt it there, though he'd never had sex with Keres. His needs were not so easily satisfied.

Behind the door, the clack of heels echoed on her wood floor.

He took a last glance at the street, though he knew he had not been followed. He had taken every necessary step to ensure his anonymity—booking the appointment under the name of a different client, taking an Uber under a false account, getting dropped off a half mile away. She had a security system, but he had cut the landline, and the cell phone jammer would eliminate the possibility of accessing help with her mobile.

Managing money for a hacker had its benefits. If you were good. And Spencer was. On the other side of the door, the sound of her footsteps grew louder. The peephole darkened. He kept his head down, though there was no way of disguising himself. Not if he wanted her to let him in.

And he did.

Desperately.

Spencer drew his breath, shutting out the sound of Bryce Scala's voice rattling in his skull. The man's visit had rocked him. And he wasn't used to being rocked. It wasn't the man himself—Spencer could have broken that man in two. It was the lingering idea that his parents could still haunt him, even though his father had died ages ago and his mother last November. He thought he had rid himself of their judgments.

But he hadn't.

Because his mother had recorded them, shared them. Her concerns about him. Her fears.

The door opened slowly. Mistress Keres wore an expression of surprise, curiosity tinged with suspicion. There had been a flash of alarm in her eyes, quickly hidden. With a subtle shift of her head, chin, and shoulders, she regained control.

Spencer kept his head down, his hands clasped in front of him— the same way he always staged himself in his church. Demurring, deferential.

He didn't stare at her, though he'd caught a glimpse of her outfit—the black leather shorts that barely covered the swell of her ass. Her short top showed both cleavage and a band of toned belly. She was disgusting. Nothing like Bella.

Anger raged in him again.

"I don't have you on my calendar today."

Actually, she didn't have him down at all, not again. He'd told himself he was through with her. It was time to move on. But then he'd read those letters. And he'd known he had to see her.

"I thought I had it right," he said. "I know it's not our normal time . . ." He forced his eyes to widen and plead. Bit his lower lip. *Please don't reject me.*

She put up a red-tipped finger and crossed the foyer, lifting her iPhone off the front table. The nails were too long. Obviously fake. Not the way she dressed for him. She knew he preferred proper clothes, a wholesome-looking woman. He'd known all the subtleties of her costumes weren't real, but suddenly, the act was garish.

From the corner of his eye, he saw her trying to get her calendar to refresh. Of course, it wouldn't. The jammer would make sure of that.

"Do you have someone else? I could just come back with this," he said, pulling out the red Cartier box. He had never brought her a gift before.

She had another john—or maybe johns—who bought her gifts. Expensive ones he'd seen on her when he'd followed her out on the town with one man or the other. Most of her johns liked to take her out. He was the anomaly.

A flash of surprise crossed her face, a flush of pleasure. He was right. The gift had been a good idea. She eyed the box, then her calendar. He already knew she had a john coming in an hour. "I don't have much time, but you look like you need me today."

He nodded. Did he ever. At home, left with the letters, Spencer had felt Scala's words batter against his mind like the waves against a ship in a storm. *Your mother and my wife were like sisters,* he'd said. *They shared everything. And I'm a minister like your father. We shared a lot over the years.*

The sharing. His parents did not share—not their attention or love. In every way possible, they had been frugal with him. But not so with others, it appeared. And then Scala's last comment, spoken with his eyes narrowed, just as his own father had done. *As a matter of fact,* Scala had said, *I saw your mother the day she died.* The way he tilted his head, the appraising look.

What did he know?

Nothing. Spencer let out his breath. He knew nothing.

He caught her studying his face.

He looked at the floor as he'd been taught. Let his eyes fill with tears. She motioned him back to the room.

Once they stood in the entryway, Spencer scanned the space again as though wakening from a drugged state. This room had held such release for him. The pain, her control. He had been desperate to feel that.

But it wasn't there. What he saw now was a cheap motel room, fake leather furniture, and the vague smell of bleach beneath layers of thick, overbearing candles.

She was holding the box.

He forced himself to smile. "It's just a little thank-you."

Keres opened its top and looked down at the thick byzantine gold rope. It was quite stunning, really. Something he had bought for Bella after Ava when he had expected them to reconcile. Not actually Cartier, but the box had been a nice touch. It certainly seemed to please the woman in front of him.

"It's stunning," she whispered, pulling it free of the box's white velvet tabs. She draped it across her neck and turned her back to him. "Will you help me?"

For the first time since Bryce Scala had rung his doorbell, he felt himself relax. "Sure. Let me see," he said. "I don't have my reading glasses." He wasn't about to touch the necklace.

His hands found the white handkerchief in his pocket, drew it out.

Her long nails clicked as she fiddled with the clasp. He breathed through the incessant noise, focused his control.

"There," she said, turning to show him.

But he grabbed her first. Wrapped the handkerchief around the necklace and jerked it backward.

Shocked, she gasped and clawed at the necklace. Her breasts jiggled in the low-cut top, reminding him of pudding.

He yanked the necklace tighter, his fingers struggling to grip through the cotton. The handkerchief slipped as he dragged her up to her tiptoes.

"You're hurting me," she said, the surprise in her voice making him smile.

He thought of Bryce Scala, of the letters his mother had written about him. A mother who had suspected something was wrong with her three- and four- and five-year-old boy. That he was broken somehow. Evil. She had called him evil. She had written those words and put them out into the world, sent them to another person.

All those years of fake love. She hadn't loved him. She had loathed him, feared him.

The anger ran in currents through his hands and into Keres's neck as though he were strangling his mother. If only he could kill her again—although not so gently—he would choke his mother slowly and watch the life drain out of her water-blue eyes. The handkerchief slipped again, and he let it fall, taking hold of the chain in his hand. He would have to take it with him now. But he didn't care.

Something broke inside his blinding fury, and the tightness in his chest loosened. He could draw a full breath.

She kicked her feet, and the shoes sailed from them. The sight of her bare toes with their faint pink polish, hidden under those hooker shoes, brought another wave of hot fury. As she reached back, nails out to claw his face, he pitched her forward and then back again, lifting her off the ground and swinging her. Then he brought her down quickly. Her feet flailed inches above the floor. She fell forward, landing on her knees and reaching out to catch her fall.

He heard the satisfying crack of her wrist, the shrill panicked cry muted by the necklace choking her. Clasping the chain tight against her neck, he drove her forward toward the floor, closing the metal on her neck. His own breath was loud, raspy with excitement above her strangled cries.

She made another struggled attempt to grab for him. A nail on her left hand snapped off against the hard canvas of his jacket. It had left a mark, he was sure. To the dumpster with this coat. *Oh well,* he thought. He'd never liked it anyway.

Straddling her now, he drove her head into the floor with the heels of his hands, cinching the necklace with his fingers. Slowly, the fight drained from her. When she began to still, he eased the pressure off the chain. Released the necklace when he was certain she was unconscious.

In case she was trying to fool him, he stood at the ready. But she lay still on the floor. For several moments, he savored her lifeless form and the thumping of his heart in his chest, the rush of adrenaline. He worried he had gone too far, but her chest still rose and fell, although weakly. From his pocket, he removed the latex gloves and pulled them on. To confirm she was alive, he pressed his fingers to her carotid and felt the *thump-thump* of her pulse.

He took hold of her unbroken wrist and dragged her to the center of the room. Then he pulled the knife from his pocket and cut off the cheap shorts and the nasty top, leaving her naked.

With rope from her workbench, he trussed her—hands behind her back, feet attached to the rope on her neck. He was not aroused by her naked body. Her control had been his aphrodisiac. What he felt now was calm, centered.

Bryce Scala was out of his head.

He was back in control.

Spencer MacDonald checked his watch and wondered how long before Mistress Keres woke.

Already, he longed to strangle her again.

2

Pain drilled through her skull. A bone saw whirred in the distance, its vibration traveling through her ribs and pelvis. Her head dulled by drugs, Annabelle Schwartzman shifted in the darkness. Something rough and thin pinned her arms behind her back, her shoulder a solid bruise against the hard metal floor. There was moisture beneath her and the faint scents of grass, dirt, and rust.

She wiggled her fingers, the metal cuffs biting at her wrists. Her hands were tied. Panic rose, cutting through the fog. Pieces of information pelted her, coming fast as she struggled to put it all together.

A long shriek of brakes cut through the darkness, and the saw went silent. Not a saw. An engine. She was in a vehicle. The hard floor beneath her felt different from the van. Had she been transferred? Where was she now? Fighting the panic, she studied the momentary silence, listening for sounds. The low drawl of a door and then footsteps on asphalt. Wet asphalt, hard-soled shoes. Boots. She held her breath. Metal clanked against metal, and a door creaked open.

Squinting, she waited for the light. But it didn't come.

She turned her head but found only darkness. Shifting her chin, she felt something rough on her face. Fabric covered her head—thick and scratchy like burlap—cutting off all light. A smell close by. An unfamiliar cologne, the stench of cigarettes.

A hand jerked her arm. She gasped, swallowing a cry as her shoulder ground in its socket. The pain was muted and distant, muffled by whatever drugs her captor had administered.

She said nothing, waited. Tried to retrieve memories from the fog. To take in her surroundings. Metal pressed hard against her wrists, her bruises tender along the carpal bones. She felt the rope threaded between her feet, the rough plastic against her anklebones. Slowly, she drew her knees upward, tucking herself into a ball.

The burlap rustled on her chin, and a flash of light hit her retinas. She lowered her head to duck out of the bag.

"No." His voice was a bark, throaty and hoarse from decades of cigarette smoke.

She turned her face away instinctively, but he gripped her neck. She felt something against her lips, pursed them closed.

"It's water. Drink." The voice had lost some of its gravel, and the words became clearer. Someone who hadn't spoken in a while. *Not Spencer.* Her captor was alone, maybe. She tried to work out how much time had passed since she'd been taken. She sensed it was dark but couldn't tell. The bruising she felt could have been two hours old or twelve.

Waiting for the bottle to touch her lips, she studied her surroundings for a second person. Only one. A man. The voice familiar somehow. But she couldn't find it in her memory. Was he someone she had worked with? A police officer? The thought was terrifying. But the voice was not Spencer's. Maybe that was good. Maybe not.

The plastic touched her lips, and she parted them slightly, feeling the wet cold strike her teeth. Swallowed a tentative sip and then drank greedily. The liquid came too fast, and she spit, choking as it went down her trachea.

He laughed as she coughed, and then he lifted the bottle to her again.

She drank again, more slowly, taking the water in until the last drops hit her tongue. Tears burned her eyes at the thought that there wasn't more. How long had she been tied up here? Her stomach lurched in nausea. "Food."

"Candy bar," he said, and the tear of a plastic wrapper followed. She smelled the chocolate and peanuts, then felt the bar against her lips. Did he know she wasn't allergic to peanuts? Did that mean he knew her? Or was it an educated guess? Despite all the buzz about peanut allergies, less than 1.5 percent of the population was affected.

The touch of the bar to her lips caused an involuntary gag reflex. She swallowed the saliva and opened her teeth to take a careful bite. Snickers. She chewed and swallowed, then took more. He was patient and silent as she ate, so she continued, buying time, thinking. How could she get out? Tied hands and feet. Blindfolded.

His one hand held her head, the other on the bar. Which meant no weapon. She twisted her feet ever so slightly, testing the strength of the rope between them. If she kicked him, could she get away? The rope bit into her ankles. She pushed harder, testing the give, but there was almost no space—certainly not enough to free one of her feet. And there was no way to run with her feet tied.

The candy bar pressed against her lips with a little force, and she took another bite. A faint breeze touched her chin, and she smelled his cologne, hints of ginger and frankincense. Her nausea reared again, and she paused to draw breath through her mouth, fighting off the urge to vomit. She needed the food and water.

The haze lifted momentarily, and she pictured the two plastic sticks on her bathroom sink.

The pregnancy tests.

She hadn't seen the results.

But she didn't need confirmation. She felt certain she was pregnant. Which meant keeping the food and water down was all the more important.

The tail end of the bar passed her lips. She closed it in her mouth and chewed slowly. The man crunched the wrapper into his hand. She felt a shift in the air. "Is there more water?"

Silence met her, and she swiveled her head as though she might sense his location. "Please," she said. "I'm still thirsty."

She smelled his breath first. Onion rings and ketchup. Heat and moisture, then his lips on hers. His tongue, warm and sour in her mouth. She twisted her face away, but he gripped the back of her head, holding his mouth to hers. She held her breath, clenched her teeth, panic building in her chest.

He stopped and laughed loud. The stench of onions filled her nose as his untrimmed fingernails bit into the back of her head. "You said you wanted more . . . Maybe next time you'll be happy with what you get."

Schwartzman drew her knees to her chest, forcing space between them.

The man released the back of her head, and the odor of onions faded slightly. He drew his fingers along her leg, his nails grating against the fabric of her yoga pants. Somewhere in the distance, an engine started.

His fingers halted. He'd heard it, too.

Another car.

"Help me!" Schwartzman screamed. "Somebody help me!"

"Shut up," he hissed as his hand clasped her leg. Those nails clawed through the fabric.

Launching her feet straight out, she connected with his body. He grunted, and she heard him fall back. The clank of something on the metal.

11

"Help me! Help!" she shouted, rolling herself toward the cold air. Her head struck something hard, and she tried to shift her course, still screaming. "Help! I need help!"

A hard, flat surface struck the side of her face. She gasped, tasting blood in her mouth. Another strike against the bone of her hip, the weapon catching the side of her ribs. She struggled to draw breath. Heard the click of the door closing.

She rocked slowly, fighting against the fear. The residual air in her lungs had been forced out with the blow; it made it hard to get that first breath. Her rational brain knew the cause, but adrenaline filled her with panic. Slowly, the air seeped into her lungs, and she drew a full, agonizing breath.

The pain echoed in her brain as she tried to get onto her knees.

His hands clasped her shoulders, and she was heaved off the floor of the truck and thrown. Like a bag of potatoes. She landed awkwardly against the wall, excruciating pain drilling her back. Tears streamed down her face, absorbed in the fabric against her skin.

He pressed her shoulders down, pinning her to the floor of the van. "Don't. Please."

Saying nothing, he straddled her, forcing her knees straight. She tried to rock against him, but he was too strong. The bindings on her feet prevented her from getting any leverage to fight back.

His weight drove her back into the hard metal floor until the ridges dug into her spine. "You want to scream?" he hissed. "I can make you scream."

"No. Please." The shearing sound of something ripping startled her, and then his hand pressed against her mouth. She breathed in the smell of plastic and adhesive just as she felt the pull of the duct tape across her lips.

Head turned, she huddled, waiting for him to leave. But he remained on top of her. Slowly, he shifted against her, grinding his hips.

She fought to close him out, to find a quiet place in her own head. *Bide your time. Find a way out.*

"That water you drank?" he whispered. "The drug'll take effect anytime."

More drugs. *No.* She thrashed beneath him, crying through the tape. He was erect against her, rubbing himself into her stomach. Panic lit her nerves on fire. Water rose in her throat. The residual taste of the candy bar was acidic at the back of her mouth. She focused on breathing, willing herself to stay awake.

But the haze descended. The rocking of his pelvis, the hard pain against her back grew more distant, less vivid. She tried to shake it off. She could not pass out. She could not be unconscious in this truck, with this man on top of her.

Her body grew light, the drilling pain on her spine far off as though it were happening in the past rather than in that moment.

His rocking rhythm seemed to slow. Everything seemed to slow. And then stop. Her head lolled, and her tongue felt too large in her mouth. There was a dull buzzing in her ears. Then she felt nothing at all.

And from somewhere in that floating blackness, she heard his words. "Sweet dreams, Bella."

3

Hal Harris paced a track from the coffee table in Anna's living room to the edge of the kitchen, while Buster sat facing the door. Every time a car drove slowly down the quiet street, Hal went to the window, and Buster stood on all fours, wagging his tail. When the car passed, Buster whined and sat, and Hal went back to pacing. He pulled his phone from his pocket and checked it again. The picture of his nephews and niece on the lock screen, with their bright gapped-tooth smiles, seemed oddly menacing. He no longer noticed the time. It was late—or early. He needed sleep, but he couldn't close his eyes.

When he tried, the panic set in—his heart raced, beating in his throat and neck, and his eyes burned as though they were on fire. Buster was no better. Since Hal had arrived at the house, the dog had kept vigil at Anna's door. Hal pressed his palm against his left pocket, feeling the two pregnancy tests inside the plastic bag.

The sound of a car slowing on the street made Buster rise to his feet, ears pointed forward. Hal watched a black sedan pull to the curb and the front door open. The dome light illuminated a curly-haired woman. Hailey Wyatt, his old partner. He forced himself to stand still, though he wanted to turn around and go back into the house, close the door.

He thought of the pregnancy tests in his pocket, longed to study the faded blue plus sign again, to confirm for himself that he hadn't made it up, that he could be a father, that Anna and he had made something. Before . . .

The car door cracked open, and Hailey stood on the street. "You up for company?"

He shrugged.

She studied him without moving. They had worked together for almost twelve years. There had been a time when she had known him as well as he knew himself. Maybe better. Still standing at the car, she asked, "If I go, will you sleep?"

He shook his head. She closed the door and rounded the car to walk up the front path. The interior dome light went black, and she was caught in shadow momentarily. He found himself noticing all the differences between Hailey and Anna. While Anna was tall, probably five eight, Hailey was barely five three. Where Anna was lean and thin, Hailey was curvy. Her hair was a nest of wild curls while Anna's was a gentle wave.

He looked away, the comparisons suddenly painful.

Hailey entered the house and sat on the edge of Anna's couch. She cranked up her chin and watched him pace. "Hal."

He looked back, and she nodded to a chair. Hal sighed and sat.

"The whole department is working her disappearance."

Hal bristled at the word *disappearance*. Anna had been abducted. He drew a slow breath and let it out. He was grateful for the response from the department. His captain, Marshall, had put out a bulletin, and the response had been overwhelming. A dozen active officers were on the case, and more than thirty off-duty personnel had volunteered to go door-to-door to talk to neighbors. But they didn't know what Spencer MacDonald was capable of. They would inevitably underestimate him.

"Roger has been in the lab all night," Hailey said. "He and Ting are sorting through the CCTV and traffic footage in a one-mile radius."

Ting was great with photo enhancement and manipulation, but finding a clear image of a face going thirty miles per hour in a white van . . . Hal wasn't hopeful.

"And I checked in with Casazza in Missing Persons. She's met with Eileen Goldstein twice."

The woman who had been struck by the white van in the neighbor's driveway. The reason Anna had left her house. The bait. Hal couldn't blame an old woman, but the what-ifs spun like webs in his brain.

Hal had spoken with Casazza, too. "White man, white van." Hal woke his laptop and checked his email. Marshall had requested FBI assistance. Hal had reached out to the Greenville police, but they weren't interested in interviewing MacDonald about the disappearance of his ex-wife in San Francisco. Hal was considering flying down there himself.

He toggled to his spreadsheet that listed the things he wanted access to—MacDonald's client list, known associates, phone records, bank and credit card records, GPS from his car, if he had a navigation system. If this were a San Francisco homicide and MacDonald a suspect, all of this would be within reach.

But Hal's confidence that MacDonald was behind Anna's disappearance was not enough to warrant that kind of access. Not officially. Hal had called in plenty of favors around the Bay Area. He'd responded to plenty as well. But across the country? In Greenville, South Carolina, of all places . . . He didn't have any kind of inroad there.

"They're sending a police artist over to sit with Goldstein tomorrow," Hailey said. "We might get something from that."

Hal said nothing. They both knew how imperfect that science was. And what good would an image do them? Facial recognition software didn't work like it did on television. There was no way to upload an image and run it through some database of CCTV footage across a city, let alone the state. And certainly not with a sketch.

16

They weren't going to get a photograph. Hal knew for a fact that the sketch Goldstein would help create was not going to be of Spencer MacDonald's face. According to the local police, Spencer MacDonald had been home in Greenville at the time of Anna's disappearance.

"Are you staying here?" Hailey asked.

He shrugged. "Maybe. I can't have the dog at my place, and someone has to watch him."

She nodded, holding her lip with her bottom teeth as though holding back a question. She opened a magazine on Schwartzman's coffee table—something called *Dwell*—and images of perfect home interiors flipped by as she turned the pages.

Hailey closed the magazine. "Roger said there was a private investigator in Greenville."

"Colton Price," Hal said, standing again. "I spoke to him a few hours ago. He's got people looking for MacDonald. There's a credit card hit at a local hotel, which doesn't make sense. He's going to call me as soon as he knows more." Hal drew the phone from his pocket again.

"Is there anything I can do?"

Hal walked the length of the room, turned back. Shook his head.

Hailey stood from the couch and made her way to the front door. "Try to rest."

He nodded. "Thanks."

After a moment of awkward silence, Hailey let herself out. Hal watched her walk back to the street and to her car. She wanted to help. He wished there was something she could do. Their friendship was built that way. During his divorce and after the death of Hailey's husband, they'd leaned hard on each other. They had been fortunate to have one another. And he was grateful.

But this time was different. No amount of leaning on Hailey was going to bring Anna home to him.

That he was going to have to do himself.

4

Pulled toward wakefulness, her head heavy and painful, Anna Schwartzman felt a strange sense of vertigo, a wave of nausea. She remembered taking a pregnancy test but couldn't recall the results. Hal was supposed to come over. Had she passed out? The room was cold, but the air was still, full of the scent of dust and wood chips. Silent.

Something was wrong.

It smelled wrong. And the surface beneath her was too hard to be her own bed. No sounds of Buster's snoring and Hal puttering around in the kitchen. No sounds at all.

Flipping mentally through her memories, she tried to recall where she'd gone. Why was it so dark? She'd been home. The doorbell rang. Eileen Goldstein had come by with a piece of mail. Had she ever opened it? No. The old woman had cried out, and Schwartzman had gone to her.

The neighbor's driveway. The white van. The smell of onions, his lips on hers. The Snickers bar, the water—she had been so thirsty. And then more blackness.

Heart pounding, she opened her eyes and blinked into darkness. Where was she? She sensed a blanket beneath her, tried to imagine the hard surface below that. Tears filled her eyes as she drew a breath, imagined the lid of a coffin above her.

Her breath caught in her throat as she reached one hand out, tentatively, into the air. No box or lid. She raised her other hand and stretched her arms. Felt around her, touched the bed below. Sheets, a mattress. Her hand found a bedside table.

She cried out in relief. She was on a bed. Hard, but a bed. Pain stabbed behind her ears as she lifted her head. The corners of her lips cracked when she opened her mouth. Dehydration.

Fighting the pain, she turned her head. Her cheek throbbed. The truck. He'd hit her. She froze a moment, holding her cheek as she sat the rest of the way up. Something whirred above her, like a window shade being released. She stilled and waited for other sounds. The quiet was resounding, completely foreign. For a moment, she feared her hearing had been damaged. She slapped the wood table beside the bed, the cracking sound a comfort. Keeping her hand on the flat wood, she held her breath and listened.

She was alone.

She had to get out of here.

Standing made her even dizzier. Nausea gripped her stomach, and her ribs ached with every breath. She drew a slow breath through her nose, then another. The soft whisper of her breath was comforting in the deafening silence. When had she last eaten or had something to drink?

Shifting her feet off the bed, her bare soles met with cold wood. Old. Dirty. The smell of dust clung in the air, and she shivered. Slowly, her eyes adjusted to the darkness. A thin sliver of deep gray shone from behind the shade of a small window on the far side of the room. *A basement*, she thought. But where?

She recalled waking in the truck. How far had they traveled?

They. She recalled the eyes she had seen. Why couldn't she place them? For years, she'd imagined being abducted. Again and again, she'd dreamed of Spencer leaping from some dark corner and grabbing her. She had always known the day would come.

But those eyes had not been Spencer's.

Surely Spencer was behind this. She sat in the darkness, listening to the silence. No cars. She was no longer in San Francisco, probably not in the Bay Area at all.

She'd been drugged, but with what?

An unfamiliar pulse drummed at the base of her sternum, and she pressed a palm to the beat. Her baby. But of course, the beating wasn't the baby. It was much too early to feel the baby. It wasn't even a baby. Not yet. An embryo, then a fetus.

Semantics.

Was she even pregnant? Could it be wishful thinking? She had never looked at the pregnancy tests. The fear was paralyzing. Fear that she was pregnant. Fear that she wasn't.

She felt it, though, didn't she? Drugged and pregnant.

"Stop." The word skidded across her vocal cords like the first tracks on a freshly graveled road. It seemed to echo across the silent room, then pinball inside her head. She was not going to think about the baby. Not now. *Figure out where you are and get the hell out.*

She twisted her head to listen again. Something shifted against her neck. She jumped at the sensation and fingered her throat. A band of hard rubber circled her neck. A collar. Taking it in both hands, she yanked and twisted, pulling to free herself. The pain in her ribs sharpened, and she cried out as the rubber dug into her neck. She winced and let go, pressed the backs of her hands against the raw skin to cool it.

Reaching up, she located a cord over her head and ran her fingers down until it connected with her collar, then up overhead. A thin cable, coated in plastic. It was surely connected to the ceiling.

When she pulled on the cable, it came loose, giving her slack to move. Above her, something clinked and grew closer, metal sliding on metal. A track.

It was a tether to limit how far she could travel. Like a dog. She worked her hands around the band, found where the thick rubber connected to the cord, and discovered some sort of bracket, a metal plate on its front. For a key, perhaps. Again she wrapped her fingers under the collar and pulled and twisted in an effort to break the two sides apart. She grunted and yanked until the collar cut into her neck. Tears burned in her eyes.

She released it and fought back her panic. Drew breaths. She gagged, her stomach heaving. But nothing came. Lowering her head, she fought to control her breath. Her mind filled with the images of a dead woman from Seattle. Zhanna Doe had been one of Schwartzman's first cases, a Russian woman held hostage in a nice Seattle building, yoked in a collar and tethered to a track.

Just like you.

Her breath came in shallow bursts. Her ribs throbbed dully. Did the Seattle police ever find out her real name? They had called her Zhanna because it was Russian for Jane.

Jane Doe.

Fight. Look for a way out. Find a weapon.

Schwartzman stood and staggered forward slowly, hands in front of her in the darkness. The metal cable zipped along the ceiling track as she walked, the pressure uncomfortable against the abrasions on her neck.

Her fingers found a wall, and she followed it in search of a door.

She gripped the knob and twisted. The door was locked. She palmed the wall in the darkness. Light. There had to be light.

She couldn't breathe; the collar was too tight. Frantic, she palmed the wall, panting and choking.

Found a light switch. Flipped it on.

She tensed, prepared for an attack, but the light flickered on with a dull brownish glow. Her eyes burned, and she blinked until the yellow spots vanished. Overhead was a single light fixture, some four or five feet above, the bulb enclosed in a steel cage. She scanned the ceiling for other devices. Surely there would be cameras.

Zhanna Doe's prison had been equipped with multiple cameras and alarms, housed inside a building in Seattle where units rented for twenty bucks a square foot. The neighbors had never heard a thing. Had she screamed out? Had her captor insulated the rooms so well that her cries were muffled?

You are not Zhanna Doe. You will not be her.

Schwartzman studied the ceiling again and saw nothing other than an ancient smoke alarm, mounted lower on the ceiling, close to the door. Its cover was missing, and the attachment to the battery hung down. Empty.

Both hands on the knob, she fought to twist it, as though she might somehow break the lock and free herself. When that didn't work, she pounded on the heavy wood door. "Let me out!"

She slapped and kicked the door, jerked on the knob, until she was winded and breathless. Her foot throbbed. Her face, her ribs. There was no response from outside. Only a profound silence broken by the sounds of her own gasps.

She was suddenly exhausted, nauseated. She wavered on her feet, both hands planted on the wall to hold herself upright. On the table beside the door was a glass of water. She lifted the glass to her lips and drained it.

Then she hurled the glass against the far wall. It struck with a promising crack.

Tugging the cable along the ceiling track, she reached the cup, still rocking on the dusty floor. No signs of a crack at all. Plastic.

Even if she had shattered it, what did she think she would do with a piece of broken plastic?

In the autopsy, Schwartzman had estimated Zhanna Doe had been held prisoner for eighteen months before she died.

Eighteen months.

In a space not much bigger than this room.

The water rose in her throat, and she drew slow, careful breaths. She couldn't afford to vomit. She didn't know when there would be more water.

She rested her hands on her knees, bowed her head, and breathed.

In her mind, she saw them again—the eyes of her captor. Blue eyes under blond, almost white brows. She knew those eyes, but she could not place them.

She drew another breath, struggling against panic.

That man was not Spencer. How she wished it had been him. She'd never considered that the unknown would be so much more terrifying. She had no idea what that man wanted with her. And worse, Hal would be looking at Spencer. Exclusively.

And if Spencer didn't abduct her, how would Hal ever find her?

5

Georgia Schwartzman sat upright in her bed. Gripping the sheets in both hands, she listened in the darkness. Someone was at the door. She fumbled for her phone on the bedside table. The screen brightened, and she read the time: 9:25 p.m. Downstairs, the doorbell rang in two quick bursts followed by three hard knocks. Who would be calling on her at this hour?

She pushed her feet into the slippers beside her bed and pulled her robe from the hook, casting it over her shoulders as she headed out of the bedroom.

Again with the knocking.

She turned on the hall light and saw the shape of a face in the glass beside the front door downstairs. A woman's face. Gripping the banister, she hesitated. Why would a woman be at her door now?

The woman waved at her. A muffled sound bled through the door as she spoke to someone else. A low reply came from a second person.

Georgia descended the stairs, patting absently at her hair. She should have checked it in the mirror, but good Lord, she hadn't even had a chance to catch her breath with all the banging and bell ringing. It felt like the middle of the night.

For her, it *was* the middle of the night. Well, she had been sound asleep anyway.

The past few years, Georgia Schwartzman rarely stayed up past 8:00 p.m. Not much to do alone at night. And it was the time of day when the house seemed too big, too empty. She'd never been much of a fan of darkness.

She unbolted the door and reached to release the chain but hesitated. Instead, she left it fastened and called out. "Who is it?"

"Mrs. Schwartzman, we're from the Greenville Police."

"I didn't call the police."

"We understand, ma'am. We received a call from the San Francisco Police Department."

"San Francisco," she repeated. *Bella.* But why would Bella send the police?

"It's about your daughter, ma'am."

"My daughter," she repeated. The words sounded strange coming off her tongue. Since her sister-in-law's funeral, she'd barely spoken to her daughter. Bella's choice, of course. As though it were Georgia's fault that Ava had been murdered. Murdered.

Her breath caught. "What's happened to Bella? Is she all right?"

"Can we come in for a moment, Mrs. Schwartzman?" The woman showed her a badge through the narrow side window.

Georgia scanned her—the sunken eyes, the puffy face. A few too many pounds around the neck and chin. She certainly looked like a detective. Not that Georgia had ever met one in person. Seen them on TV, certainly.

Georgia unchained the door and opened it.

The air outside was cool, and the wind cut right through the thin robe. She liked the house at seventy-five degrees—day or night, winter or summer. She waved the officers inside and pointed toward the living room, closing the door firmly and shivering as she followed them.

The male detective—he'd just given his name, but she couldn't recall it—was heavyset as well and a little older than his female partner. He was balding heavily on top and had a few side pieces combed over and sprayed down with what looked like lacquer. Her husband had had a full head of hair when he died. Her father, too. The detective would have been better looking if he'd just cut the hair short. Someone ought to tell him.

The detectives settled into the two large chairs. The woman detective, Marjorie Small or Thrall, held a closed notebook in her lap. She pressed her palms against it as she leaned forward. "We understand your daughter works with the San Francisco Police Department?"

Georgia nodded. "She's a—" But she couldn't get herself to say *medical examiner*. And the word *coroner* was worse. "Yes."

"Did you talk to your daughter today?"

"Oh, no. We don't talk that often."

"Your daughter was last seen yesterday morning. Her friends aren't able to locate her."

"What do you mean, *locate her*? She's an adult. She's probably out of town for a few days."

The two detectives exchanged a glance.

"When was the last time you spoke to your daughter?" the woman asked.

"Over the holidays," Georgia replied, then wondered if it was true. She'd received a gift from Bella—a lovely cashmere blanket in a soft gray. It lay draped over the corner of the couch on the other side of the living room. And there had been a book, too. But suddenly she couldn't remember what it was.

Georgia had sent a gift as well. One of those enamel Hermès bracelets—gold with white. It would be stunning on Bella. She tried to recall the conversation. If Bella had called, they would have spoken on Christmas or the first day of Hanukkah. When Bella was growing

26

up, they had celebrated Hanukkah and Christmas, but after Sam died, Georgia felt like she hardly celebrated at all.

They didn't speak on Hanukkah—she'd never taken that for her own—so it must have been Christmas. Surely. But now Georgia couldn't remember. She'd gone to church Christmas morning and helped set up for the community dinner. Then she had gone to wrap some of the donated gifts for the children the parish had adopted for the holiday. And then . . . she'd gone to service that evening. Surely she'd talked to Bella at some point in the days around Christmas . . .

"Mrs. Schwartzman?"

She looked up, feeling slightly dizzy.

"Can I get you some water?" Detective Small offered.

Georgia started to shake her head but then nodded, dabbing the back of her hand against the cool moisture above her lip. "Yes, please. The glasses are just to the right of the sink in the kitchen."

As his partner left the room, the man shifted forward in the chair. "When you last spoke, did your daughter seem afraid in any way?"

She shook her head. Since the day she'd left her marriage, Bella had acted bulletproof, like nothing from the past mattered.

Detective Small returned with a glass of water, and Georgia took a long drink.

"Thank you." She held the glass between her hands. "What has happened? Do they think Bella's in trouble?"

The detectives exchanged another look. "We're here as a courtesy, really," Small said.

"Obviously, your daughter is an adult, and she was seen yesterday morning," the male added. "Her partner is concerned because she left the house without her purse or keys and hasn't been home since. Does that sound unusual?"

"Her partner?" Georgia asked.

Small opened her notebook. "A detective by the name of Hal Harris."

She'd never heard the name. But of course, she wouldn't have. She and Bella didn't talk about her work.

"Does that sound like something your daughter would do?"

Georgia stared at him. "What?"

"Leave the house without her keys and purse and be gone overnight."

"I don't know. Surely her colleagues have more information on her whereabouts than I do. She works all the time."

"The detective seemed to think that your daughter's ex-husband might be involved."

She pressed her hand to her chest, wishing Spencer was there now. He would be so much better at handling these questions. "Did you speak to Spencer?" she asked.

"We wanted to eliminate any other possibilities before we bother Mr. MacDonald."

Georgia nodded. Greenville's chief of police was a client of Spencer's. The DA, too. Or maybe it was the mayor. Spencer knew them all. He always had a knack for handling politicians. Her husband, Sam, had no patience for them and dreaded it when his cases butted up against local politics.

"Well, I don't know where she would be," Georgia said after a moment. "But I'm sure Spencer would be happy to answer your questions. I have his number if you'd like to give him a call."

The two detectives shared a look again. The male detective rose from the couch, and Small stood a moment later. "If you hear from your daughter," the man said, making his way toward the door, "give us a call, please."

"Of course."

The two detectives left, and Georgia locked the door. Only then did she notice that she held a business card in her hand. Detective Leonard Hardy.

She checked the door again, set the card on the entry table, and made her way back up to bed. Tucked under the covers, she wondered why they didn't want to talk to Spencer. Surely he'd been through hell with the trial and all, but he would want to clear up any confusion. He would want to help find Bella if he could.

Wouldn't he?

She sat up in bed and turned on the lamp. Putting her readers on, she unlocked the phone and texted Spencer. Have you heard from Bella? The police were here. She sent the message and then started to type a second one. But what else would she say?

As she was thinking, she saw the line of three dots. A wave of relief washed over her. He would respond. Of course he would. Spencer was gracious and kind.

She looked down at the phone, but the dots were gone. She waited for his message to drop in. Usually, they were so fast. She watched the phone for several minutes. Maybe there was something wrong with the connection. His message would probably be there in the morning.

Her eyes burned. She removed her reading glasses and set them and the phone on the bedside table. Reaching for the lamp, she yawned.

She really was exhausted. She would talk to Spencer tomorrow. Then she would call the detectives and tell them that he had nothing at all to do with this.

By then Bella would probably be back.

Leave it to her daughter to get everyone all worked up in the middle of the night for nothing.

6

Schwartzman woke to the feeling of light on her face. Her head ached, and her neck was stiff. She blinked into the dull light, remembering. A sob caught in her throat as she touched the collar on her neck. Not a nightmare. Reality.

She was a prisoner.

She opened her eyes. Sunlight cut through curtains on a narrow window, centered on the far wall. Daylight.

Her mouth was cottony, and her tongue stuck to the roof of her mouth. How long had she been out? Eyes burning, she closed them again, pressed the heels of her hands against the pain.

Her fingers found the cable, and she pulled it down, the whirring of the metal clip running across the track above. She sat up, experiencing a head rush as her blood pressure dropped momentarily. The plastic cup, the one she'd thrown across the room, sat on the bedside table. It had been returned to the table, refilled. She crossed her arms over her chest, chilled. Someone had been there.

She froze, listening to the silence. Whoever had been there was gone now.

She lifted the glass and sniffed the water. There was no strange smell, no chalky film along the edges of the glass, no drug residue in the bottom. And yet, she was certain she'd been drugged. She had no memory of falling asleep. She hadn't woken when someone had entered the room. She wasn't a heavy sleeper, and she certainly wouldn't be expected to sleep well here, collared and locked up.

The water was the most obvious choice—the man in the back of the truck had drugged her that way. She shuddered at the memory of the smell of onions and cologne with his lips pressed to hers. He was keeping her here. He would be back.

The panic suffocating, she gripped the collar and pulled at it, wincing as it dug into the bruises on her neck. Forcing her fingers to release the collar, she pressed them to her forehead. Drew slow, even breaths. *Panic will not help you.* An increase in blood pressure, the rush of adrenaline, would only increase her metabolism and make her hungrier, thirstier. She needed to remain calm.

Examine everything. Then make a plan.

Nothing was impossible. Not even this.

First, the drugs. She had to know what he'd given her and where it was coming from.

With her sleeves pushed up, she stared at the blue veins beneath her pale skin. No needle tracks. But there were a thousand places to inject a human body, and her abductor had injected her with something when she was first taken. Still, the drug now was most likely in the water. Her abductor would know that her thirst would win. Given a choice between dying of thirst or ingesting drugged water, she would drink. Anyone would.

She considered what drugs he was using. Rohypnol was easy enough to get and caused near-total blackout but not unconsciousness. She winced at the memory of an autopsy she'd performed in her first month in San Francisco.

A thirty-six-week-old fetus who'd died after his pregnant mother had been drugged with Rohypnol and raped. The bartender had put the drug right into her cranberry juice. There'd been no underlying cause for the fetal death.

A side effect of Rohypnol was that it could cause spontaneous abortion.

Schwartzman pressed her palm to her belly. Squeezed her eyes. No cramping. No signs of trouble with the pregnancy. *If you're pregnant,* said a voice at the back of her head.

No second-guessing. She would go on as though she were pregnant. Rohypnol was also said to cause tremendous headaches. Her head didn't hurt, not today. Not much anyway.

So likely not Rohypnol. She tried to believe it. *You have to.* The reasoning was as close to scientific as she could get. He might have given her some form of benzodiazepine, the easiest sedative to obtain. Most were reasonably safe in the first trimester of pregnancy. Depending on the dosage. First trimester. That gave her, what, four or five weeks?

God, she couldn't be here that long.

Think. Plan. Move.

Upright in the bed, she scanned the room. The glass of water caught her eye again. Her fingers itched to grab it. Her throat burned for the cold sensation. But she left it. She would drink the water only if she had no choice.

She struggled to orient herself, wondered how many days had passed since she'd gone running into the neighbor's driveway to save Mrs. Goldstein. Again she saw those eyes—familiar but not. He'd used her name. He'd known her. She'd been thrown into the white van, felt the piercing stab of a needle. And then?

She rubbed her hand over her arm where the needle had penetrated when she was in the back of that van. No sign of a scab. Her ribs were less sore today, and the swelling in her face had gone down as well. She guessed it had been a couple of days—three on the outside.

Find a way out.

She put her feet on the floor. The sensation of dirt and the smell of dust, the cold air, reminded her of waking in Ava's garage. Tied up. Spencer. He was not the man in the van, but surely this all came back to him.

She crossed to the door, moving too quickly. The cleat caught in the track on the ceiling and stuck, yanking her backward. She stumbled, gripping the cord and working it loose before moving again. The collar left an ache in her throat. Swallowing was painful.

Again she thought of the water. Not yet.

She took hold of the knob, surprised to feel it turn in her hand. It had been locked before—she was sure. Doubting herself now, she opened the door slowly and gazed into a narrow hallway. What she had initially assumed was a basement was actually a bedroom. The walls outside the room were made of horizontal logs, like something from *Little House on the Prairie*. A cabin—an actual log cabin.

She shuddered in the doorway. Under different circumstances, the cabin might have been quaint. Above her, the track cut through a notch between the doorways, enabling her to exit the room. Tugging the cleat along the track, she stepped across the threshold cautiously, one hand holding the cable above her and the other braced against the wall.

To her right was a small bathroom. A shower curtain that had once been white hung along a rusted bar. Above her head was another notch where the track continued into the bathroom. She stepped in and palmed the mirror over the sink, praying for the strong, sturdy feel of glass—something she could break and use to cut her collar. Or something she could use as a weapon.

Like the water glass, the mirror was made of some sort of plastic. In its reflection, her face was gray and muted. Beside the sink lay a flimsy plastic toothbrush and a small container of Colgate toothpaste, unopened. She brushed her teeth without water and washed her face, holding her breath and sealing her lips to avoid getting the water in her mouth. She used the toilet. Uncertain when someone might come, she kept her movements quick and efficient.

The small bathroom made her claustrophobic, the sensation of the collar more oppressive there, if that were possible. She experienced a measure of relief when she emerged to the hallway. The cabin was empty. No sounds from inside, not from anywhere. She reached the end of the hallway and studied the main room.

The space was maybe ten by fifteen and had three windows, two of them flanking the door on the other side of the room. On instinct, she moved toward it before turning her eye to the ceiling and confirming her fears. The track did not reach the door—not even close. Even when she drew the cable out as far as it would go, she was still three or four feet from the door. Perhaps her kidnapper had measured the cord for her specifically. On a second glance, she realized that even if she were a foot taller, the cord wouldn't be long enough to reach the door.

Studying the ceiling, she realized the setup took planning. Meticulous planning, the kind she would expect from Spencer. Was someone else as diabolical as her ex-husband?

Turning back, she worked the metal clip along the track to keep the cord from choking her as she moved to the kitchen. A counter stretched along the far wall, with a sink at its center. Above the counter were cabinets, and a single window over the sink let in the room's only natural light. Beyond the counter was an ancient-looking stove at the far side of the room, maybe fourteen inches wide, with two spiral electric burners on top. She imagined starting a fire, burning the place down.

But what then? Would the track come loose from the ceiling before she died of smoke inhalation or burned to death? Anthony DiMalio came to mind, a man she'd autopsied only a few months earlier. He'd died in his bed after falling asleep while smoking a cigarette. The smell of burned flesh had stuck in her nose for weeks.

No. No fires.

A small dining table dominated the center of the space. A stainless-steel band ran around the rounded outer edge of the tabletop. She tested the steel band with her nail, but it was tight. What would she do with a metal band?

No. She had to think creatively.

Check everything. Every single thing.

The surface of the table inside the band was pale-pink linoleum, worn and scratched but clean. She pushed against the table, but it didn't shift. The table legs were bolted into the wood floor.

Two chairs sat at the table, dark-green and lightweight plastic, the kind that beach establishments left outside and that were sometimes carried off by a strong wind. She turned them upside down, searching for anything metal or sharp. Nothing. On the table, someone had placed a cup, a single bowl, and a plate made from the same indestructible plastic as the cup in the bedroom. Unsure what she was looking for exactly—a tool, a weapon—she moved on. In the cupboard beside the oven, she found a cast-iron fry pan with a wooden handle. Maybe six inches across and covered in a thick layer of rust, it was the first thing she'd found that might be used as a weapon. But it wouldn't help her break the collar.

She opened the cupboards around the sink, one at a time, and found them empty. Drawing the cord from the ceiling to create slack, she ducked to look under the sink and found a small container of dish soap, a sponge still in its plastic, and an unopened roll of paper towels. As though the cabin were an Airbnb she had rented instead of a prison.

She continued searching cupboards and drawers. A drawer to the left of the refrigerator contained only a handful of plastic spoons, individually wrapped. No knives, no metal.

Her legs trembled beneath her.

Nothing she could use to cut or fight.

The table had been bolted to the floor. The chairs were cheap and lightweight. The mirror was plastic.

They had taken precautions. They had planned.

Someone had planned for her stay.

But for how long? And then what?

7

Spencer MacDonald had been up since 4:30 a.m. Not that he'd slept much. He was not himself—timid, nervous. But this was it. He only had to endure this memorial, and then he was heading to the airport. His suitcase was in the trunk of his car. Too agitated to sleep in his own bed, he'd stayed in a hotel the night before. The security guy he'd hired to stay at his house looked enough like him to fool people from a distance. If someone came to the door, the man would say he was just looking in on the house, that Spencer was traveling for work.

Which he was. Today.

Spencer checked his phone for a message from Caleb, wondering if there had been an update on Scala's activities regarding the letters.

Nothing.

Hackers were notorious for going dark just when you needed them. Spencer started to compose a text to remind Caleb how crucial Spencer's role was but stopped halfway through to erase it. Caleb wouldn't take the bait. He never did.

Since the first message Spencer had received from Caleb, Spencer had been cautious about what he asked of Caleb. Caleb had been a faceless investor for all these years—one who always had tips, whose insights made them both a lot of money. And as they had gotten to know one another, Caleb had started to provide Spencer with access to his very unique skill set, most notably, access to Bella's life.

Spencer's charm helped him raise money for Caleb's special projects. He played the market well enough to go unnoticed by the SEC vultures. Lose a little, win a little. Play the smaller stocks—none of the big ones. Mostly foreign entities, companies Caleb could manipulate. Make a few dollars per share, across a few thousand shares in a hundred or so dummy accounts. Caleb handled the back-office paperwork, tax forms, and the IRS. As long as Caleb made money and Spencer showed his clients the returns they expected—or better ones—everyone was happy.

As in all relationships, he preferred that the debt be in his favor, particularly when his partner was a cipher. He charged his normal rates, orchestrated the trades with aplomb, keeping Caleb's greed in check to keep them both safe. But that was before Bella's rejection. Before her unfortunate choice to attempt to frame him.

By then Caleb needed him much more than Spencer needed Caleb. But slowly, Spencer spent through the goodwill that had built up in those first years. Over the past few months, he'd asked even more of his secretive partner. This past week, the debt had definitely shifted in Caleb's favor.

Caleb knew that Spencer was moving but little more. He wasn't someone who asked questions, a commonality between the two men. For their joint venture to continue, Spencer had to be sure he wasn't leaving any loose ends. Bryce Scala felt like a loose end. When he'd asked Caleb to run a thorough check on the man, Spencer hadn't explained why. Caleb's full search on Bryce Scala revealed a limited online presence—a barely used Facebook account, an AOL email address—and no mention of Spencer anywhere. And aside from the call inviting Spencer to this service, there had been no other communication.

You're in the clear.

He wanted to believe it. As he made the turn onto Saint Mary's Court, he felt the familiar tension in his neck and shoulders. He tried to bring back the release he had felt with Mistress Keres's neck in his hands, the pressure of her skin between his fingers. But even that joy could not overpower the trill of panic he felt as he pulled to the curb behind the churchyard.

He scanned the headstones dotting the grass, eyed the Southern live oak with its skeletal fingers that stretched across the churchyard. How long since he'd been here? He'd promised himself he would never be back. The street where he'd grown up was a block away, three turns from the church. Mornings, Spencer and his father had walked together, past the church and west two blocks to the elementary and middle schools nestled in a cul-de-sac.

While other children were shuttled to and from by mothers in station wagons smelling of biscuits and gravy or in big yellow buses rowdy with childish energy, Spencer had walked beside his silent father. Walked as he had been instructed—head up, eyes forward, alert and wordless. The closer the school grew, the more Spencer longed to abandon his father's austerity and sprint toward the other children. But he never did. His mother might have encouraged those small rebellions that would grow a flame inside him, if she'd had the courage. Instead, she'd taught him to follow, to obey. Coward.

And his father didn't just walk to the end of the block and let him go on alone. He'd walked Spencer through the school grounds, down the hall, and to the door of his classroom, where he'd looked down his long, narrow nose at the other children and teachers alike. When he'd finally left Spencer alone, his father's suffocating presence still remained, the severity of him like a black cloud, crackling with the threat of lightning, the boom of thunder. A storm that could brew in a single moment. In half a moment. Once his father left, Spencer worked every moment to charm them—his teachers and peers—to undo the impression his father left. He wanted to be a brilliant light that would blind people, blotting out the memory of his father.

Beyond the church, the tower of Spencer's office building rose from the skyline like a thin, distant flag. How he longed to be there now. The red-hot pride he felt in that office rushed through him, how he looked down on his father's little church, on this street, on his past.

From that window, he was immune to the deadening hate in this place.

He checked his watch. His mother's service was to start in fifteen minutes. He'd felt so much lighter after her death. Those moments in her room had been electric—the anger surging through him as he'd finally confronted her. All those years of tamping down the fury, of never speaking his mind, and he was finally free. Able to voice his rage at her spinelessness, her blind obedience to his father, and her own cold manner. He hoped his parents could see him from the depths of their hell, when he was in his home in Greece with his bride and his own son. They had failed to hold him back, to thwart him. He would have his castle, his triumph, despite and in spite of them.

So soon, he would be the master of his domain.

Reluctantly, he shifted his attention to the present, staring up at his father's church. He hadn't been inside since his father died. Church now was a way to show his face in the community, to see and be seen by clients, so when he attended three or four times a year, he went to the Baptist church close to his home in the wealthiest parish in Greenville. Baptist light, some of the parishioners called it, more palatable than many. Not that he noticed. He could sit in those pews and focus his attention like a laser on the outside of the minister's left ear and never hear a word.

That was the one thing he'd learned spending hours after school every day—and all day in the summer—inside the walls of that church. He learned to close off his mind from the words that echoed against the stained glass and the old stones and fill it with his own words. His own thoughts. Translate his father's hate into a hate all his own.

And he would do the same thing now.

Play the role. His childhood had been ample preparation for pretending to be someone else—the charming banker, the country club boy, the gentleman. He attended fund-raisers and took women on dates—one or two dates but never a third—all with the pretense of being open for love to strike again. Which he was not. He wasn't even certain it was love that had struck with Bella. Though what he felt now burned with a passion that some might compare to love, he knew better.

What he felt was far more powerful than love.

He still appeared on Greenville's list of most eligible bachelors, though he'd been passed over during his imprisonment. Now, of course, the story only served to heighten his appeal. A good man wronged was a better story than a good man.

He shut off the engine and smoothed his hair without checking in the mirror. As he cracked the door, he smelled the rot of old wood and wet, slick stones. This place was no different from any of the churches he'd visited in the last twenty years, he told himself. So what if it was the actual structure he'd entered in his youth? His father wouldn't be there, nor his mother. Just a group of old people he hadn't seen in years and a man he didn't know. A man whose wife had kept letters from Spencer's mother. Letters in which she'd confessed to having a son she thought might harbor evil.

Is it possible for a child to be born of the love between two of God's chosen people and still be wholly evil?

It should have made him laugh—his mother and father as God's chosen ones, that he was a product of love.

When Bryce Scala had rang his doorbell about a week earlier, Spencer had been looking for things of value. Not garage sale value or sentimental value but real value. Were there clues that would give the detectives looking for Bella any hint of her whereabouts? Those had to be eliminated. Was there something that he might leverage to make his future more comfortable? He went through potential weapons, items that might help him create the ambience of home for Bella. Their new home.

The survey of the living room had yielded nothing that warranted a second look. The last of the remaining valuables were in a safety deposit box at a branch of Wells Fargo that he never visited. Cash and bearer bonds—they would be the last things he would pick up on his way out of town.

These were the final days. If nothing else, the daily search reminded him of how well he had planned for his own disappearance. How ready he was.

From Greenville, he would be going to Dallas to meet the wealthy few individuals who planned to invest in Caleb's project. Caleb himself was unable to make a personal appearance, so Spencer would be the face. With that completed, he would retrieve Bella and say good-bye to this country and this life.

Spencer remembered how when the doorbell rang, a gray-haired man he didn't recognize had looked at him through the small window. In his hands, the man held a bundle of folded papers, maybe three inches thick, secured with a rubber band. Like letters. No choice now, he'd opened the door.

"Spencer MacDonald?"

"Yes."

The man had smiled. "I'm Bryce Scala. I was friends with your father and mother."

Spencer had put out his hand. "So nice to meet you, Mr. Scala." He hadn't opened the door to invite Scala inside. He'd wanted the exchange to be brief.

"I was so sorry to hear about your mother's passing."

"Thank you," Spencer had said, casting his eyes downward. "It is hard to imagine that she's really gone." Of course, he had seen it happen, so imagining it was unnecessary. He need only recollect the sensation of driving that needle into her ear, of watching her faculties fail. Her lips stumbling on words, her hands flopping around like fish tossed on land. And then the wonderful relief as she went silent. All of it was still fresh enough to relish in his mind.

But then Scala had asked to come in. And Spencer had no choice but to comply. The two men had sat in the living room, Spencer noticing how sterile it seemed, how obvious that he was preparing to leave this place. Bryce Scala eyed the room and Spencer as he explained how his wife and Spencer's mother had been wonderful friends—pen pals.

"We were living in Asia at the time." Scala had handed over the letters. "I thought these might be of interest," the man had told him. But his voice had been measured, his gaze steely. Spencer knew, even before reading them, that the letters contained something that made Spencer vulnerable.

"I'm hosting a memorial for your mother," Scala had announced, the letters sitting on the empty coffee table between the two men. "Monday," he'd said, as though telling Spencer was a courtesy and nothing more. "Hope to see you there."

Spencer should have said then that he'd be traveling. But he couldn't. The old lessons of his childhood took over—honor your parents; respect your elders.

He stood behind the church, as frozen now as he had been then, staring at the back entrance. He'd rarely come in the front as a child, always ushered through this entrance instead.

As much as he resented the complication Bryce Scala's arrival had imposed, Spencer knew it might have been worse if he hadn't faced Scala in person. At the very least, Spencer had the opportunity to present the facade of the grieving son. He would have to sell it inside the church, pretend that, even as an adult, he had looked for guidance from his wise mother. Share a story or two in the company of a few of his parents' friends, too distraught to speak but wanting to share what they had been to him.

Spencer walked around the church to enter from the front steps. He ascended slowly, holding a serene and somber expression as he moved through the sea of people who'd congregated just outside the doors. Voices called his name. He shook hands, seeing nothing but dark suits and church dresses and the blurred circles of faces.

As he looked up at the stained glass Jesus looming beyond the pulpit, the dark shadow of his father encircled him, and it was all he could do to make his way down the aisle for the chains constricting his chest.

8

Hal was on his way back to the office after interviewing a potential witness on a case when he received a relayed call through Dispatch. Dallas
FBI had picked up Spencer MacDonald in the airport there on his way
into town. They were holding him for questioning. With Hailey's help,
Hal had convinced Captain Marshall that someone from San Francisco
PD should be involved in the search for Anna. She was their ME, after
all. Marshall got special dispensation from the bureau to include one
of SFPD's inspectors on the case, and Marshall agreed that Hal could
go for a few days. Hal never had to mention that he was going with or
without permission. Having the blessing of his captain and the bureau
was certainly preferable.

Twenty minutes later, Hal was at home, throwing clothes in a bag.
Fifteen minutes after that, he'd booked a flight. A local agent would
meet him at the airport. En route, he made arrangements for Anna's
neighbor to watch Buster and asked one of his friends who lived down
the hall from his apartment to check in on his cat, Wiley. Hailey and
O'Shea would cover for him at work.

After four cups of coffee, Hal made his way through the sea of
faces toward security, groggy and out of sorts. The phone in his pocket

beeped, a nudge from the hourly alarm he'd set to remind himself that another sixty minutes had passed since Anna had been taken.

This would be hour forty-seven. Forty-seven hours since that van had backed into the driveway and struck down an eighty-five-year-old woman. Forty-seven hours since Anna had come to Mrs. Goldstein's assistance and been abducted.

He placed his shoes and belt in a bin with his wallet and phone and watched it float down the conveyer belt.

A hand touched him from behind. He wheeled around to find a woman in a skirt suit and stockinged feet. "You're up." She motioned him toward the X-ray machine. He stepped through, and the machine bleated.

"Are your pockets empty, sir?"

"Yeah," he said. "I put it all . . ." But then he felt the hard lump in his front pocket. He removed Anna's keys from his pocket and stared down at them. He'd been carrying the keys since finding them on the entryway table. In his downtime, he worried them between his fingers, like rosary beads. He'd driven her car a half dozen times before without noticing the small silver heart on her keychain, a Tiffany thing. He wondered where it had come from. Not the sort of thing she would buy herself.

"Sir," the TSA agent said again, pointing back through the machine. "You have to go back through."

The woman in the business suit pushed past him with an exasperated sigh as he returned and dropped the keys in a dish. He walked through the machine in silence and retrieved his things, returning Anna's keys to his pocket before putting on his belt and shoes. He felt a strange vacancy at his waist where his gun should have been. He was not allowed to take the department-issued weapon. Or any weapon. As he made his way toward the gates, his phone rang in his pocket. His pulse batted against his chest and ricocheted in his neck. The phone trembled in his hand.

Every time it rang, it was her voice calling to him. He no longer checked the screen. Her phone was with Roger, being searched for evidence. No one was calling from her number. "Harris."

"Hal, it's Harper."

Harper Leighton. Hal hadn't spoken to the Charleston detective since MacDonald had been released from prison more than a year and a half earlier. He choked on the inhale, unable to speak for the cork in his throat. The Southern accent was more pronounced in Harper's voice than in Anna's. He stopped in the walkway.

"Hal?" Harper said, drawing his attention back.

"I'm here."

"I heard about Anna."

"MacDonald's in Dallas," Hal said. "I'm heading there now."

"There was someone here, watching MacDonald, right?" Harper asked.

Hal thought about Colton Price and his inane excuses. "Yeah," he said.

"So how—"

How did he get Anna? And where did he take her? "I don't know."

"Hal," Harper said in a hush that felt like a blow to his gut. "What can I do?"

"I don't know."

She started to speak again, but he interrupted. "I've got to go now, Harper. I'll keep you posted."

"It's going to be okay."

He ended the call without responding. Would it be okay? How? Could he survive if something happened to Anna? He refused to consider it.

What he knew was that Anna wouldn't survive losing that baby.

He waded through the sea of people. Business travelers wheeled their luggage past him, trailing clouds of perfume and aftershave, followed by families with small children. He saw Anna's face everywhere—in the woman who stood bouncing a mewling newborn, in the dark-haired gate agent calling for the premium cabin to board, in the woman riding by on the white cart, her leg in a cast. He watched the white cart until it was out of sight.

The white van. There had to be something memorable about it, but Eileen Goldstein couldn't recall.

Hal knew that Spencer MacDonald was behind this. He couldn't wait to look him in the eyes, the bastard. All this time, Hal had never stood face-to-face with the monster who had tortured Anna. He should have done it years ago. Should have made the trip to Greenville when MacDonald had gotten out of prison. Or when Anna had gone home to deal with her aunt's murder.

Hal would face him now, that son of a bitch.

Anna had been so afraid of him. Hal recalled how she'd pushed him to teach her how to fire a weapon. They'd gone to the range together a few times, and he'd been relieved when her interest had dropped off. He wished now that he'd pressed her to take self-defense classes. How had someone gotten her into the back of that van? How hard had she fought? Had she almost gotten away?

If only he'd been there . . . The thought was a continuous loop in his brain.

Hal studied the monitor and confirmed his gate assignment. Twenty minutes until he boarded. In four hours, he'd be landing in Dallas. In five, he would be interviewing MacDonald. Hal would get the truth out of him. He might be the only one who could. MacDonald wanted Anna, and Hal knew her intimately. He would use everything he had to crack MacDonald.

Did MacDonald know that she and Hal had been intimate? That they were a couple? Had he been watching them?

They hadn't told anyone. It had seemed premature.

Roger knew. Roger, who had come straight to Anna's house after Hal called, who had gotten in touch with the Crime Scene Unit to process Anna's house. Roger had been the one to find the positive pregnancy tests. His team had spent as long in Anna's house as they did any active crime scenes. Hal had no doubt that Roger would give this case everything he had.

But there was nothing in Anna's house to suggest what had happened to her.

Hal had known there wouldn't be.

Anna had been entered into NamUs, the US Department of Justice's National Missing and Unidentified Persons System, within two hours of the discovery that she had been abducted. The department had also put out a BOLO—a Be on the Lookout alert—and issued an EMA, an Endangered Missing Advisory. They'd used the photograph from her work badge on the flyer, and her expression was neutral, professional. No sign of the smile he loved. And why would there be?

Even with all the people participating, he still felt Anna slipping away from him. He took the keys from his pocket and worried them in his fingers. The gate agent called his group on the intercom. He straightened his shoulders and joined the line, feeling the seconds sliding by one by one. *Patience,* he reminded himself.

He'd get MacDonald. Find Anna and bring her home. Or he would die trying.

—

The plane had been stuck on the tarmac for an extra twenty minutes, and Hal had spent the three-hour flight from SFO to Dallas in a middle seat between two women who'd shared life stories across his lap and a passenger in front of him who repeatedly had tried to recline his seat, banging painfully into Hal's knees.

Hal arrived in Dallas ready to blow. He'd kept his phone on during the flight, taking surreptitious glances at the screen despite the lack of a signal. As the plane descended, he'd found himself praying for news.

But the only message on his phone was from the FBI agent meeting him at the curb. Telly Azar was his name. The only thing worse than his name was the fact that Telly was twelve years old. Or he looked it in his picture on the bureau's website.

As Hal got into the unmarked Chevy Impala, he hoped the kid was just the ride to the department. But this was his agent, the one who was supposed to help him break Spencer MacDonald.

"Telly Azar," the agent said, offering Hal a small hand with a surprisingly firm handshake.

Telly. Anna's life might depend on a guy named Telly. No fucking way.

The agent tried to make small talk on the way to the bureau, but Hal remained silent, buying his time until he could let loose on whoever had assigned Anna's case to a child. The agent seemed to pick up on Hal's cues, and they spent the majority of the ride in silence.

When they arrived at the bureau's Dallas office, Hal excused himself and called San Francisco's supervisory senior resident agent, a man he'd gotten to know in a few shared cases over the years.

"You're putting Anna's fate in the hands of a sixth grader?" Hal growled.

"He's the best in his class."

"Best in his class?" Hal repeated. "What? Last year's class?"

The SSRA didn't respond.

"This is Anna," Hal whispered, his voice breaking. "Dr. Schwartzman," he corrected, clearing his throat.

"He's your contact, Hal. He's got the full support of the bureau behind him. Don't underestimate him because he's young. You were young once."

And an idiot, he thought. Hal blew out his breath. "What's with the name Telly?"

"You should ask him."

Hal fell silent. He wasn't going to make small talk with that kid. They weren't going to be friends. The kid could go to the playground with someone else. "Forget it."

"His full name is Telluride."

"Telluride," Hal repeated.

"Like the ski resort in Colorado."

"Christ. There has to be someone—"

"Listen, Hal, give him a chance. I'm told he's very good."

Hal ended the call and pressed his face against the cold tile wall. Named after a fucking ski resort. Jesus H. Christ.

When he emerged from the restroom, Telly Azar had them set up in a conference room. "There's coffee there if you want it," Telly said. "MacDonald is here for our interview when you're ready."

Hal ignored the coffee and remained standing. "I'm ready. I know exactly how I'm going to handle him."

Telly's finger hovered over a button on the phone. He pulled it away slowly, shaking his head. "I can't let you do that."

"Do what?"

"I appreciate how hard this is for you," the agent said.

Hal stared at Telly, a kid with his unlined face and his sharply pressed suit. "You do? You appreciate it?"

"We're on the same side," Telly said softly.

"I know this guy. I know how he works."

"And that will be helpful. Later."

"Later." Hal shoved his hands deep into his pockets so he didn't wrap them around the agent's neck.

"We have to do this by the book. That means I conduct the interview."

Hal drew a deep, slow breath, battling to keep his voice even, calm. "He wants Anna, and I know her. I can use that to—"

"No, that's not how I'm running this. Emotions make things go sideways. I don't want this going sideways. Do I need to do the interview alone?"

"No," Hal said quickly, feeling a rush of heat. He would not miss the opportunity to see MacDonald in person. Even if it meant taking a backseat in the interview.

Telly watched him. The two men didn't know each other. The agent had no reason to believe him.

"I need to be in on this," Hal said. He had to hold himself still, to fight against the desire to beg. "Please."

Something in Hal's expression—desperation maybe—must have convinced Telly to agree. The agent nodded, and Hal released the breath from his lungs, the air hot and dry as it passed his lips. He'd given up control of the interview. *You had no choice.* But what if MacDonald played the agent? He played everyone else.

The thought of sitting by while MacDonald evaded the questions . . .

"You ready?" Telly asked.

"Absolutely," Hal lied.

However it went down in there, Hal was coming out with some damn answers.

9

The panic that came from searching the cabin drained Schwartzman, forcing her to retreat to the bedroom. It was a few hours before she rose and willed herself to return to the hunt. *Don't think. Just take it all in.* Something would come to her. Some idea. It had to.

Back in the kitchen, she studied the ancient appliances. The small refrigerator reminded her of Hal, the way he had to stoop to get into her refrigerator, the image of him leaning down to reach a bottle of Guinness from the lowest shelf.

Where was Hal now? She wrapped her arms around herself. Had he gone to her house? Had he seen the pregnancy tests she'd left in the bathroom, the ones she'd never looked at?

Again she had to force the thoughts away. The panic came so quickly, like a tap just below the surface. She drew a slow breath. "Don't waste your energy." The sound of her voice was soothing. Longing wasn't going to solve her problem. Nor were thoughts of Hal.

Survive and escape.

Hunger made her belly ache. She opened the refrigerator and found milk and juice, some fruit, and lunch meats. Food. Schwartzman almost buckled in relief, remembering the heavy padlocks on the refrigerator and cupboards in Zhanna Doe's kitchen, her weakened and emaciated frame.

Zhanna's captor had locked away the food, leaving her collared and hungry, like a dog.

Using Zhanna's nails and hair as a measure of her malnutrition, combined with bone density, Schwartzman had estimated that she'd likely been starved for most of her captivity. She'd found evidence of extensive sexual abuse, and it appeared that she'd suffered at least one abortion—likely performed in the apartment. In the end, Zhanna had looped the cord around the bedroom doorframe and hung herself.

Dying had become the easier option.

You will not die here, Schwartzman told herself, turning her attention back to the room.

She opened the refrigerator again and pulled out the carton of milk. It was good protein and would fill her belly. She checked the carton. It had not been opened. Turning it upside down, she confirmed it was still sealed. She squeezed gently. A drop slid down the side of the carton and hit the floor, then another. She traced the drops to the underside of the fold at the top of the carton. Turning it sideways and viewing it under the light, she saw the puncture mark.

The right size for a needle.

The milk was drugged. She grabbed the orange juice and turned it upside down, squeezing harder now as the frustration built. A slow drip came from a puncture mark in the same place. Drugged. She noticed the small puddle of water beneath the liter bottle of water on the bottom shelf. Drugged.

She stared at the kitchen sink. Surely if they'd taken the time to drug the liquids in the refrigerator, then they'd drugged the tap water, too. Dragging the cord along the track, she crossed the kitchen to the sink. On her tiptoes, she studied the scene out of the fogged window. Behind the glass, a set of heavy wrought-iron bars, like a prison, lay stark against the whiteness beyond.

At first, she couldn't make sense of the view. She tried to find the edge of the white, expecting it to take shape as a building or a warehouse. But slowly, a pine tree emerged, its dark spine and needles buried beneath a layer of white.

Snow.

Everything outside was buried in snow. She tried to imagine where they might be but couldn't. North was all that came to mind. Maybe somewhere in the Sierra Mountains; maybe out of California entirely. How long had they traveled?

Shivering involuntarily, Schwartzman pressed her fingertips against the cloudy windowpane above the kitchen sink, surprised to find the surface wasn't cold. She studied the ground again. That was definitely snow on the ground. She wiped the surface of the window, expecting to clear the fog on the glass, but the window looked the same. Checking the slack in the cord above her head, she climbed up onto the countertop and pressed the whole of her hand to the window.

Like the mirror and the water cup, the window was made of a thick plastic.

Unbreakable.

Even if she could pull the window out and get past the bars, she would freeze to death. She had no shoes, no coat.

The dull buzz of a baseboard heater kicked on in the other room, and she jumped. Drawing a breath, she tried to calm herself. *Work. Think. Focus. One thing at a time.*

Using a chair from the table, she climbed up to the sink to get a look outside. On the counter, she balanced one knee on either side of the metal sink. Her face pressed against the thick plastic as she studied the frozen ground outside. How was the water drugged? Fighting the stubborn casement, she slid the window open and leaned out until her cheek was pressed to the cold iron bars. From there, she spotted a small plastic bottle similar to the ones that hung from the side of a rodent's cage. The bottle hung from a fence stake. A thin plastic tube ran from it and wrapped around a curved pipe that led toward the house.

Shivering, she closed the window against the frigid air and climbed back down off the chair. Pulling the cord slack, she lowered herself again. One hand on the cord, she opened the cupboard beneath the sink to study the pipe that rose from the subflooring.

Using her fingernails, she dug into the opening around the pipe, loosening the old, flaking caulk to reach the lower part of the PVC. It was too dark to see. Returning to the bedroom in fits and starts as she pulled the cord along the track, she retrieved the bedside lamp and retraced her steps into the kitchen. There, she plugged the light into an outlet by the sink and let it hang upside down over the counter.

Winded, she dropped again to her knees, the collar choking her. Eyeing the ceiling, she saw the clip had caught above the table. She scrambled to get hold of the counter and pull herself up, her breathing tight and panicked, and she spent a few moments calming herself. Then, careful to create slack in the cord, she lowered herself again. With the added light, she peered down into the narrow opening around the pipe.

There, at the back, maybe two inches below the surface of the flooring, a thin tube fed into the main pipe. That had to be the drug. If she could push that tube off the pipe, then the drug wouldn't reach the water.

She wedged her fingers into the space between the flooring and the pipe, stretching them toward the tube. But it was too far. Retrieving a plastic spoon, she held the rounded side and tried to maneuver the handle to pry the tube away. With the handle wedged under the spot where the tube entered, she pushed slowly, trying to break it free. Instead, the spoon snapped at the base of the rounded end, and the handle vanished under the floorboard.

She broke two more spoons in the same way. Fighting frustration, she yanked the lamp off the counter and held it above her head. Panting and exhausted, she considered slamming it into the floor, imagining the wonderful crash it would make. But the base was smooth, rounded metal not porcelain. Other than the thin slivers of glass from the bulb, there would be no useful tool from the breakage.

And she might need the lamp.

Calming herself, she lowered it to the floor and leaned against the cupboard.

Breathing through her nose, she tried to ignore her parched tongue, the way it stuck to the roof of her mouth. She could not lose her temper. Now she was thirstier than ever.

She crossed to the refrigerator and opened the freezer. She pulled an ice tray out, staring at the cubes. Maybe they had filled the trays before the water was drugged. Using one finger, she pushed on a cube. It wasn't frozen solid. The drug had decreased the temperature at which the water would freeze.

Which confirmed that the tap water was drugged. So were the ice cubes.

She returned the tray to the freezer, shut the door, and leaned her forehead against the cool surface.

She would have to drink. The milk and orange juice were drugged, as was the kitchen tap water. Did that mean that the water in the bathroom was safe?

You have no choice. To stay alive, you need hydration.

Filled with dread, she tugged the cord along the track to the bathroom. There, leaning over the small grungy sink, she drank until her belly was full.

10

In the bathroom mirror, Georgia Schwartzman made another adjustment to her hair. There was nothing to do about how tired she looked. She'd checked her phone a half dozen times over the course of the night, hoping for a message from Spencer. It seemed an unfair irony that by the time life had slowed down enough that she could sleep in, her body no longer had the ability to shut down completely. Last night had been particularly bad. And she'd found herself fretting around the house all morning, getting in the way of the household staff.

She'd tried to make herself useful. Twice, she had called Bella and left messages—the first short, the second longer. She felt remiss that they hadn't spoken on Christmas, though she still wasn't certain they hadn't. Phoning her daughter always stirred an uncomfortable sadness, made her feel testy and defensive. By the end of the conversation, she usually wished she hadn't called. As though every time she reached out to Bella, it was a reminder of what she hadn't done right.

She couldn't imagine her own mother ever feeling that way. Guilty? Never. She certainly hadn't been coddled the way kids were today. But Bella didn't want coddling. Did she?

How was it possible to create a child and raise her to adulthood and still know so little about her?

As she had puttered through her morning routine, Georgia found herself checking her phone every ten or fifteen minutes, staring at it as though the device itself were at fault. Finally, she forced herself to leave the house.

It was early afternoon when she got in the car and thought about running to the market to pick up a few things. Maybe she'd make a side trip down to the boutiques along Augusta Road. But she couldn't stop thinking about Spencer. The dots had appeared after she'd texted him . . . Didn't that mean he was on his phone? Then why not answer? She wasn't a slave to her phone the way some of her friends were—and certainly not the way the young people at the club were, barely looking up to avoid running into people poolside. But to expect a return text after more than twelve hours didn't seem unreasonable. And it wasn't like Spencer. He was always so prompt. Unless something was wrong.

That was ludicrous.

They were hardly close friends. He owed her nothing. But he was her financial adviser. They spoke quarterly or so . . . or they had. She tried to remember the last time he'd called.

She couldn't remember.

She stopped at the left turn toward Augusta Road and changed her mind. She would go by Spencer's office. Then, if there was still time before the 4:00 p.m. garden club meeting, she'd go shopping. In fact, it might not be a bad time to ask him about these new tax laws. She tried to follow the changes in the news, but she had no idea how they would impact her. Sam had made sure she would always be taken care of, but it was never a bad idea to check in.

At his office building, she found a parking spot shaded by the tall building and rode the elevator to the top floor. As she stepped into the foyer, a young woman greeted her from behind a desk. "Hello. How can I help you?"

"I'd like to speak to Spencer MacDonald, please," she said, noticing that his door at the end of the hall was closed.

"I'm afraid Mr. MacDonald is traveling this week."

Georgia smoothed her hand along the side seam of her pants. "Traveling?"

The woman nodded but said nothing.

"Perhaps I can speak with Jenny."

A little shake of her head. "Jenny?"

"Jenny Fontaine," Georgia said, scanning the hall for a sign of Spencer's assistant.

A second woman appeared behind the first. A decade or so older, she was probably mid to late thirties. Her dark hair was pinned into an oversize bun that looked too large to be natural. Georgia noted her long fuchsia nails, the strange way they were shaped, almost into points.

"I'm afraid Ms. Fontaine no longer works here," the second woman said.

Surprised, Georgia looked around the space as though she might know someone else. She'd been a client for thirteen or fourteen years. Jenny had been here that whole time. Longer. She had come to Bella and Spencer's wedding. "When did she leave?"

"A few months ago."

"Why?" Georgia asked.

She watched as the younger woman eyed the older one, who slid her a quick look. "I'm afraid I don't know," the older woman said. "If you'll excuse me, I need to get back to work, but Crystal can help if there's something you need." As she turned, the heavy bun swayed across the back of her head. It made Georgia think of a big fat ass. Women loved those now, too. Another thing she did not understand.

Then the woman was gone.

Georgia looked at the younger woman. "Crystal?"

"That's me," she said, smiling to display her teeth. Georgia noticed that two of her front bottom teeth overlapped slightly. "Would you like to leave Mr. MacDonald a message?"

"Do you know when he'll be back in the office?"

Crystal studied the computer in front of her, frowning as she clicked her mouse. "Hmm," she said with a glance over her shoulder. But the woman with the bun was on the phone now, her back to them. "Actually, I don't. For some reason, his calendar is blocked off."

"Blocked off?"

"It just means we can't access it. Usually, it means someone will be out for a few months—like maternity leave," she added, her eyes momentarily bright.

Georgia gave her a moment to think about what she'd just said, but it didn't seem to occur to Crystal that she had implied Spencer was out on maternity leave. If he was taking an extended trip, wouldn't he have told his clients? Did this have anything to do with Bella? But of course not. She thought of how Jenny used to keep her company when she was waiting for her appointments with Spencer. How odd to think she was gone.

She'd probably retired. Georgia seemed to recall Jenny had a couple of children of her own. They were probably grown by now.

"Ma'am?"

Georgia shook her head. "I'll just get out of your hair." She leaned in closer to the desk and lowered her voice. "But before I go, do you happen to have a contact number for Jenny Fontaine? I'd love to reach out to her."

"Oh."

"I would imagine you have her details in the company contacts. Then I'll be going."

"Sure," Crystal said. "Let me just look here."

More clicking and frowning, and she seemed to locate something. "I only have her address."

"That would be fine."

Crystal lifted a yellow sticky note off a pad and began to write.

A moment later, the bun stepped out of the back room and into the small reception area. As she bent over Crystal's computer, the room felt suddenly crowded. "What are you doing?"

"I'm just getting Jenny Fontaine's address."

The bun reached over and took the mouse from Crystal's hand. "No," she said. "No." She looked suddenly flustered, casting a forced smile up at Georgia. "I'm sorry. We really can't give out contact information. It's against company policy."

"I didn't mean to get anyone in trouble." Georgia pressed a hand to her throat.

"No worries," the bun said, glancing at Crystal, who was also growing red.

Georgia stole a look at the Post-it Note, the big round letters easy to read. *Dominic Court,* she thought it said. *Yes, 128 Dominic Court.*

When she looked up, the bun was staring at her.

Georgia forced her own smile. "I just love your ring." She pointed to a cheap band with a heart bent into the metal that Crystal wore on her pointer finger.

"Thank you," Crystal said, looking genuinely pleased.

"Sorry to bother you ladies," Georgia said.

"Did you get what you need then, Ms.—" the fat bun asked.

"It sounds like Mr. MacDonald's calendar isn't working, so I'll drop him an email," Georgia said, ignoring the question about her name. "Spencer is good with responding to those. Much better than I am," she added with a little laugh.

The bun said nothing, the smile on her face suspicious. Crystal offered a little wave. "You have a nice day."

Georgia made her way through the foyer and back into the elevator. When the doors had closed and she felt the little bump of the box beginning to descend, she realized that the encounter had been oddly unsettling. She sent a text to herself with Jenny Fontaine's address so she'd have it. But what did she plan to do? Show up at her house? Of course not.

Out in the fresh air, she was happy to put the incident behind her. She would send Spencer an email. Maybe something was going on with his mother in Florida. There were lots of reasons why he might take a few weeks off, even if she'd never known him to do it before.

Enough, she thought. The police showing up, the lack of sleep—she was starting to invent things. With her car unlocked, she stopped to check the dashboard clock. She still had plenty of time to go to Augusta Road before the garden club meeting. A little shopping was exactly what she needed.

11

Despite the bright midday sun, Schwartzman felt the lethargy she equated with her days of chemo. The water in the bathroom was also drugged. The aftereffects dulled her senses like a thick fog, and her head ached. Eyes closed, she tried to discern whether there might be another source of the drug. Was it possibly in the air as well? Or in the sheets? In her clothes? She'd read a case where a victim had been drugged through a chemical infused in her mattress. It was possible. She turned her nose to the sheet, but there was no off odor. She couldn't be certain.

And there was also the fetus. In the early weeks of her first pregnancy years ago, she'd felt profoundly tired, needing rest after only a few tasks. She opened her eyes. The glass of water by the bed was full again. She rose, keeping a hand on the cord as she moved from the bed. Although she hadn't changed out of her own clothes—yoga pants and a flannel button-down—a new stack waited for her on the small bureau, gently worn but clean and fresh-smelling. Someone had come into the room. Did he watch her? Did he . . . No.

Surely she would know if she'd been touched. The man had been aggressive in the back of the truck. Now that he had her here in this cabin, why leave her alone?

Or maybe it was just a matter of when he would return.

"No." The word was sharp and hoarse in her ears. She rarely went so long without talking. She said it again. She would not think about what might happen. There was only the mental space to work her way through the problem of finding a way out. Anything else was not relevant.

She had not been raped, which meant right now, she had to focus on escape. Nudging the cord along its track, she went into the bathroom and checked the ceiling. Nothing looked like a camera or an opening or a place where one might be hidden.

Why did he need a camera? He had access to her every time she was drugged and unconscious. She studied the collar in the mirror, realizing she hadn't taken a close look at it after trying to pry it loose. The locking mechanism was at the back, so she twisted the collar around her neck, the rubber chafing her skin. The cord in her face, she tugged it gently to create slack and tried to get a clear view of the back.

The light in the bathroom shone painfully dim. Located just above the mirror, it cast a long shadow from her chin down onto her neck and chest, making it impossible to see.

She yanked on the collar in an effort to bring it closer to the mirror, the rubber digging into her skin. She coughed and stopped moving, worked to catch her breath and swallow the uncomfortable lump in her throat.

Don't think about the collar. Just for a few minutes, do something else.

Drawing a deep breath, she turned to the shower and pulled back the curtain. Despite the ugly color, the shower and tub appeared clean. She cranked the water on and tested the temperature until the water felt comfortably hot on her hand.

Using the sleeve of her shirt, she cleared the steam off the bathroom mirror. She checked the door. Certain it was locked, she unbuttoned her shirt and stripped off the yoga pants. In the stream of the water, she let the spray strike her scalp and the water run down her face. The heat felt amazing. Even working around the awkward collar and the cord, she felt calmer.

For a moment, she had the sense that this was just a test and she could beat it. Yes, she was locked up, but at some point, there would be an opportunity to escape.

And she would be ready.

As she wiped the water from her eyes, she caught sight of something on her skin. Thinking it was a bug, she started and shook her arm. It didn't move. Through the water, she saw a strange block print across her forearm.

Stepping out of the spray, she wiped her eyes again. Looked down and felt another wave of nausea. She froze in horror at the six digits printed on her left arm in black ink—*212345*. Like a Holocaust tattoo. Tears burned her eyes, and she scrubbed at the skin with her opposite hand. The ink blurred, the numbers fading from black to gray, but they were still visible. Inked on her skin.

She studied the print, noting that it was thick and bold as though written slowly, with care. And yet the writing was messy, almost childish. She grabbed the bar of soap and worked a lather over the numbers. Using her nails, she rubbed and washed until the skin was red and sore. The numbers were faint but still visible.

The Holocaust.

That was when she remembered the man who had worked in her morgue, the man who had threatened to hurt her and said he would enjoy cutting her. His words played in her head. *"It would be fun . . . Because you're a fucking kike, and I hate kikes."*

The man whose eyes she'd seen, the man who had abducted her. It wasn't Spencer. It was the morgue attendant. Roy Butler.

Butler had attacked her in the morgue. That was over a year ago. Why had he come for her now?

She shuddered at the thought that followed. Hal would never think of Roy Butler. Fighting her panic, she stepped back into the water to rinse off the soap and found the water had gone cold. Doing her best to rinse, she ducked in and out of the water until her teeth were chattering audibly and her body was quaking. She wrapped herself in a towel and dressed quickly in her own clothes, the thought of someone watching in the front of her mind.

In the bedroom, she removed her shirt and took a gray hoodie from the stack, pulled it on. Traded the yoga pants for a pair of baggy sweats. Zipping up the hoodie, she noticed the sky had darkened. She made her way to the bedroom window and scanned the window frame. Thick white flakes fell from the sky. Snow.

Water.

What she needed now was a way to collect the snow. She studied the side of the house. There—a beam jutted out a foot or so beyond her window.

Taking pains to move carefully across the room on her leash, she retrieved the water glass from the bedside table and carried it to the window. After she worked the small window open and dumped the drugged water outside, she used the sleeve of the sweatshirt to wipe out the glass.

Then, body pressed to the wall, she stretched her arm out as far as she could and balanced the glass on the beam. Shivering in the cold, she shut the window and watched with a measure of pride as snowflakes drifted into the cup.

She returned to bed and told herself she would sleep until the glass was full. But lying on her back, staring at the track above the bed, her cord draped loosely like a hangman's noose before the drop, all she could think about was Roy Butler.

12

Telly pressed the intercom button, turning to speak into the mike. "You can bring in MacDonald."

Several moments later, the door opened, and Spencer MacDonald was escorted into the room by two men in charcoal gray suits that were a near match. Either one looked twice as qualified as Telly. Hal said nothing as he studied MacDonald's face.

MacDonald wore a comfortable smirk that Hal wanted to slap right off his face. That this man had ever been with Anna. That he had hurt her, then hunted and stalked her. He had killed her aunt, her aunt's friend. As though by instinct, Hal's fingers made their way to his belt.

There was no weapon there. In Texas, he was a boyfriend, a friend— at best, a colleague. Outside of California, he was helpless. He felt the pressure of a hand on his arm and glanced down at the fingers, up at the face. Telly.

Hal nodded, and Telly removed the hand. "Why don't we all take a seat?" Telly pulled out a chair.

Hal sat beside the agent.

Again MacDonald smirked. "Here is fine." He took a chair at the opposite end of the table and adjusted his seat at an angle to the door. Hal glanced behind him, wondering if he was expecting someone to join them.

As though this were a chat among old friends, MacDonald crossed his legs and folded his hands together on one knee. "How can I help you gentlemen?"

Even if he couldn't participate in this interview, Hal refused to play MacDonald's game. Somehow this man had Anna. But he was here in Dallas. In fact, the day Anna was taken, MacDonald had been in Greenville. Recorded at a bank ATM and on CCTV. Hal didn't care. No cell in his body believed that Spencer MacDonald wasn't ultimately behind this plan. He was.

But his presence in Greenville during her disappearance in San Francisco meant someone was helping him. That was going to be Hal's way in, the weak link in MacDonald's plan. An accomplice was never foolproof. Whoever was helping MacDonald either had a financial interest in kidnapping Anna or an interest in Anna herself. The latter would mean that MacDonald had agreed to share her.

Hal did not believe MacDonald had any intention of sharing Anna with another man.

Which brought Hal to his next question. Would he have left someone alone with Anna, someone who might hurt or rape her without MacDonald's knowledge or permission? No. So perhaps the accomplice was a woman. But once that woman realized what Anna was to MacDonald, she would be on the outside. Maintaining that balance would be difficult for MacDonald, and from what Hal knew of him, MacDonald was not a man who did nuance well.

The second possibility was that the accomplice was in it for money or some sort of payment. MacDonald had hired someone. Hal hoped this was the case. People did insane things for love, and that made the situation less predictable. Money was powerful but, in Hal's experience, not as prone to motivate people to the extremes that love did.

With MacDonald, Hal knew he was dealing with love. Or perhaps love's bedfellow, hate. But if Hal could locate the accomplice . . .

Telly flipped open his notebook, the cover landing against his hand with a little slap that Hal had already tired of in their ninety-minute relationship. "When did you arrive in Dallas, Mr. MacDonald?"

"Today. Just a few hours ago."

"You came from?"

"Home."

Telly waited.

"Greenville, South Carolina."

"And what are you doing here?"

"Business meetings."

"Our records show that you booked several different destinations."

"I did. Five, to be exact."

"Why was that?"

MacDonald glanced at Hal as though taking stock of his reaction. "I have business meetings."

"What kind of business meetings?" Telly asked.

"Private ones."

Telly shook his head. "I'm afraid I'll need more than that."

"Why should I disclose anything about my meetings? You haven't even told me why I'm here."

Telly flipped the notebook closed again. "Are you aware that your ex-wife, Annabelle Schwartzman, was abducted from her San Francisco home on Saturday?"

This was the part Hal wanted to see.

"I did not know that." MacDonald turned to hold Hal's gaze. He tipped his head ten or fifteen degrees to the side. "Are you a friend of Bella's?"

Hearing that nickname made Hal's insides curl. The name that had haunted her. The reason she'd taken to introducing herself as Schwartzman—only Schwartzman. It was the one name that Spencer MacDonald hadn't owned or manipulated. It also was the one name he'd despised—her Jewish surname.

"How about we ask the questions?" Hal said.

MacDonald smiled a full grin as though thrilled to hear Hal's voice. "No."

Hal felt himself rise in the chair and had to focus all his energy on restraining himself.

"Do I need to repeat the question, Mr. MacDonald?" Telly asked.

MacDonald seemed amused.

"Then I'd appreciate an answer before we start looking at obstruction of justice," Telly said.

MacDonald tittered, looking at Hal as though to share a moment of humor at little Telly's big threats.

Hal glared.

MacDonald shook his head. "I have not seen my ex-wife since she attempted to frame me for murder."

"And that encounter occurred in Charleston, North Carolina?" Telly asked.

MacDonald opened his mouth to speak and then shook his head as though to say, "Nice try." "No. That was in Greenville. I was not in Charleston during that time."

Hal leaned back and interlaced his fingers behind his head. Every atom of him fought the desire to launch himself across the room.

Telly leaned toward MacDonald, cutting off Hal's view for a moment. Enough time to pull himself together.

"You're saying the attack in the garage belonging to Dr. Schwartzman's aunt never happened?" Telly asked.

"Never," MacDonald repeated. "It was a figment of her imagination." His gaze slipped to Hal. "She's got a very active imagination." He looked back at Telly. "I spent five months in jail for those accusations. The only time I've seen my ex-wife, Bella . . ." He drew out the nickname as though knowing exactly what it did to Hal. ". . . was when she broke into my home and planted evidence there." MacDonald rocked back in his chair and then stood. "And I'm sure you are both aware that I have been totally cleared of all charges related to the deaths of those women in Charleston."

Telly watched him, saying nothing.

MacDonald straightened his suit jacket, pulling it down with both hands before brushing off the arms, as though he'd picked up dirt from the FBI's office. "Is there anything else I can help with, Agent Azar? Detective Harris?"

"Not at this time," Telly said without rising.

MacDonald rounded the table and headed for the door. When he reached it, he gripped the knob and turned back. "I'm a big believer in karma. I'm sure things will work out with Bella exactly as they should."

With that, MacDonald slipped from the room in a way that made Hal think of a snake.

Hal burst out of his chair and charged at the closed door. He halted inches away. Fists raised, he trembled as he held himself from pounding on the door.

"That went well," Telly said, standing from the table and closing his notebook with a little slap.

Hal swung back, staring at him. "What?"

"He's cocky, self-assured."

"And that's a good thing?"

"Yes," Telly said without flinching at Hal's mounting fury. "It means he's overly confident. He'll make a mistake."

"He's been stalking her for eight and a half years, and he hasn't made a mistake yet."

"I'm sure he has. Just not one that anyone caught."

"And that's different now? Because you're involved?"

Telly gave a curt nod. "Because we're involved."

Hal wanted to feel the confidence Telly did. Or maybe it wasn't confidence but the blind faith of youth. But Hal didn't have either.

He had seen Spencer MacDonald slip through their fingers too many times.

13

She woke with pangs of hunger and sandpaper in her mouth. The bedroom was quiet, the light waning. Maybe late afternoon, early evening. She listened to the silence as memories of Roy Butler assaulted her—the sound of his voice when he'd called her a kike, the smell of him in the back of the truck, his long nails pressed into her neck. His smells, his hate. The collar seemed to grow tighter on her neck. Why did he bring her here? What did he want with her?

She pinched her eyes closed and forced him away.

Turning in the bed, she stared at the square of gray sky through the window. Her throat closed at the sight of snow falling in the sky—relief and also longing. Snow was water, clean water. And it was Hal. Memories of Thanksgiving together, of walking through the streets of the suburb of Sacramento where his sister lived. It had been snowing, a rarity for that part of the country. She held herself, remembering Hal's arms around her. His touch, his kiss.

Forcing herself out of bed, she retrieved the cup from the ledge and made her way into the kitchen, where she dumped the fresh snow into her kitchen cup. She carried the empty cup back into the bedroom and returned it to the ledge. Moving through the cabin, edging the cord along the track, felt like an intense workout. Her legs and back ached. She was likely dehydrated, and without sufficient water, her body was unable to flush the toxins.

What she needed was more snow. She scanned the ground below the window, the snow a deep blanket of white. If only she had something she could use to reach for it, to scoop it in through the window. She mentally sorted through all the items in the cabin, but there was no such tool.

For several minutes, she watched the flakes of snow drift into the cup. Drug-free water. The snow fell at a steady rate, but it would be hours before the cup was full again. There was no way to collect more as the ledge was too narrow for anything larger than the single cup. She reminded herself that some snow was better than none. It would be enough to last her awhile. If the snow continued to fall, she would continue to flush the drugs from her system.

She stopped herself from thinking too far ahead. One step at a time.

Returning to the kitchen, she felt more energized. She took a yogurt from the refrigerator and removed the lid. She tested the edges of the plastic liner to be certain there were no gaps between it and the yogurt. After peeling off the plastic liner, she emptied the container into a bowl. Next, she washed the liner and the container and then returned to the table. Without touching the yogurt, she raised the liner to the light, peering at it. She shifted it in her hands, bit by bit, until she had examined it completely. No needle hole.

She repeated the same for the container. Again no hole.

The yogurt appeared drug-free.

She ate the contents of the bowl, finishing it completely. Then she drank the melted snow. Now she would wait an hour before eating anything else. As a test.

To pass the time, she organized the food in the refrigerator, taking note of which items were most likely to be drug-free. Yogurt, lunch meats, cheese. The rest was questionable. Certainly the liquids—milk, water, and orange juice—were drugged. How much work had he done? She did the same with the food on the counter. The bread, Cheerios, and peanut butter were probably fine. Apples. Oranges could be easily drugged, although she could examine them for needle marks as well.

She lifted a plump orange to her nose, the smell making her stomach growl. But she set it down again, reminding herself to make one decision at a time. Treat the food like a case, like a body. One organ at a time. Measure the results and then move on.

As she'd done before, she poured milk into the glass and dumped it down the sink. Did the same with the orange juice, then rinsed the glass and sat at the table to study her body. Her head felt clear. Her focus was good. She lifted a hand and made a fist, raising it and lowering it in front of her. No signs of trembling, no impact to her motor skills. At least not yet. Maybe the yogurt wasn't drugged.

She wanted another. Could she assume they were all drug-free?

No. She would have to go through the process with each one, with everything.

As though Hal's voice was in her head, she thought, *Your only job is to keep away from the drugged water and maintain your strength.*

And find a way to escape.

For the first time, she studied the end of the track on the ceiling just beyond the oven. There, a small cap held the clip on the track. Both hands gripping the collar, she backed away, using her body weight to try to yank the cord free. But the track ended too close to the wall. She didn't have the right angle to pull it out. She drew one of the flimsy plastic chairs to the wall past the oven and climbed on top of it. Leaning into the wall, she pulled with both hands, trying to pull the cord free. The end cap didn't budge.

Down from the chair, she jerked the cord across the kitchen and checked the drawers for something to pry it off. Nothing but a few pieces of plastic cutlery. Although she already knew the contents of every corner of the cabin by heart, she checked each cupboard again, standing up on the counters, her fingers scouring with the hope of the desperate.

There was nothing.

She opened the freezer and pulled out two trays of ice. Threw them across the room and listened to the plastic trays clatter against the floor. They did not break.

She fisted her hands and slammed the freezer door shut, over and over. Suddenly, the slack on the cord reversed into the track, jerking her backward. She let out a cry as it dragged her across the floor. Both hands gripped the collar that choked her. Up on her tiptoes, she fought with the cable that threatened to hang her. Her throat burned. Her eyes felt as though they would burst.

With one foot, she hooked the leg of a chair and dragged it across the floor. It tipped, and she let out a sob, stretching her fingertips to right it as black holes ate into her field of vision. Moving by feel, she yanked the chair close. The black was almost complete as she clambered up onto the chair, creating slack in the cord. Bits of her sight returned.

She could breathe. Tears streamed down her face. She gripped the cord in both hands, terrified to let go.

Her throat was raw. Her chest burned. Shaking, she remained on the chair, drawing slow, deep breaths. She tested the cord and felt it give. Drew out the slack until she had several feet of it loose at her side. Slowly, she sank to her knees on the chair.

Then put a foot tentatively on the floor.

She studied the clip in the ceiling, the cord. Had the cord simply retracted because she had pulled too hard, too far?

Or was someone watching her, playing some cruel game?

Huddled on the chair, Schwartzman tucked her knees to her chest and listened to the silence, afraid to know the answer.

14

After the interview, Hal had gone outside to watch MacDonald exit the building and make his way down the street. There was no question MacDonald was taunting him, and Hal had felt himself rise to the bait. Only Telly's presence had prevented him from going after MacDonald physically. "We'll get him," Telly kept promising. "But we've got to get him the right way, so we can make it stick."

It all sounded good to Hal. But slow. There wasn't time for slow.

Hal had to give it to Telly. For a young guy, he was remarkably focused. Unfortunately for Hal, Telly's focus was paperwork. After their brief meeting with MacDonald, Telly dug into the data—background reports, cell phone records, financial transactions. He had reports spread across his desk like he was making a collage to hang on the wall.

In the bureau bullpen around them, agents shouted across the room and phones rang, but Telly appeared oblivious to the noise. With a small spiral-bound book tucked under his right arm, he read and jotted notes, filling page after page. Hal understood that Telly needed to get caught up on Spencer MacDonald, but Hal already knew everything he needed to know.

MacDonald had Anna, and they needed to find out where.

"Telly, he has to be communicating with someone about Anna."

The agent didn't look up.

"Telly!"

Telly put his finger on his place and lifted his face to look at Hal. "Did you know that MacDonald's mother died?"

Hal exhaled. "I couldn't care less about his mother."

Telly shook his head, frowning. "It just happened. Right after Thanksgiving. A local Florida law firm has filed an application for probate."

Hal tried to imagine what MacDonald's mother had to do with Anna. "And?"

"I'm not sure yet," Telly admitted, scanning the page with one finger. "She was living in a retirement home. Death certificate was issued by a local coroner. Cause of death is listed as natural—atherosclerotic cardiovascular disease. She was eighty-two."

Hal put both palms on the desk and leaned forward. "Where is he right now?"

"Still in town." Telly returned his attention to the report.

"Who is watching him?"

"A couple of agents."

"What's he doing?" Hal asked.

"Meeting with clients, from what we can tell," Telly said, pointing impatiently back at the report.

"Are you running background checks on the clients?"

"We're collecting names and identities, watching for anything unusual."

Hal dropped his head back and stared at the ceiling tiles. They were much cleaner than the ones in the SFPD's Homicide Unit. "We're missing something. He can't just be seeing clients. He has to be up to something, communicating with someone."

"That's what I'm looking for."

"It's not in there," Hal snapped, upright again. "It's where we can see his face, watch him. We won't figure it out just reading through damn paperwork."

The room hushed around them. Hal rubbed his face.

Telly's cell phone rang, and for the first time all day, he answered the call. "Yes."

Hal watched as Telly's eyes narrowed on the wall opposite them. A nod.

Hal felt his own spine straighten. Something was up.

"Yes, please," Telly said. "Thanks."

"What is it?" Hal asked when Telly lowered the phone.

Without a word, Telly rose and nodded toward the hallway. Hal followed him down a short hallway, where the agent cracked a door and peered inside. Confirming the room was empty, he walked in and closed the door behind them.

Hal felt like he might jump out of his skin. "What?"

"We're getting some off-the-books help," Telly said, pulling his phone from his pocket.

"Off-the-books help on what?"

"A friend of mine is dating a girl who works at the Andrew Hotel."

Hal felt the hitch in his breath. "Where MacDonald is staying."

Telly nodded, scrolling across his phone as Hal watched over his shoulder.

"What kind of help?" Hal asked.

"She runs the front desk."

"And?"

"And when MacDonald went out today, she happened to need to check the radiator in his room. It was acting up." The agent's expression gave nothing away as he focused on his phone, swiping the screen. Telly stopped scrolling and used two fingers to zoom in on an image. Hal leaned in closer.

It was a standard hotel room. Bed made, a suit coat hung over the back of the desk chair. A laptop sat centered on the desk, closed and plugged in.

Telly flipped to the next image. A bathroom sink, toiletries lined up on top of a white washcloth. Hal scanned them, momentarily struck by how mundane the details were. Even a monster like Spencer MacDonald brushed and flossed his teeth.

The images changed. On top of the dresser sat a single penny—darkened with age and years of handling. A phone charger was plugged into the wall. Nothing written on the hotel notepad. Another penny lay discarded beside it.

"What are we looking at, Telly?"

"The room."

Like Hal didn't know that. He kept watching as Telly scrolled through the images.

A picture of the trash can followed. Inside was an empty white sack, like the type from a convenience store. In the next shot, the sack was gone, and they could see to the bottom of the trash can, empty other than a third penny. Telly scrolled again to display a hand holding a small white receipt. Zoomed in, Hal saw it was a cash purchase in the amount of $24.99.

What had MacDonald bought?

Telly scrolled, but that was the last of the images.

"I didn't see a briefcase or computer bag," Hal said.

"He might have it with him. Or it might be in the closet."

There were no pictures of the closet. Or inside the drawers.

"She was probably worried about getting in trouble," Telly said, his thoughts in line with Hal's.

It made sense. The hotel employee had taken images only of what was in plain sight and in the trash, which left them nothing to go on other than a white plastic bag and a single receipt. "Scroll back to the pictures of the room."

Telly slid his finger across the screen, reversing the images.

Twenty-four dollars and ninety-nine cents. Maybe a bottle of something? "You see any glasses? Any sign of a bottle of booze?" Hal asked.

Together, they studied the images again. A glass sat on the bathroom counter, an inch of clear liquid still in the bottom. Almost certainly water.

"You're thinking about the receipt," Telly said.

"Twenty-four ninety-nine. That's not a candy bar."

"No," Telly agreed. "A bottle makes sense, but no sign of it anywhere."

"Might have been in the trash and was emptied when the room was cleaned earlier."

Telly shook his head. "Room has a 'do not disturb' on it. It wasn't cleaned."

MacDonald wouldn't want anyone in his room. He'd made his own bed, tidied his own things. Of course he had. Spencer MacDonald was a man who liked control, which made Hal second-guess the idea of alcohol. "I doubt MacDonald is much of a drinker. Maybe an expensive Scotch once in a while."

"Right," Telly agreed. "Doesn't match his personality."

They looked back through the images a third time.

Hal thought about what he'd seen. Something struck him. "The pennies."

"Yeah," Telly agreed. "Three of them."

"And all in different spots," Hal added. "I hate pennies."

"I always leave them in the little dish."

Hal nodded. "Me, too. And there are three here. One on the desk, one on the bedside table. One in the trash. If you buy something for twenty-four ninety-nine, you only get one."

The two men were quiet a moment, both thinking. "Which means he's bought more than one."

Hal nodded, scanning his mind for the kinds of things that cost twenty-five bucks and could be bought at a convenience store. There was no indication that MacDonald was buying clothes or hats. If what Telly said was true, he'd been watched all day, and there was no sign of him trying to hide his identity. Maybe he'd bought a pair of sunglasses, but three? And why not use a credit card? Who carried cash these days?

"Multiple purchases of the same thing," Telly added, scrolling back to the picture of the bathroom. "No sign of any medications . . ."

"Twenty-five bucks is some expensive medication, not likely over the counter," Hal said.

"Something he would need three of, in the course of two days," Telly added.

"Right," Hal agreed. "Something like . . ."

"A burner phone," the two men said simultaneously.

Hal started for the door. "We know where he is now?"

Telly eyed him.

"Do we know where he is?" Hal pressed.

"He's at dinner at a place called Sapphire, about two miles from here."

Hal glanced at his watch, still on California time. The face read 4:40 p.m. "When?"

"His reservation is at six thirty."

That was now. "Let's go." Hal opened the door and started down the hallway.

Telly followed. "What are you going to do?"

"Eat dinner. I'm ravenous," Hal added.

Telly's eyes narrowed. "You can't touch him, Hal."

"It's food, Telly. Aren't you hungry?"

The agent nodded, his expression reluctant. "I could eat," he said finally.

"Good," Hal said, slapping Telly on the shoulder. "I've got just the place."

"Is it Sapphire?" Telly asked.

"You guessed it." Hal felt almost hopeful.

15

Schwartzman must have drifted off again. She woke drowsy and parched. Her throat was raw, and her neck ached. She fingered the collar that had almost strangled her, wincing as she swallowed. She listened to the silence, stunned at the lack of any noise. No whirring machines, no cars—nothing but the occasional whisper of snow falling from a tree branch and the occasional purr of the baseboard heater.

The window was growing dark. Not yet night but closing in on it. This far north, the dark sky could mean 4:30 p.m. or 8:00 a.m. She longed for a way to measure time, for something to help her keep track of the lost hours. It was not the most important thing, she told herself. First, water.

She put her feet on the cold wood floor and dropped her head between her legs to stretch out her spine, careful to pull the cord down to give herself slack. The cord moved slowly through the track as though the mechanism were half-asleep.

At the window, she retrieved the cup of snow from the ledge. Stretching her fingers, she scooped the snow within reach, adding it to the cup before closing the window. The snowflakes that fell were light now, crisp and fine. She stared at the sky. She'd never lived where it snowed, but she was familiar with the drizzle of Seattle, and this felt like the equivalent. Like the snow could stop anytime.

Her breathing grew shallow, and she fought against growing panic.

Moving into the kitchen, she again peered out the small window. The clouds were thin and separated, exposing the blackness behind them. The sky felt too dark, like the world had been sucked up from all around her. It was so much blacker than in the city. No light pollution, which meant no one would hear her scream. No one to help.

You have to help yourself.

She turned on the small light on the old stove and glanced at the clock. The dial to change the time had been broken off, and the minute hand now lay between the five and the six at the base of the clock. But the hour hand appeared to be moving. At the moment, it sat between the two and the three.

Two thirty in the morning? It was possible, but she doubted the clock was right. Earlier, she'd noticed the hour hand between the ten and the eleven, though the sky felt like afternoon.

The best she could figure, the clock was behind by four or five hours, which meant that it was somewhere between 7:00 p.m. and 9:00 p.m. Or maybe it *was* 2:00 a.m. Perhaps someone had set the clock this way to mess with her, to make her feel more out of sorts. The room Spencer had designed in his house was like that—a room specifically to torment her. The video of her in Ava's garage, the images of the ultrasound, the pulsing noise of a beating heart.

This felt like Spencer's doing.

But then, where was he? Why hadn't he come for her? Why would Spencer allow Roy Butler access to her? And if Spencer knew Butler, did that mean Spencer had planted Butler in her morgue? Or had Spencer met Butler after he'd left the morgue? If Hal could connect them, if he learned that Butler was connected to Spencer somehow, it might help Hal find her.

84

It had been more than a year since Butler had disappeared from the morgue, but it felt like something Spencer might have orchestrated.

But how would Hal know that? What clue would possibly point him to Butler?

She had to fight the rising panic. *Focus on what you can control.*

She poured the melting snow into the cabin's only bowl and returned to the bedroom, dragging the cord along the track, and set the cup back on the ledge outside.

In the kitchen, she studied the bowl of snow as though she might make it melt faster. She could put it on the stove and warm it, but she didn't want to risk any evaporation. She needed every drop.

Working the cord loose from the track, she pulled a length and wrapped it around her hand to avoid being choked again. The burning in her throat still felt raw and tender. She forced her gaze away from the bowl. Watching it was maddening.

Instead, she thought of Hal. Was it dinnertime in San Francisco? Or the middle of the night? Was he there? Would he be staying in her house or at his own home? She closed her eyes and pictured Buster. She hoped they were together. Hal would make sure that someone was caring for the dog.

When the snow melted, it filled only a third of the bowl.

Not nearly enough to survive on.

She did her best not to drink the icy water in one long swallow. The snow was frustratingly light and fluffy, perfect for skiing but not useful when one needed water. And worse, it had stopped snowing. The sky out the kitchen window was black and cloudless, the constellations dancing behind the white fog of the Milky Way.

It reminded her of walking Buster to the park up the road from her house. She wondered if she'd see Buster again. Or the park.

Or Hal.

No. She would not think that. She turned her attention to the ceiling in search of something that would feel productive. She took slow, deep breaths and tried to make a plan.

She caught sight of the end cap on the track and recalled the sensation of being strangled. She was afraid to try again. The idea that someone could push a button and kill her with the collar was terrifying.

It was random. It had to be.

She refused to believe that someone was watching her every move. If that were true, they knew she wasn't drinking the milk or the orange juice, that she was trying to work out how they were drugging her. Even the melting snow wouldn't be a secret then.

"No," she said aloud. She rejected the idea that she'd made no progress, that they knew exactly what she had already learned from her environment.

Her fingers found the collar, tested its thickness, its bend. The locking mechanism was impossible to see, and she couldn't imagine finding a way to release it. The only option would be to cut through it. But there was nothing sharp enough.

Getting the cord off the track seemed like the best bet. But without any tools . . . Her thoughts circled around the limitations. She went back to the bathroom and studied the room from the doorway. Soap. Would it work to soap up the end cap? Maybe that would loosen it? She moved along the track into the bathroom and was pulling back the curtain when she heard the clinking of metal on metal.

The curtain rings. She stood on the edge of the tub and reached overhead to unfasten one of the metal loops that connected the shower curtain to the rod. Gripping it in her hand, she returned to the kitchen and teased the cord back through the tracks to the far side of the room, dragging a chair along with her.

Hope and fear warred in her chest as she climbed back up onto the chair. She held the cord under her arm, waiting for it to retract into the ceiling. Nothing happened. It was possible that everyone was asleep now, which meant maybe someone did control it.

Gathering her courage, she jammed the metal ring into the tiny gap between the end piece and track, but the ring was too thick. Next, she experimented with wedging the ring between the track and the ceiling to pry it loose.

Her fingers stung, her wrists cramped, and the metal ring bent and twisted. She turned it in her hand and tried the other side. Tried and tried until the ring was unusable.

She stepped down from the chair and pulled the cord loose, dropping to sit in the hard plastic.

She was never getting out of there.

Hal would never find her.

Roy would kill her.

Her pulse pounded in her throat. Tears streamed down her face. *I'm so tired, Hal.*

Fight, Anna, came his reply in her head.

16

Monday, 7:28 p.m. CST

Telly drove to Sapphire faster than Hal would have expected for a guy who had calmly spent hours studying paperwork at his desk. While Hal scanned for a parking spot on the street, Telly pulled up to the curb and put the car in park. The valet gave the Impala a distasteful look before taking the keys.

Telly glanced at the valet's name tag and pulled his wallet from his pocket, flipping it open to show his badge as he passed over the keys. "Please be careful with it, Damon. It's not much, but it belongs to the FBI. Something happens, I got to explain it. You know what I mean?"

The kid's expression shifted. His back straightened ever so slightly, and his gaze slid toward Hal, who nodded slowly.

"Yes, sir," Damon said, and Hal waited for Telly to catch up before pulling open the restaurant door and letting the agent enter first.

The hostess looked grim when Telly admitted they didn't have a reservation. Hal scanned the crowd. No sign of MacDonald. He also noticed that he was the only black man in the place. He wondered if, in Texas, his skin color might work against their getting a table. But the hostess offered them two seats at the bar. "Last spots in the house," she said.

"We'll take 'em," Hal responded without hesitation.

"May I take your coat?" she asked.

Telly wore only a blazer, but Hal had layered a windbreaker over his sports coat. "Yes, thank you."

Hal shrugged out of his jacket and watched as the hostess ducked behind a thick velvet curtain.

A coatroom.

She returned a moment later and handed Hal a small white ticket stub. As she lifted two menus from a stack and turned toward the bar, Hal put his phone to his ear and covered it with his free hand. "It's the wife. I'll be right behind you."

Telly gave him a look but said nothing, following the hostess across the room.

The moment the hostess turned her back, Hal ducked into the coat closet and slid his phone into his pocket. The room was dark and cramped. Two racks of coats hung on thick white plastic hangers, one row on each side. He scanned them as though he could intuit which belonged to MacDonald.

His pulse thumped against his throat. No guessing, he told himself. Just move. He dug in, starting with the coat closest to his right hand. Putting one hand on either side of the coat, he ran them top to bottom. His big hands stretched across the coat in two swipes. No lump, he moved on. Next coat. Something soft. Gloves, maybe. He didn't stop.

Some were clearly women's coats, but he was moving too quickly to distinguish. Halfway through them, he felt a hard rectangular shape in a black wool coat that turned out to be a box of Altoids mints. Damn it. He shoved the tin back into the pocket and kept going. The closer he got to the end of the coats, the more desperate he felt. *Come on, MacDonald. Fuck up. Fuck up so I can find Anna.*

His heart pounded as he passed his own jacket, counted six more. Pat, slide left, pat, slide right. As he reached the last coat, he sensed motion behind him. He reached back, fingers finding his wallet in his pants pocket.

The hostess stood in the open curtain. Her eyes narrowed, her mouth an unattractive line.

Hal smiled widely and held up his wallet. "Was going to be hard to have dinner without this." He nodded toward the room. "No reason my friend should have to foot the bill, right?"

Her lips turned into an uneasy smile, although her eyes remained flat and accusatory, pretending to believe him but not quite. He reached past her and pulled back the curtain, pocketing his wallet as he waved into the room. "After you."

She stepped out of the closet, and he followed, reaching out to palm the last coat. Nothing.

If MacDonald was carrying an extra phone, he had it on him.

Hal settled into the chair beside Telly and scanned the room. There was still no sign of Spencer MacDonald.

"He's behind that wall," Telly said, reading his mind. "Can't see him from here."

Hal shifted his bar chair so he'd see when MacDonald walked by. Then he lifted the menu and tried to decide what to eat.

The two men ordered twenty-five-dollar hamburgers and a fifteen-dollar order of truffle fries to split. They ate in near silence. Telly watched a couple of women at the far end of the bar while Hal kept an eye on the wall where MacDonald was.

"You can't approach him," Telly said again as Hal chewed another bite of burger. He had to admit it was pretty good. Texas knew its beef.

"You mentioned that," Hal said, reaching for more of the truffle fries. He liked regular fries better.

He was eating slowly. No way was he going to finish his meal before MacDonald did. He had just taken another bite of burger—three bucks' worth, maybe—when Spencer MacDonald emerged from behind the wall, heading across the restaurant. Beside him was an elderly woman, her hand on his arm. For a moment, Hal wondered if it was a relative, but then he saw the stones on her necklace, the rock on her left hand. More likely a client.

Hal set his napkin beside his plate. "I've got to use the bathroom." He didn't wait for a response from Telly. Instead, Hal strode across the room, aimed directly for Spencer MacDonald. Telly called something out to him, but Hal didn't hear and didn't turn back.

MacDonald might have heard Telly. At that moment, MacDonald turned his head. Hal was maybe three feet away. MacDonald flinched, his shoulders drawing up around his ears. His feet tripped over themselves as he backed away, looking like he might knock his dinner companion over to escape Hal's path. "What—"

Hal grinned his biggest, dopiest grin and grabbed MacDonald's elbow, playing it up. All around them, conversation slowed and quieted, and heads turned. Hal jerked MacDonald toward him, smiling all the while, and clasped his right hand. "Goddamn, man. It is great to see you."

MacDonald's mouth dropped open, incapable of speech.

"How are you enjoying Dallas? Beautiful, ain't it?"

MacDonald's eyes narrowed.

But Hal pumped MacDonald's hand, resisting the urge to clamp down on the fingers like a vise and break them. As he let go, he brushed his arm across MacDonald's blazer. Against his forearm, he felt the lump of a phone in MacDonald's breast pocket. One phone.

"What are you doing?" MacDonald hissed, reaching into his pocket to pull out the phone.

Hal brushed his hands across MacDonald's shoulders. "I love this jacket, man." He turned to the old woman. "He looks sharp, doesn't he? I mean, wow, right?" He whistled.

The woman shuffled away, trembling slightly as her mouth stitched itself into a distasteful scowl.

Hal swiped his palms across the bottom of MacDonald's blazer, pretending to straighten it. Feeling the pockets in the process. Empty. "You are looking very sharp." Hal was still grinning.

"Let go of me," MacDonald snapped, raising his phone toward Hal.

Hal grinned into the camera, certain he was being recorded. He gave MacDonald a light slap on the shoulder, all smiles, and nodded at the old woman. "I just wanted to say hello," Hal said as he squeezed between MacDonald and the woman, allowing his hand to graze past the backside of MacDonald's pants. One pocket had contents. The right side. His wallet, surely. Nothing else. No second phone.

Without another word, Hal glided away and strode toward the bathroom.

Inside, he checked that he was alone and drew slow, even breaths, struggling to release his rage. His hands twitched with the need to strike something. Instead, he washed them thoroughly, using too much soap, then patted water on his face. After a few minutes, he exited the bathroom and returned to the main dining room. There was no sign of MacDonald or his dinner guest. As Hal walked back to the bar, he pulled out his phone.

Telly stared at him wide-eyed.

Hal punched his contacts list and dialed MacDonald's number that he'd gotten from the file. A moment later, the familiar voice answered.

"Great to see you, Spencer," Hal said.

"I don't know what you think you're doing," Spencer MacDonald hissed. "But you can't assault me in public and get away with it."

Hal lowered his voice, the sharp edge finally bared. "I think you're confused, Spencer."

"I am not," MacDonald snapped.

"But you are. Believe me, you'll know it when I assault you." Hal ended the call and set the phone on the bar. Some of the guests glanced in his direction, and the two women at the far end of the bar sat huddled across their table, clearly talking about him. Hal turned back to his plate and reached for a handful of truffle fries, shoving them into his mouth. He decided he hated truffle fries.

"You want to tell me what that was about?" Telly asked.

Hal swallowed. "I was checking to see if he had a burner phone on him," Hal said. "But he only had one phone, and it was his regular line. No burner."

He turned back to face the bar, the adrenaline draining out of him as frustration mounted again.

He told himself he'd rattled MacDonald. That had to count for something. If only it made him feel better.

17

Spencer was not a man who did public confrontation. After the interaction with Harris in the restaurant, Spencer had attended to his octogenarian client, helping her find her coat and ushering her out of the restaurant.

She had moved at a glacial pace, which had made him feel antsy and slightly sick to his stomach. In hindsight, he was grateful for how slow she was. He'd been richly rewarded for those extra minutes.

The restaurant manager had seen the interaction with Harris and had come outside to make sure they were all right. The owner, too, emerged from the kitchen, and then a senior attorney with the DA's office who had been dining with his wife and daughter joined them. All eyes were on his client, but it was Spencer's hand the men shook.

"Did you know that man?" They asked his client about Harris.

"No," she replied, her hand pressed to her bosom as though ready to swoon.

When they asked him, Spencer didn't mention the interview with Hal earlier in the day. "I think he's a police officer from California somewhere. The other guy is local. FBI, maybe."

The men spoke among themselves, the assistant district attorney promising to make phone calls. And then Spencer put his client in her Town Car with her driver and sent her on her way.

Spencer parked himself in his rental car and waited. Staring into the dark night, Spencer dreamed of all the ways he could drive Hal Harris insane.

There were so many.

He felt suddenly more alive than he had since his visit to Mistress Keres.

Torture was a game at which he was particularly good. Not physical torture. That always struck him as rather banal. Plus, Hal Harris was a beast. Bodily harm would be too expected. A goon like Harris had probably been in his share of fights. Men that size always brought out the Neanderthal in other, smaller men. As though beating up a man like Harris would prove something.

Not Spencer. But he did want to hurt him. Oh, so much.

The interaction with Harris inside the restaurant had rattled him. After his mother's service that morning, inside his father's church, the effect had been magnified. He was suddenly thrown back to the days after Bella first left him—raw and unsure. He was not himself.

Nineteen months had passed since he'd been released from prison. Every day since that one, he had climbed steadily toward this next step. Every step was an ascent, and he was so close.

But then Bryce Scala had appeared at his door with those letters and a plan to throw his mother a memorial service. Did Scala know how Spencer had killed her? Could he possibly have proof, proof that he would bring to the police, and some Neanderthal like Harris would show up to put him back in prison? It was almost as if God was punishing him. Or that was what Spencer would have thought if he believed in God.

He did believe in Hell, though. And he was certain his father was there, watching over his shoulder as he let Scala into his living room, laughing at this latest twist in his son's fate. Imagining his father's thin-lipped smile, the right side of his mouth twisted upward in a sort of snarl, filled him with rage.

He had felt so much rage that he'd felt unable to guide himself through the most basic of tasks—dressing, meals. He was supposed to go to the office, but he was too raw, too close to breaking.

Instead, he'd headed to the home of Mistress Keres, thinking that seeing her might be enough. All those months of letting her dominate him, he'd shown supreme control over his anger, but he had known his control would not last. So he had allowed himself to let go.

It had been a lot to manage with the cleanup and body disposal. But he was a clever man, and she was not a large person. Afterward, he could think clearly again. With a calm mind, he convinced himself he could sit in that church and listen to Scala heap praise on a woman who'd never even loved her own child.

Scala had asked Spencer if he wanted to participate in the ceremony, give some sort of eulogy for his parents. "I'm afraid I'd be too emotional," he'd told Scala, working up a frog in his throat.

Yes, he'd thought the visit to Florida was the long-awaited closure to his parents' hold on him. He could surely handle a two-hour memorial.

Even inside his father's church.

But he'd underestimated how that place could bring him to his knees. He was a child there—lowly and awkward and hated. Even as an adult. Even as a powerful man, he'd felt himself curl in against the very air. The smells lashed out at him like tiny barbs—wax, fire, the dust on the tapestries that hung high on the stone walls, depicting scenes of Jesus's torment.

It was as though his father stood beside him, the man's long pencil-like fingers pressing into Spencer's young shoulder as he whispered about the power of Jesus's suffering. "It is suffering that builds men," he would say, blowing his stale breath. "Suffering that tears them down. Will you not rise to be something?"

Over and over again. The tone of his father's voice changed over his childhood until Spencer's defeat was as set in stone as the Ten Commandments.

And it was as though Bryce Scala knew exactly how his parents had felt about him. Scala barely mentioned Spencer in the eulogy, focusing instead on his mother's love of God and of her God-worshipping husband.

He thought again of his mother's letters, how she had heaped the blame on Spencer. A child. Not once did she write about the influence of his father or his use of religion to repress and control his son.

Spencer kept his gaze on the bright blue Sapphire sign above the door, waiting for Hal Harris to emerge. He touched the back of his hand to his temple, surprised to feel sweat on his skin. Starting the car engine, he turned the air on high. It was truly in the past now. Ten days from now, he would be in Thessaly, Greece, where no one would ever disturb his household again. He would have Bella. *His* wife. *His* life. He had only to finish off these investor visits and return to Greenville to empty his safe deposit box, something he'd planned to do before Scala's visit derailed him. It didn't matter, he reminded himself. But the fact that he had forgotten something so important made him question his fortitude. He would have to be strong until they were settled in Greece.

He rolled the car window down a few inches and let the cool night air blow in before shutting the engine off again.

In the rearview mirror, he confirmed that the Uber was parked behind him. Now it was just a waiting game. It took longer than he'd expected, but a little after nine, Hal Harris and the FBI agent stepped out of the restaurant and into the night air. Spencer gripped his phone in his right hand, aimed it out the window.

Spencer's estimate had been almost dead-on. It took Harris about six seconds to see him. As soon as their eyes met, Spencer put his hand outside the car and patted the driver's door to give the sign. Behind him, the Uber's car came to life.

Without a sideways glance, Harris strode toward him. The Uber driver pulled into the street, accelerating smoothly as Harris stepped off the curb. Harris glanced at the car, hardly noticing it until it was within feet of him. The driver handled it perfectly, easing toward Hal foot by foot.

When the Uber was three or four feet away, Hal halted, turned to the driver, and raised his hands. "Hello," he shouted at the driver.

The car continued forward at a snail's pace.

"It's like he doesn't even see you," Spencer said. "It's like you're the invisible man."

Hal's gaze focused like a laser on Spencer, who gave him a wide grin. Hal stared at Spencer as the Uber continued to ease forward. The car stopped just inches from Hal, who jumped as though he'd been hit, his expression filled with surprise and rage.

Spencer let out a loud, bark-like laugh. Being confronted by Harris inside the restaurant had startled him. Just the sheer size of the man coming at him was momentarily terrifying. He'd been overcome by a desire to run. Like a child.

In the end, the others assumed that his response to Hal Harris had been exactly appropriate. They'd seen him look bewildered and a bit startled, and they'd felt anger on his behalf. Harris had acted frenetic, his energy that of a man on drugs.

Hal turned back to the Uber and raised both hands. "What the hell are you doing?"

The Uber started filming Hal through the windshield, motioning to Hal as though to usher him out of the way.

Hal slapped the hood of the car.

A gasp from several patrons echoed outside the restaurant.

Spencer said nothing but also continued to film. The Uber driver stepped out of his car. Then Harris's FBI buddy was in the street, too, trying to pull Hal away from the car. Hal strained against the FBI agent's hold, shouting back at Spencer. "You're not going to get away with this, MacDonald."

Spencer laughed again, making sure the sound carried. "I have no idea what you're talking about. Absolutely no idea."

After Harris and the agent had left, Spencer paid the Uber driver the negotiated fee. Six hundred dollars had seemed steep, but as he reviewed the footage of Harris, it was worth every cent.

Still parked on the street, he watched and rewatched the videos of Hal Harris—his own and the one the Uber driver had sent him. The anger on the man's face barely covered the terror there. Pain.

Spencer froze the screen and studied the creases etched in the inspector's forehead, the downward curve of his lips. The way his eyes flashed wide and his nose flared in anguish as he turned to look at Spencer. Hal Harris looked like a man on the edge.

He imagined showing the footage to Bella.

Yes. This would work very well.

Satisfied, Spencer pulled away from the curb and headed toward his hotel. Soon he would be in Denver, one step closer to Bella.

18

Schwartzman dreamed of water. Tall glasses of it that lined a crystal lake, a waterfall. Inside her head, she heard the gurgling sound of a brook. When she opened her eyes, her head ached, her throat lined in sand. Outside, the sky was an explosion of tiny white lights on black. Not a cloud. Forcing herself from bed, she went to the window and stared out at the darkness. Some of the stars she saw were dead now, but their light still traveled toward Earth. What would happen if she died? Where would her light go?

A single star dropped through the night sky, scoring the sky with a thin white line. She closed her eyes and made a wish. *Help me get home safely.* Home. San Francisco was home. Hal was home. Never had she felt that more clearly than these past days.

She retrieved the cup from the outside ledge. In it was an inch or two of snow. It would melt into an ounce of water. Maybe. And there was no indication that it would snow again anytime soon.

You have to think of another way.

She carried the glass to the kitchen, dizzy and exhausted. Setting the glass on the table, she sank into the flimsy plastic chair, pulled the cord loose, and laid her head on her hands. Her thoughts reverted to

Zhanna Doe. They'd found evidence that Doe had had an abortion, but she also had a Pfannenstiel incision scar. It looked like a C-section scar, which could imply that she'd given birth. The tricky thing about those types of scars was that they could also be from an open oophorectomy, a hysterectomy, which Doe hadn't had, or some other low pelvic procedure. In many other countries, a midline incision, not a Pfannenstiel incision, was used for a C-section, so the scar itself was not enough to say whether Doe had had a child. Still, it made Schwartzman wonder. Was it possible that Zhanna Doe had a child who was still alive somewhere?

Closing her eyes, Schwartzman thought she'd do anything to protect her baby. What if Roy kept her here for months? It wouldn't be long before the pregnancy showed, especially as she lost weight. If Roy did rape her, then he might believe the baby was his, at least for a while. Would being raped somehow keep the baby safe?

No. It was unthinkable. It felt like giving up, and she was not ready to give up. There had to be a way out of here before it came to that.

She swirled the cup, the snow melted enough to drink. She raised it to her lips and tipped it into her mouth as though it were a shot. The water stung her dry throat and barely wet her mouth. Holding the empty glass, she imagined the baby inside her growing desiccated.

Numbers from medical school streamed across her mind like ticker tape. An average adult was 60 percent water. A human baby was 75 percent water. Amniotic fluid 98 percent. The heart and brain 73 percent.

A lack of water would kill the baby. Kill them both, for that matter. The effects of the drug were less known but likely less dangerous. The drug wasn't lethal to her or the baby—at least not immediately. She glanced at the kitchen sink. Drugged. The bathroom sink, too. But the shower?

There was only one way to find out for sure. On her feet, she dragged the clip along the track to the bathroom and turned on the shower. There, she filled the cup, drinking it down quickly and refilling it again. She drank three glasses, filling her belly until it was uncomfortable.

Then she left the glass on the sink and returned to her bed, waiting for the drug to affect her.

Her heartbeat was erratic. Her eyelids heavy. Was that the drug or the effects of adrenaline and fear? Questions bounced about her head—how she would continue if the only option for water was from a drugged source. What she would do. Lying awake, her throat burned as though by some invisible poison.

At some point, she fell asleep and dreamed of a young man with large blue eyes and a gentle raspy voice with a lisp. His hands felt a little moist, the fingers thick and short against her own.

"Come on out of there, Roy," a woman said to him, her voice tired but kind.

Schwartzman jerked awake, flinching at the sensation of being touched. The room was empty, the sky outside light. She went back through her thoughts, trying to determine what made her feel as though she had been touched. It was just a dream, she told herself. A nightmare. The shower water was drugged, and the dream was a side effect.

But was it only a dream?

If the drug was a benzodiazepine, it shouldn't have been strong enough to sedate her through a physical assault. She squeezed her eyes closed and focused on her body, finding nothing unusual. And yet, it was there, the vague sense of fingers on her face.

Roy.

She pitched her head over the side of the bed and vomited on the floor. Then, wiping her hand across the sleeve of her hoodie, she began to undress. Her fingers fumbled with the zipper. Everything here had buttons or zippers—the shirt, the hoodie, a pair of men's small plaid pajamas, a new addition to the stack of clothes. With the collar, nothing could go over her head.

Someone had thought through the details. She felt another wave of nausea and paused to lean over the bed again. But she didn't throw up.

Stripped down, she examined her skin, studying it in small quadrants the way she would a victim's in the morgue. Her gaze froze momentarily on the faded handwritten numbers on her arm before she yanked her sleeve down and kept looking. As much as she pulled and twisted, the only imprints she found on her skin were consistent with the folds of her clothing.

She re-dressed more slowly, trying to calm herself.

The dream had left her unnerved, but she couldn't say why. The Roy in her dreams was gentle and sweet and nothing like the man in the van. She smelled something unfamiliar, a mixture of soap and dirt. Except for the pajamas someone had added to the stack of clothes, the room appeared the same, the glass empty on the bedside table.

Stepping carefully, she made her way into the bathroom and returned with tissue to clean up the floor. Pulling out the cord, she bent slowly. Something shiny under the bed caught her eye. She reached out, and her fingers touched hard metal. She lifted it and sat back, one hand keeping hold of the cord.

In her hand was a gold-toned key, like the kind that might fit a front door. She turned it over in her hand. Had someone dropped it? Or was it some sort of test?

But what kind of test would it be? The key was no good if she couldn't reach the door. She needed a way out of the collar, and the key was clearly not to the collar. If it even had a key, it was some tiny thing, the size of a bobby pin. She wished she had something like that. She didn't even own a bobby pin.

She set the key aside and cleaned up the mess on the floor. Outside, the sky was growing lighter. She collected the toilet paper and took it into the bathroom.

When she returned to the bedroom, she reached down for the key and held it in her palm. First, she needed a way out of the collar. Then she could use the key.

She looked around the room for a place to hide it. She had no idea what they did in that room when they came. Who came or where they looked, what they touched. The idea made her feel another wave of nausea. *They don't touch me.* So she would keep the key close.

Back on the bed, she pulled off the corner of the sheet and the mattress pad and found a buttonhole in the corner of the mattress. There, she worked the key under the button until all but the top of it was hidden. Carefully, she replaced the mattress pad and the sheet, laying her pillow on top of the bump.

The key wasn't much.

But it felt like something.

19

Wednesday, 9:10 a.m. CST

Now that he was a persona non grata in Dallas, Hal was grateful they were heading to Denver. After the encounter in the restaurant Monday night, Telly's SAC had gotten phone calls from three different sources complaining about Hal. It turned out that Sapphire was the spot where very powerful people ate, including several members of city and state government. Not to mention that MacDonald's client was heir to a crane-and-freight-elevator fortune. The irony didn't escape Hal—another reason to hate elevators.

At least Telly had convinced his SAC not to pass the complaints on to Captain Marshall in San Francisco, but that was only if Hal managed to fly completely under the radar for the remainder of his time in Dallas. Which meant Hal was hamstrung. Even Telly wasn't to go anywhere near Spencer MacDonald, and all detail had been pulled off him. Despite his SAC's warning, Telly had managed to get a couple of agents to tail him at a distance. It turned out, even in his short time at the bureau, Telly had earned some favors.

While two agents tracked Spencer MacDonald at a considerable distance, Hal and Telly locked themselves in a conference room and pulled data—lists of known associates of MacDonald's. Not an easy task in any situation but made more difficult for several reasons. One, as best as they could tell, the only person MacDonald knew in Dallas was the older woman he'd been at dinner with. The second challenge was the nearly impenetrable shield MacDonald had from the folks in Greenville. The police department was strangely protective of a guy who'd been to prison.

Telly had been able to gain the assistance of a single FBI agent in Greenville. While she was both efficient and competent, the agent worked on her own. Originally from northern Virginia, she was an outsider to the folks in Greenville. Her every attempt to gain information had been thwarted, and though she'd tried to obtain warrants, there wasn't a judge in town who would give her access to MacDonald's dealings.

It didn't help that the mayor of Greenville was a client of MacDonald's and did not take kindly to insinuations of MacDonald's guilt. Tuesday evening, Hal put in a call to Harper, but as of 10:00 a.m. Wednesday, he hadn't heard back. He'd left a message for the PI Anna had hired, Colton Price, but that one, too, had gone unanswered.

While Hal focused on MacDonald, Telly put together a comprehensive list of cases Schwartzman had worked since her first days in Seattle through her time in San Francisco. A data team would sift through the lists and see if anything stood out. Hal couldn't help but feel like reading through her cases was a waste of time.

But he knew what it took to run a successful investigation. Throw the net wide, cover everything, and then reel it in carefully so you don't lose anything.

Midmorning, Telly and Hal sat in on a briefing from the pair of agents who'd been watching MacDonald for the past two days. A couple of old guys, heavy and barrel-chested, they were similarly rounded with fleshy noses and full lips—a sort of strange twin phenomena. But one was bald and tall, the fingers on his right hand yellowed from smoking. The other had fiery red hair and a row of tiny pointed teeth that reminded Hal of a mouse. The mouse stood about six inches shorter than his partner.

In the conference room, the two men struggled to work the projector, bumping around each other like Tweedledee and Tweedledum. Once they sorted out the technical difficulties, they presented Telly and Hal with a ten-minute slideshow filled with images of the back of Spencer MacDonald's head in front of one building or another. The two men didn't look capable of catching the old woman MacDonald had dined with, let alone MacDonald.

After they left, Telly went back through the photographs, sitting on the edge of the conference table a few inches away from the projector screen, studying the images. Hal wondered if his mother had warned him about sitting too close to the television.

No one seemed able to find a single hair out of place on that bastard's head. And yet somehow, MacDonald had managed to steal Anna right from under Hal's nose. Again the blame came around to strike him squarely in the face.

But MacDonald had pulled stunts like this before. He had successfully seduced a woman into killing for him. He'd managed to get access to Anna's medical records. He'd killed two women and escaped prosecution.

MacDonald would not get away with this. Hal would not allow it.

He sank into a chair and dropped his head in his hands. *Where is he holding you?* He refused to believe she wasn't alive. MacDonald was too obsessed with her. At least there was that.

MacDonald was getting on a plane late that afternoon, heading to Denver. Hal was going, too. And Telly. The FBI had promised the San Francisco Police Department that they'd provide resources until she was found, and Hal was going to hold them to it.

MacDonald would be in Denver for two days before he moved on to Detroit, then Cleveland, Richmond, and finally back to South Carolina. Hal would follow him to every destination. He would walk on MacDonald's heels, breathe down his neck until MacDonald took him to Anna.

Because the thing Spencer MacDonald wanted most was Anna herself. Maybe he also wanted to punish her, but he wanted her to pledge herself to him, to beg for her life, to profess that she couldn't live without him.

MacDonald wouldn't be able to stay away from her, not forever.

And when he went to her, Hal would be there.

If Hal couldn't find her before MacDonald went home, Hal would go there, too.

Could he be holding Anna in South Carolina?

Hal kept coming back to the question of how he had transported her. Human trafficking was rampant on the freeway system. At that moment, she might be in the trailer of an eighteen-wheeler, a thousand miles away. She might be even closer.

Or she might be headed to Alaska.

Or to Peru.

Hal sprang from his chair. "I can't sit here. I've got to move."

Telly nodded without looking up. "I'm going to stay here and finish reviewing these. Flight's at five, so we'll leave for the airport about two thirty." Telly glanced at him. "Meet you back here?"

"Sure," Hal said.

"Hey, Harris."

Hal stopped and looked back.

Telly was still focused on the report. "We're making progress."

Hal left the conference room.

People glanced up as he passed, but fewer paid attention to him now than they had Monday. Now he was a familiar face. He didn't want to be a familiar face. He wanted them to look at him, to focus on why he was there. As soon as he lost his newness, the search for Anna would, too. And with that came a loss of focus and energy.

He strode down the hall, letting his rage out in the speed of his walk. In the empty elevator bank, he smacked the down button hard enough to feel the sting in his palm. He stood in the center of the elevator and hardly noticed the descent. He would not give in to his fear.

Not his fear of elevators.

Not. Any. Fear.

He shoved open the glass door and walked into the Dallas air. The cold wind whipped across his face, clogging his throat and pressing on his chest. He shivered in his light jacket, yearning to turn back inside. Instead, he charged forward, taking the steps to the street by twos and turning randomly in one direction. He started to walk.

His phone buzzed in his pocket, and he pulled it out without slowing. Hailey's number. He halted and fumbled to swipe the screen. "Hailey?"

"Has Marshall called you?"

He froze, his feet rooted to the pavement. The fear almost doubled him over. "What's happened?"

"There's a new case."

He could hardly breathe. A case meant a murder. What was she saying? He choked the word out. "Anna?"

"No," she said hurriedly. "No. It's not Anna."

Something shifted in his chest, enabling him to draw a shallow, uneasy breath. "Does it have anything to do with Anna?"

"No. It's nothing about her."

He didn't care about any case that didn't involve Anna. Why would he?

"There was a double homicide in Union Square."

Hal could only imagine the public outcry. Union Square sat right in the downtown shopping district, a stone's throw from Neiman Marcus and Tiffany. The city erected its hundred-plus-foot Christmas tree there. San Francisco worked hard to keep the area aesthetically pleasing for tourists, not an easy task considering the number of homeless people who slept on the square.

"You still there?" she asked.

"Yeah."

"Homicide is short-staffed. Marshall requested I come back from the task force to work it. Kong is managing their other cases on his own."

Hailey had been working the past year and a half on a domestic abuse joint task force. Kong and O'Shea were normally a team. "Where's O'Shea?"

"Called back to Boston. His mom was diagnosed with stage-four liver cancer. They don't think she'll make it through the month."

Hal searched for something to say. He felt for O'Shea. He would also trade O'Shea's mother for Anna, no question. He closed his eyes and rubbed his head. He was a terrible human being for even thinking the thought. "You okay with that?" he asked. "Working the case, I mean?"

"Sure. I want to help."

Anna's name went unmentioned, but she was there, at the center of the conversation. "Have you heard anything?" he asked.

A silence.

"Hailey," he barked, fear taking hold again.

"No. There hasn't been any word here."

The words sank in like a slow, steady burn. No word. He read it to mean that no one was working her case. What about Roger? What about all the volunteers who had gone door-to-door? But he couldn't bring himself to ask. He shook his arms to free himself from the cold and began to walk again.

When Hailey spoke, her voice was soft, delicate. "Are you and she—"

At Anna's house the other night, Hailey hadn't asked. Hal and Hailey had an awkward history around discussing their relationships.

He hadn't been a fan of her husband, John, who had been killed almost five years earlier. For her part, Hailey hated his ex-wife, Sheila. They had each let their feelings known, and as a result, a divide had grown between them.

Since her husband's death and his divorce, they had managed to close the distance. She was still a close friend, though her new role in the task force meant he saw less of her.

"It's none of my business," she said.

He thought about the baby, his baby. He wanted to tell her. He wanted to celebrate the news with his old partner. When he'd spent time with her two daughters over the years, she'd always said he'd make a great dad. And now he was. Or he might be. He would have to tell her. Eventually. Either way. He squeezed his eyes closed and prayed he would be able to share the joy of holding his own child. Finally, he said, "Yes."

The line fell silent briefly. "Yes, it's none of my business?"

"We are together."

"Hal," she said, her voice a long, sympathetic whisper.

He imagined all the things she could say. She had lost her husband, her children's father. She knew about grief and fear. But he prayed she'd say nothing. He didn't want to talk about John's death. He didn't want to talk about death at all.

"Listen, I should get back," he said.

"Uh, Hal?"

"What?"

"Marshall's calling you back," she said. "We need you on this case."

"I'm on leave," he said. "I'm not coming back until I find her."

Marshall's voice boomed in the background. "Is that Harris?"

"I don't—"

Hal was interrupted by his captain's voice. "I need you back here."

"Captain, I can't."

"I need you back here now."

Hal gritted his teeth. "I'm not coming back to work."

"The hell you aren't," Marshall snapped. "I'm not asking you."

"Captain, I can't come back now, not without An—"

"The FBI is working on locating Dr. Schwartzman," Marshall said, cutting him off. "They've assured me that they're pursuing every angle. You don't work for the FBI, Inspector. You work for me. And I need you here. Tonight."

"Tonight? There's no—"

"Tomorrow morning, then, Harris."

Hal drew a breath. He was light-headed and nauseated. How many days could he go without sleep? What had he eaten today? He shook his head to clear the cobwebs. "Captain, I don't think you understand."

"No, Harris," Marshall growled. "I don't think you understand. We're all worried about Dr. Schwartzman, but I've got a department to run. And I've got the mayor on my ass, and I'm not going to tell him one of my best inspectors is chasing a runaway medical examiner."

Hal flinched. "She did not run away."

"It's not your case."

Hal shook his head, trying to come up with another way to explain to his captain that he wasn't coming back. He couldn't. He clamped his mouth shut, walking faster. What choice did he have? He could insist on taking his vacation time, but with O'Shea out, Marshall wasn't going to approve it.

Which left . . . what? Was he going to quit his job? He'd quit in a second if quitting would bring Anna home. But if he was no longer working for the department, he wouldn't have access to the resources he needed to find her. He wouldn't be able to work with Telly. He wouldn't be able to track MacDonald or run background reports on the people around him.

"This double homicide," Marshall said. "This case is yours and Wyatt's."

Damn it. A double homicide, with all the extra attention from the press and the city, would bury him in work. Every waking hour would be occupied, stretched to its limit.

"I need that case solved," Marshall went on. "And you two are what I've got available for the job. I'll expect to see you tomorrow by noon. We'll get you caught up then."

With that, Marshall ended the call.

Hal stared down at his phone and slowed his pace. Go back to San Francisco or lose his job. He had no choice. He needed access to law enforcement to find her.

Hal closed his palm around the phone and squeezed until he thought it might snap in his hand. Replacing the phone in his pocket, he turned around and started back to the bureau to inform Telly that the agent would have to go to Denver on his own.

20

Outside, the sky was a deep magenta. Fat cumulus clouds marked the sky, their undersides reflecting the light. Looking out the window, Schwartzman would have sworn the view was fake, like a painting of heaven. But this was no heaven. And the pink sky meant no snow. Which meant no water.

Her fingers found the key hidden back in the mattress. She had tried for hours the night before to cut the collar with the rough edge, but she'd barely made a dent. Her arms and neck were stiff and sore from the effort.

She would have to drink again today. Already, she felt light-headed. Her lips were cracked in the corners, and a hint of metal floated in her mouth from the blood that seeped from the small cuts. Roy had drugged the water in the shower as well. Which left her . . . what? Toilet water?

She thought about the yellowed inside of that bowl. If she contracted a parasite, it could be harmful to the fetus—potentially more harmful than whatever sedative they were using to drug her. Plus, there was no guarantee that the water that ran to the toilet wasn't also drugged. If that was the case, she risked the drug *and* whatever parasites were in the toilet water, and the combination could cause her to terminate the pregnancy.

No. She wasn't willing to take that chance.

Despite her thirst and the accompanying dizziness, her thoughts felt clear. Before she could drink, she had to work on an escape. Once she gave in to the thirst, the drugs would make her sleep.

She gave herself one hour to find water or a way to cut herself out of the collar. One hour.

Out of bed, she heard the click of the baseboard heater go on. The main room had a forced air vent. The bedroom was the only room with a baseboard heater, which meant the room may have been added after the original structure. It was the second time she'd heard the heater click on in the last ten or twelve hours. The temperature was dropping. If she were to get free, she'd have to have a plan for finding shelter, too.

Again she considered how she might cut through the collar. She listened to the rustling sounds of the hot air and wondered about the heater. Rising from the bed, Schwartzman dragged the cord to the farthest wall of the bedroom, below the window. Pulling out sufficient slack to allow her to sit on the floor, she got on her knees beside the baseboard heater and tucked a length of cord under her leg. She tested the metal housing, not yet hot to the touch.

She opened a corner flap to display the controls and turned the dial to "Off." The control cover was a piece of plastic, worthless for her purposes. But the heater itself was metal. She pried off the bracket at the end of the heating unit. She sawed its edge against the fabric of the sweatpants, but it was too smooth to cut. She thought about trying to wedge the bracket up under the ceiling track to pry it loose, but the bracket didn't seem strong enough. Setting it on the floor, she pressed down on it.

It bent with the slightest pressure. If the shower curtain ring didn't work to bring down the track, the bracket certainly wouldn't.

Setting the bent metal aside, she returned to the unit itself. The top of the heater was mounted to the wall. Below it, the small metal slats of the vent ran perpendicular to the unit, hundreds of them. She fingered them, testing again for their ability to cut. With her fingers wedged between two, she tried to pull one loose, but the slats were too close together, too firmly in place. Removing one would require pliers. Moving lower, she ran her hands across the slat that stretched along the length of the unit. By wrapping her fingers underneath, she was able to loosen the cover.

With a little work, it came free. A three-foot-long piece of flat metal. The bottom was curved to fit under the unit, but the top was straight-edged and thin. She rubbed her elbow along the top and felt the metal through the fabric of the hoodie. It might be sharp enough to cut. She stood slowly, careful as the slack of her cord retreated into the ceiling mount.

Setting the cover on the bed, she lowered her neck to the straight-edge. Shifting her torso left and right, she searched for an angle that would enable her to use the sharp edge to cut the collar. No matter how she turned, her chin was in the way. Twice, she sliced the skin along her jaw before the edge reached the collar.

Frustrated and winded, she sat back on her heels. It was the most activity she'd had since she'd been abducted. Her arms and shoulders ached. Catching her breath, she stared at the metal, thinking it through. *Come on. There has to be a way.* She tried several more times without success. The length of the metal made it too unwieldy to hold and impossible to maneuver, especially so close to her face.

The metal was too large, too solid not to work for some purpose. She thought she might bend it, break it into something smaller, but she had another idea first. With her cord gathered in one hand and the metal in the other, she climbed up onto the bed and studied the track. Maneuvering the metal slat beneath it would require both hands. She swallowed against the fresh terror of strangulation.

With no choice, she slowly released the cord until it ran in a straight line to the ceiling cleat. Then she lifted the metal cover. On her first try, the slat was too close to the track, the angle wrong. She pulled out slack in the cord and backed to the head of the bed, kicking the pillow to the other end and standing with her back against the wall. There, she released the cord again. The tautness of the collar against the back of her neck brought a wave of nausea. Drawing slow breaths, she raised the metal cover and tried to work the thin straightedge under the track on the ceiling.

The work was slow and awkward. The curved bottom of the metal meant she had to hold it by one corner to try to get the metal into the narrow slot between the track and the ceiling. Outside, the pink sky had faded to a bluish purple as the sun rose over the horizon. Her hour was almost up. She tried not to think about her thirst, which felt overwhelming and oppressive.

Covering her hand with the sleeve of the hoodie, she used the heel of her hand to hammer the metal corner under the track. But she managed to wedge only an inch or so of the slat's corner successfully between the ceiling and the track. When she twisted the slat to try to pry the track from the ceiling, the slat corner bent immediately, the metal as soft and malleable as the corner bracket piece had been.

She created slack in the cord and lowered herself to the bed. Exhausted, she lay back and closed her eyes. There had to be a way to use the metal to help. As a weapon? She supposed she could swing it at someone, but it would take both hands, which meant letting go of the cord and risking strangulation. And even then, the slat was hardly heavy enough to do much damage.

Standing from the bed, she turned back to the heater. Through the window, the sky was a brilliant blue, all the traces of pink bleached away. She glanced down at the way the light hit the snow on the ground, making it sparkle like diamonds. All that water. So close.

But maybe . . .

She opened the window, shivering as the frost bit her face. She studied the snow piled against the outside of the house, maybe four feet below the window. She lifted the slat and stared at the one bent corner. Pressing it against the floor, she bent the other side until the two corners were almost touching. Like a scoop. Checking the slack on her cord, she eased the slat out the window and lowered it slowly until the metal hit the crisp snow. She punched through the hard top layer and pushed it forward until it came free again.

There, at the end of the slat, was a pile of fresh snow.

Cautiously, Schwartzman pulled the slat back in through the window. Clearing off the bedside table, she dumped the snow on the hard surface and scooped it into a small, firm pile. Then, laying the slat carefully on the bed, she went to the kitchen and retrieved every container that would hold water—the cup, her bowl, the fry pan, the ice cube holders, the empty yogurt container still in the trash. In the bedroom, she filled each one with snow, packing it down until it would take no more.

Then she hid the slat under the bed and moved the containers to the kitchen. She wanted to shove the snow in her mouth, but still frozen, it would dehydrate more than help.

Instead, she took the fry pan, filled to the brim with snow, and set it on the stovetop. Now she could spare a little water. She turned the stove on low and waited for the ancient coils to glow red.

In the meantime, she shuttled the rest of the containers back into the kitchen and searched for anything else she could use to collect snow. She could empty the orange juice and milk, but she didn't know how much of the drug might have leached into the containers.

She scanned the collection of vessels she'd assembled. They held at least thirty ounces, and with the stove, she could melt the snow quickly. She returned to the stove, but the coils were still black, cool to the touch. She tried turning on the oven, but it, too, remained cold. No heat.

Tears burned her eyes. She needed water. Waiting even ten more minutes seemed impossible. There had to be a way to get it to melt. She turned to the kitchen faucet. The water wasn't drinkable, but it did get hot.

She put the stopper in the sink and ran hot water into the basin until the bottom was covered with a thin layer of steaming water. Then she set a cup of snow in the water, holding the top of it until she was confident it wouldn't tip. She added a second cup and the bowl and pulled a chair to the sink to watch the snow melt.

After five minutes, she retrieved one of the cups from the hot bath and wiped the water off the bottom with her sleeve. Then she lifted the cup to her lips and tasted the pure joy of icy water.

A sob caught in her throat. She had water. At least temporarily. She drank until the water was gone and only snow remained, then replaced the cup in the hot water and lifted the bowl.

She continued this way until she had consumed twelve or fourteen ounces of water, and then she went back to the bedroom to reload while the rest melted. Back and forth, she gathered snow and worked to melt it, planning how to spend the waiting time. Scour for the makings of a tool that would cut. Make a plan with a clear head. Think of Hal and their baby. Yes, especially that. Free of Spencer's invisible fingers inside her brain, dulling her senses, anything was possible.

21

Georgia Schwartzman was not feeling herself. She couldn't remember the last time she'd missed a Wednesday lunch at the club. Wednesday was women's day, and a group of twelve or thirteen of them had a standing date. Plenty of the women missed weeks—some for months at a time—but Georgia was almost religious in her attendance. Her life was exactly conducive to being there without fail. No husband, no grandchildren, a daughter who was thousands of miles away. Or maybe not thousands of miles away. Did anyone know where Bella was? Had she turned up at home, and no one had thought to let her mother know?

She'd left Bella two messages, but it wasn't unusual for her daughter to take days or even a week to phone her back. "It's been a crazy week at work." Her daughter's standard excuse for the delays.

Spencer was still out of the office and had yet to return either of her voicemails or any of her texts. Georgia had spoken to the Greenville detective who had come by the other night, but he had nothing new to report. No word on Bella. No reason to think Mr. MacDonald had any part in her disappearance.

"Disappearance," he'd said again. "If it was in fact a disappearance."

When Bella had left Spencer, she'd changed her phone number and didn't give her mother the new one for some time. It had been several weeks before Georgia learned she'd been staying with Ava. Since then, Bella had gone through a few other phone number changes.

Surely this was just another one of those. But someone should know where she was. If not her mother, then her job, certainly.

Georgia knew she should call the San Francisco inspector. She'd written his name down after the police visit—Hal Harris. When she searched him on Google, the results all referenced homicide. Why was a homicide inspector involved in her daughter's . . . If it wasn't a disappearance, then what was it? She sat at the kitchen island with the avocado toast she'd made herself. She had no energy, but she also had no appetite. She took a small bite of the toast and chewed slowly. What she longed to do was go back to bed. But she'd been sleeping for days.

Maybe she was coming down with something. She didn't have any pain, and she wasn't feverish. She could call Dr. Hayes, but getting an appointment was always such a process. She didn't even have the energy for that.

And Dr. Hayes always asked the most probing questions. Was she having any negative thoughts? Was she sleeping? Drinking too much? In the last few years, it seemed like the man wanted to open a door straight into her head. Had it started around the time Bella left Spencer? All these years, she'd convinced herself that Anna and Spencer's split had been a private affair. What things would other people possibly have to gossip about other than their divorce?

But then there was Spencer's arrest. Even that had been hushed. Certainly, no one ever talked about it with her. Maybe she should have been thinking more about her own head. How had she imagined that people weren't talking behind her back? An ex-son-in-law in prison? What bit of gossip was juicier than that?

How many Wednesday lunches had she attended during which women watched her and silently wondered how she'd let her daughter marry such a man? But she'd never thought that. She had always believed Spencer was innocent. That the miscarriage had broken something inside her daughter. That the only way Bella could handle the loss was to blame Spencer.

That was the only thing that made sense.

But after the police had been at her house and she'd had that strange visit to Spencer's office, she began to wonder if she was wrong. And the thoughts became a new weight she carried, pressing down on her. So at Tuesday's bridge group, she'd found herself asking the others if they invested money with Spencer. She was surprised to hear how openly they discussed her ex-son-in-law.

"I think we used to," Patrice had said. "But Bill moved the money after Spencer was arrested."

The table had gone silent momentarily, every woman gripping her cards and holding her breath. But Patrice reached across to pat Georgia's arm. "I know he was cleared of all the charges, but Bill is Bill."

"A change can be good," Evelyn had added, rattling the ice in her empty vodka soda glass. *Her second,* Georgia thought, although she'd been a few minutes late, so it might have been her third. "It must be a little strange working with your daughter's ex-husband?"

Georgia thought it had been the most natural thing in the world. And suddenly, she couldn't for the life of her recall what had made her think that.

"I'm surprised he hasn't been snapped up again," Cheryl Ann said, looking directly at Georgia. "I mean, aren't you?"

Georgia nodded, taking a sip of her wine. She'd asked for the chardonnay, but it was suddenly too thick on her tongue, too warm.

"I heard he took out Montgomery Swann's middle daughter," Evelyn said, raising her empty glass and shaking it to get the attention of Cheryl Ann's maid, who did not normally tend bar. Still, the maid retrieved the glass and carried it to the side bar to fix another. "They only went out twice, but Emory—that's the daughter—she thought it was going great. She was falling for him. But two dates, and he never called again."

"Same thing happened to Diana Heathrinton's daughter," Patrice said, waving an empty hand. "What's her name? Caitlin or Catherine or . . ."

"They call her Kiki," Cheryl Ann said.

The maid handed Evelyn a full glass, which she promptly drank down to two-thirds.

"Maybe he's still in love with Annabelle," Patrice said, raising her eyebrows.

"I hope you don't think it's rude, Georgia, but he does strike me as a little strange," Evelyn said, continuing to make her drink disappear.

Her own hackles were up. She thought of Jenny Fontaine, who had worked in his office all those years.

"No stranger than my sons-in-law," Cheryl Ann said dismissively. She shook her head toward Georgia as though to say, *Don't pay her any mind. You know how she gets after a few drinks.*

"Well, Tamara Rogers said she sees him at the club all the time, and he's very friendly," Patrice went on. "But then she ran into him down near the community college." She waved her arms and added as an aside, "We all warned her not to go down there. It's not safe. But her grandson is a freshman. And who did she see when she stopped for gas but Spencer? She was parked at the pump next to him. He had to have seen her, but when she got out of the car and said hello, he walked right past her, got in his car, and drove away without a word. Like she wasn't even there."

Georgia was looking for an excuse to leave when Patrice got a call that Bill was being taken to the hospital with chest pain. This was not particularly unusual for Bill, although only Evelyn commented on its regularity. The rest of them ushered Patrice off, and once she'd left, the party broke up quickly. Georgia thanked Cheryl Ann for hosting and ducked out before Evelyn could corner her again.

Both Patrice and Cheryl Ann had called her the following day, but Georgia didn't answer. She did send an email to Patrice to be sure Bill was all right. He was. But since leaving Cheryl Ann's, Georgia found herself sticking closer to home. And while she'd assumed that she would attend the lunch, she couldn't find the resolve to go, even when she told herself she could easily avoid the bridge ladies. There were always at least three tables to choose from, but she felt certain that the conversation from their bridge night—the speculation about Spencer's recent dating and about his strange behavior—would have made the entire loop by now.

Not that she could blame them. She would have done the same in their place. But suddenly, she felt like an idiot for never asking these questions. He'd been so solid, so successful, not to mention handsome.

A perfect groom.

A perfect husband.

And Bella had been—well, young, for one. And so totally destroyed by her father's death. And then there had been her insistence on going to medical school, something she'd never talked about before. Georgia had felt certain this wild idea had been a side effect of the grief, an impulsive decision she would regret later. All those years of school would put her life on hold. It would be impossible to get married or start a family while she was getting her degree.

Then Spencer had asked Bella out. At that first date, Spencer had come to the house and brought Georgia flowers. Not that she was swayed by a bouquet of flowers—though they were beautiful.

But she had been swayed. Spencer had made Georgia believe he could heal Bella. She missed the daughter who listened to her, who liked the things she liked, who enjoyed spending time with her. Not that she was wrapped up in her daughter like some mothers were. No, she had a life outside of Bella, her weekly lunches and managing the upkeep of her house. But it felt lonely, too, and somehow she thought Spencer might be able to bring the two women back together.

Now she didn't know what she thought.

A week after his first date with Bella, Spencer had invited Georgia to lunch. "I've got a favorite spot," he told her. "It's a quiet little place where we won't be disturbed."

Georgia had not accepted on the phone. She said she would let him know. It seemed odd that he'd reached out to her at all. After all, Bella had said the date didn't go well. She'd seemed too upset even to talk about it, so why would Spencer want to see Georgia?

Georgia had probed a bit more about the date, but Bella had remained tight-lipped and quiet. Georgia, in turn, had made no mention of her lunch date with Spencer. He'd called again, two days later. "It's only lunch, Georgia," he'd said in that buttery voice.

So she had accepted.

For two days, she'd built it up in her mind—what he wanted, what she would wear. The closer it drew, the more she'd let the crazy ideas go to her head. There had been no one in her life since her husband's death. The thrill of a date—it wasn't actually a date, she told herself. But the thrill felt like a drug, and no amount of reason could wash it from her system.

She'd laid out a yellow sundress with white flowers and a thin band of eyelet at the waist and along the bottom edge of the skirt. She'd spent an hour in front of the mirror, doing her hair and makeup. Put on a pair of Chloé ballet flats. She had felt twenty.

Seated in the living room reading, Bella hadn't even noticed her mother when she'd left the house. Georgia had snuck out like a teenager and driven to lunch, blaring music much too young for a woman her age.

And when they were seated, Spencer had ordered a bottle of expensive wine, a white burgundy. After the glasses had been poured, he'd raised one, clinking it against Georgia's. "To the woman I want to marry," Spencer had said.

A rush of heat had moved through Georgia, head to toe.

He'd clinked his glass against hers, and before she could respond—thank God, it was before she'd said anything—Spencer had said, "To our Bella."

22

Schwartzman felt better than she had since she'd arrived. She was clearheaded, alert. The drugs were surely flushed from her system. The speed with which she'd metabolized them made her think it was likely a short-acting benzodiazepine. She recalled a case in which a woman had been drugged with Halcion and held captive for two days prior to her death. When the body came to autopsy, Schwartzman had found no trace of triazolam, the active ingredient in Halcion, in her urine or blood. It was only by chance that the Crime Scene Unit had happened upon a sample of the drug that had spilled at the scene. Triazolam was a hypnotic agent with a short plasma half-life, somewhere in the range of two to six hours, if she remembered correctly.

By her estimation, she had been flushing the drugs from her system for about nine hours, which meant Halcion was a possibility, as were some of the other shorter-acting benzos. Rohypnol, on the other hand, had an elimination half-life of ten to twenty-five hours. She didn't believe she had been roofied.

With easy access to water, she now ate the foods she'd been avoiding for their high sodium content—cheese and meat. Her stomach had shrunk after days with little or no food, so she made herself eat every hour. The rest of the day, she melted snow and drank. While she waited for the next cup to be ready, she canvassed the farthest corners of the collar's reach for anything she might have missed in her earlier state—nails, pins, or any sliver of metal that might cut.

She found nothing.

Satiated with food and water, Schwartzman spent the remaining hours of daylight filling up all her containers with snow and hiding them in the oven to melt, in case someone should visit during the night. By the time she had filled every available cup and bowl, the snow that was easily accessible from the bedroom window was almost out of reach.

She would need another source soon. The bathroom window was too high, but maybe she could reach out the kitchen window. For the night, she returned the slat onto the baseboard heating unit. With the bent end and the missing bracket, it hung slightly crooked, but someone would have to be paying attention to notice. So far, it didn't seem like anyone was paying that much attention.

Seated at the kitchen table, nursing a glass of melted snow, her thoughts returned to Roy Butler. She tried to remember who had hired him, but that had happened while she was dealing with her mastectomy and the chemo. Roy just seemed to appear one day.

That was impossible, of course.

If her being in this cabin had been Roy Butler's plan from the start, then how did he come upon her? Were female medical examiners his choice of prey? Some combination of power and death that merged into an ultimate, twisted fantasy?

She found herself searching for things that might have lured Roy Butler to her morgue. Newspaper articles always mentioned her involvement in various cases, and the name *Schwartzman* would have stuck out to someone who made a point to hate Jews. And her appearance, too—the dark wave of her hair, the prominent nose. She looked Jewish. If she'd had her mother's looks, would she be collared inside this cabin?

Surely it wasn't just luck that she'd been chosen as the plaything for another crazy man. Spencer was behind this. He had to be. But then why hadn't he shown up to claim her? How long would he let her sit here? It had been four days, by her guess. Four days under the power of a strange man, a man Spencer would find despicable. Why risk it? What could Spencer possibly be doing that was more important than being with her?

And how long did she have before he arrived?

Rising from the table, she went to the sink and looked out the window. Through the metal bars, all she saw was snow. The source of the drug she'd seen when she first arrived was now buried. She scanned the view beyond the bars—just a field of white interrupted by the occasional tree, like a handful of tally marks on a sheet of notepaper.

Climbing up on the counter, she reached through the open window, took hold of the bars, and tried to rattle them. They were solid. The snow outside this window was thicker than the layer she'd been harvesting outside the bedroom window, which got more sun. Getting the makeshift scoop out through the bars was possible, but only if she held it vertically. The bars were too close together to allow for the slat to go horizontally, which meant scooping the snow would be nearly impossible unless she could somehow hold the slat out past the bars. But then how would she get the snow back inside?

The light leached from the sky, blue growing to indigo toward black. She pressed her face to the cold bars and thought about what was out there. All she needed was one little break. A tiny tool that would help her escape. An idea.

It was there somewhere.

She shifted on her knees and turned to sit down on the counter. To the right of the window, tucked just past the bars, she noticed a long, thin icicle. The lightest shade of blue, it was almost transparent. Up on her knees again, she edged closer to the window and reached for it, pressing herself against the window. If the collar retracted, the pressure against the bars would easily break her arm. She held her breath and wiggled her fingers slowly, cautiously, until she could touch the hard, cold surface. Then she walked her fingers up along the icicle, stretching her arm until the window cut uncomfortably against her shoulder.

Gripping the icicle in a tight fist, she twisted her wrist. Felt it snap in her hand.

With slow movements, she brought her arm back toward the bars, shifted the icicle to the other hand, and set it carefully on the sink before getting down from the counter. She closed the window and held the smooth, cold column across both palms.

She could drink it. It might be another 150 ml of water.

But the sharp end suggested it might be more useful another way.

Moving slowly, she headed to the freezer and tucked the icicle at the very back of the box, where it settled in a small channel, almost invisible.

A weapon.

For the moment, she had clean water and a weapon.

23

From the San Francisco airport, Hal was tempted to catch a bus that would take him to Bryant Street and the Homicide Unit. He glanced at the clock on his phone. It was almost 11:00 p.m. here, 1:00 a.m. in Dallas. Nothing he could do at the department at this hour. While he waited at the airport curb for an Uber to take him to Anna's house, a quick call to Roger caught him up on the search. No leads, no suspects. Hal couldn't imagine going home to bed. He knew he wouldn't sleep. He hadn't slept since she'd been taken.

Being awake, he preferred to keep busy. Odd how his perception of time had changed, how it mattered only if the hour meant he had access to other people—to the labs and crime scene techs working the evidence from Anna's house; to Telly, who had gone on to Denver without him; to the FBI agents in the Dallas office who'd run reports on MacDonald and were now expanding the search to everyone Anna knew, every case where she had presented evidence in a trial.

They didn't need to bother, Hal told them. If they turned MacDonald inside out, they would find Anna. He was certain.

But they insisted on protocol. Telly would listen, though. He kept the focus tight on MacDonald. And Hal would have to depend on Telly now.

Hal texted Hailey that he was on the ground. Headed home. Suggested they meet early so she could fill him in on the case. He waited to see if she would reply, but his phone remained quiet. To pass the time as the Uber driver made his way north on the 101, Hal opened the email app on his phone and read a report on Penny Moore, the woman MacDonald had dinner with two nights earlier. Her late husband, Patty, had started with nothing and built an empire. At the time of his death—he'd died of an aneurysm last year—his net worth was estimated at something north of $2 billion. The report referenced some shady dealings and a handful of lawsuits against him, but aside from those, there was nothing much on Moore. Was it possible Spencer MacDonald was her money manager? Why had she sought out a man from North Carolina to take over her husband's holdings? There had to be a manager as capable as MacDonald in Texas.

He thought of MacDonald, sitting in that car across the street from the restaurant. What was he planning? Spencer MacDonald was just a man. One man.

Then again, MacDonald had pulled off some impressive stunts before, seemingly on his own.

Forcing MacDonald from his mind, Hal opened the initial report on the two homicides in Union Square—both gunshot wounds, same caliber, almost certainly the same gun. The victims were found about twenty feet apart, three entry wounds in one and a single wound in the other. Hailey's notes suggested the second victim might have been collateral damage. Nothing connected the two victims, and so far, nothing in either's background suggested an obvious motive. Even as he read the notes, shifting his focus to a regular case felt impossible.

He looked up as the Uber driver exited the freeway and turned toward Anna's house. He hadn't heard back from Hailey. She would be fast asleep. He would have to wait until tomorrow to get caught up. More waiting. He scrolled back to the message that had come from Telly while he was on the plane.

We're making progress.

That was becoming Telly's buzz line. What the hell did it mean? What progress? What, specifically? It was like politicians saying how well things were going under their leadership. From where Hal stood, he didn't see any progress at all. Once again, Hal reminded himself that Telly was a kid. But a smart kid. And he'd seen young officers solve complicated crimes.

Leaving Spencer MacDonald felt like leaving Anna. And he didn't know what he'd do if Telly screwed up tailing MacDonald to Denver. No. He knew what he'd do. He'd kick the kid's ass.

The rush of anger flattened back into fear. He focused on what he'd do if Telly screwed up, trying to stir the heat of rage back to life. Fear was cold and empty, its icy tentacles slowing him down. It made him want to sleep, and then it made sleep impossible.

How had Anna survived so many years of living in fear?

As the driver turned down Anna's street, he thought about Buster. Wished he could have picked the dog up from Helen's house. He would have liked the company. Too late now.

The Uber stopped at Anna's house. Hal's Toyota was still parked in the narrow spot behind her SUV. There were parking tickets on both cars. *Bastards*. He reached the front door and took out her keys, his fingers worrying the little silver heart on her keychain. He closed his eyes and rested his head on the door, steeling himself for the assault of her that would confront him.

Her smell, her things . . . he both dreaded and longed for them.

The times when he was inside Anna's house, with Buster beside him, were the closest he felt to her. Tomorrow he would call Helen and pick up Buster. Reaching down without opening his eyes, he let the door fall open and inhaled her—her perfume, her laundry detergent, the geranium dish soap she used in the kitchen.

He stepped inside.

"Hal."

He started at the woman's voice, eyes open. His mind spun momentarily. *Anna?* But no. The voice was out of place. The small table light went on, and his mother rose from the couch. Buster rose behind her, trotting to Hal's side.

He swiped at his eyes. "Mom? What are you doing here?"

"You're not calling me back."

"I—"

"I don't want to hear it." She walked past him toward the kitchen. "I'm putting on tea."

"How did you get in?"

"Helen next door let me in, brought this guy back." She nodded toward Buster.

Hal dropped his bag and got down on his knees to nuzzle the dog.

The teakettle was shrieking before he'd finished greeting Buster. Middle of the night, and his mother had the teakettle going. Waiting for him. For how long?

She poured water into a mug already holding a tea bag. He recognized the blue tag dangling against the side—Sleepytime Tea, which meant she'd brought the tea from home. Suddenly, he knew exactly what had happened. "Hailey called you."

His mother added a dollop of honey, stirred the tea, and offered it to him.

He took the mug. "You didn't have to come."

"Like hell, I didn't. Your sisters would be here, too, if I'd let them. I told them to stay home. For now." She started back into the living room.

"Mom, there's nothing to do here. We just have to wait."

She sat down on the couch and folded her hands in her lap. "Then I'll wait right here."

He thought about arguing with her, but he knew better. "I can sleep on the couch."

"I'll stay in that back room," his mother said. "My things are already in there. I'm sure you could stay in Anna's room."

He'd forgotten about the guest room. At the back of the little house, he'd always found it too far away from her, even before they were together. He rubbed his chest.

"You'll find her," his mother said.

He opened his mouth to respond when his phone rang. A glance at the screen. Dispatch.

"Harris," he answered, holding his breath.

"It's Officer Conrad at the desk. Inspector Wyatt said to call you in on this one to find out if you were back from Dallas."

Hal exhaled. "I'm back. What've we got?"

"Man knifed on Stockton Street."

"We caught it?"

"That's what she said."

"Where on Stockton?"

"Near Sutter. I can text the address."

It was two blocks from Union Square, close to the two gunshot victims. "A connection to our other case?"

"Don't know," Dispatch said.

Hal watched his mother listen intently while pretending to read a *Smithsonian Magazine* she'd brought with her. Just like when they were kids. The woman didn't miss a beat.

"Should I tell Inspector Wyatt you're on your way?"

"Please." Hal ended the call.

His mother looked up from her magazine. "You have to go?"

"I caught one."

"Those shootings near Union Square?"

He nodded. "You should go home, Mom."

"I'm not worried about any shooter." Her mouth twisted unhappily. "You hurry home."

He leaned over and kissed her forehead. "Don't open the door for anybody."

"I am no fool, Hal."

"No, ma'am."

24

Schwartzman woke disoriented by the wedge of light that cut through the bedroom window, as bright as daylight. And yet the dark edges in the room suggested it wasn't yet morning. Thoughts arrived through a thick fog. A dull headache thumped in the posterior of her temporal lobe, and she detected the slightest smell of orange in the air. Easing herself up in the bed, she considered the strange smells and the head pain and wondered if the drug had affected her sense of smell.

But she had found a source of clean water. Why would she feel the effects of the drug now?

Drawing excess slack above her collar, she rose from the bed. The partial moon was like a sliver of a flashlight aimed through the window, the sky around it bright and clear. Not a cloud in the sky. The weather in the mountains changed quickly. Just because it wasn't snowing now didn't mean . . .

But the fear was already building in her chest like a cough. She tugged the metal clip along the track to the window. The snow looked lower than it had under the window. A wet sheen glistened on its surface. She told herself it couldn't be that much lower, but the spot where she'd shoveled through the window was now lower than an outdoor spigot. One she'd never seen before because it had been under the snow. *You can still reach it.* Even in her mind, the words reeked of doubt.

Not allowing herself to hesitate, she removed the slat from under the bed and guided it out the window. Pressed to the sill, she stretched her arms through the bars and reached down. The slat waved awkwardly in her extended hands.

With her torso partway out the window, the slat touched the surface of the snow. Pressing, she tried to dig in, but the top layer was crusty and stiff. She shoved harder, extending her arms until she held only the bottom three or four inches of slat. Finally, the metal broke through the ice, and the release pitched her forward. The cord caught against the frame, tightening the collar on her neck. The familiar choking startled her. A whir filled the air as the cord jerked upward. The collar bit into her trachea, making her gasp.

In her panic, she grabbed hold of the collar. The metal slipped from her fingers, and the slat dropped, landing short-end first into the snow. She let go of the collar, stretching to grab it. Her fingers grazed the end. The collar tightened again, and she was yanked onto her tiptoes.

She stumbled back, both hands gripping the collar as the cord retracted into the ceiling track. Her feet barely touching the floor, she swung one foot onto the bed and then the other. The collar loosened as she yanked on the cord to slow its retreat. The cord stuck, no longer shortening, and she looked out the window to see the slat had tipped sideways. Its long, thin edge cut through the snow, and the slat was now almost invisible in the white crust below. She stood on the bed, shaking, the cold air stinging her skin. She couldn't reach the window to close it, and she was not yet ready to move back to the floor.

After some tugging, the cord released from the track, and her heart rate slowed. She was able to draw full breaths. Slowly, testing the cord, she lowered herself back onto the floor and closed the window. Her face to the glass, she looked down on the only remnant of the slat—a thin line in the snow where it had broken through.

Rubbing her neck, she moved away from the window. The water glass on the bedside table was full. After it was gone, there was only one more cup of melted snow, hidden in the oven.

Already, she could feel her thirst building again.

She reminded herself of how much she'd had to drink the day before. Still, she was light-headed and panicky. She closed her eyes and filled her lungs. One thing at a time. She should sleep, but the adrenaline had filled her bloodstream, and it would be at least twenty minutes before the sensation ebbed. She would return to the kitchen and check the snow level out that window. If the snow were lower, maybe she could find another way to disconnect the source of the drug to the pipe.

She carried the water to the kitchen and thought of the icicle in the freezer. Her weapon. She would drink it if she had to.

She set the water glass in the center of the dining table and tried not to think about it. Each time her gaze was drawn there, she reminded herself that the human body could survive without water for five or six days. But it would almost certainly kill the baby. Out the window, she could just barely make out the plastic bottle and tube that housed the drug. It was too dark to see how much liquid remained in the plastic bottle.

Turning back to the kitchen, she took stock of the food items in the house. Her back ached as she stooped to check the refrigerator, noting with a wave of panic that the shelves were starting to look bare. Again. Had it been two days now since new food had appeared? Three? She'd lost count. Even the milk that she'd been dumping systematically down the drain was almost gone. What then?

They knew she had water. There was no immediate risk of her dying.

She thought again of the container of drug she'd seen out the kitchen window. Was someone restocking that as well? If they hadn't been here to replenish her food, maybe they hadn't tended to the drug supply either. How long would it feed into the water before it ran out? At the kitchen sink, she cranked the water on high and watched it spurt into the basin. Leaving it on, she returned to her place at the dining table.

Holding the cup of melted snow in both hands the way the parishioners did when taking Communion at her mother's church, she lifted it to her lips and closed her eyes. The back of her throat seemed to absorb the cold water before it slid down her throat, leaving her with only a moment of icy relief.

She stared at the empty cup, longing for more. If the water ran all night, surely the drug container would be empty. She could run it for a full day. If she could wait sixteen or even just twelve hours to drink, the water should be drug-free.

Checking that the tap was open as far as it would go, Schwartzman felt the last bits of adrenaline leave her system. Keeping hold of her collar, she headed back to the bedroom to sleep.

25

Despite the late hour, the area around Union Square was still busy
with pedestrians. The bars closed at 2:00 a.m., and the streets were
dotted with drunken people trying to hail cabs and waiting for Ubers.
As he always did approaching a crime scene, Hal scanned the faces of
the crowd for any who seemed especially interested in the scene or in
the police presence. A dark-haired woman caught his eye. She stood
with her side pressed to the outside of a building, her coat over her
shoulders. She was Anna's height and build. The dark coat and slacks
similar to what Anna wore. His pace slowed, and he waited for her to
turn so he could see her face.

It couldn't be Anna.

And still, he couldn't draw his gaze from her. Unlike most of the
people out at this hour, she didn't sway but stood upright and still, a
phone pressed to her ear. The police barricade was approximately fifty
feet ahead, but Hal would go crazy if he didn't see her face. Crossing
the street, he changed course, heading toward her. The air was cold and
his jacket lightweight, but in the twenty steps that it took to reach her,
sweat collected at the back of his neck. He slowed as he approached,
his throat closed, his eyes burning. Her hair was just the right shade of

brown, a long wavy piece stretched out on the back of her jacket, its sheen caught in the light of the streetlamp. He was almost to her when she lowered the phone and looked up.

She had dark skin and eyes, rounded features that were nothing like Anna's.

"Sorry," Hal said. "I thought you might be someone else."

She blinked and said nothing, her expression startled and uncertain.

He hesitated momentarily with the thought that he should explain himself or at least show his badge, but his thoughts were jumbled. And he could come up with no way to tell her what he thought he'd seen. He rubbed his head with his hand and tried to shake off his body's reaction to thinking he had seen Anna. Telly was working on it. Hal touched his phone through his pants pocket. He hadn't heard from Telly since he'd arrived in Denver. He had promised he would call as soon as he had an update. Hal had to hold the faith. It was harder than usual.

As Hal approached the crime scene tape, two bystanders turned to vomit, almost in sync. From the look of them, it was hard to say if the vomit was caused by alcohol or if they had somehow gotten a look at the victim behind the makeshift barrier. Approaching the scene, he felt a familiar sense of calm. He knew how to do this. The police had barricaded an area of Stockton Street around the sidewalk where the victim lay, but without detouring traffic, it wasn't enough of a buffer to prevent drunken onlookers.

The victim lay in a puddle of blood. That meant the attack had been aggressive, and the victim had likely exsanguinated in a matter of minutes. Hailey was squatting beside the victim. Next to her was a figure in a Tyvek suit, like the one Anna always wore. Though he knew it wasn't her, Hal swayed momentarily at the sight of the suit. Hailey caught his eye and turned. The figure in white turned, too.

Inside the Tyvek suit was a thin black man with charcoal glasses that made his eyes look too large for his face. His skin was darker than Hal's, and he wore his hair in tight curls that faded into his neckline and grew maybe an inch long on top. His face was clean-shaven, and with the hard part on his left side, he looked young enough to be in college. But then Hal reconsidered the Tyvek suit. He was here as a medical examiner, in Anna's place.

"Hal, hi," Hailey said, waving him in to the scene. "This is Scott Theobold. He's working the scene." She spoke the words carefully. Avoiding the term *medical examiner*. Avoiding mention of Anna.

Hal's ribs seemed to topple on one another until they were bone on bone, constricting his lungs. His heart rattled against the solid sheath of his sternum. He couldn't inhale, as though drowning in the night air. The department needed someone to fill in for her, he told himself. It wasn't permanent. The department had to believe she would be found. They couldn't accept that she was gone forever. She was not gone forever.

"Hal?" Hailey asked, concern in her voice.

Without answering, Hal lowered to his haunches beside the body, noticing the open wound on the victim's neck. The whiteness of exposed vertebrae glowed under Hailey's flashlight. An aggressive attack didn't begin to describe what Hal saw. Whoever cut this guy had almost severed his head. "What do we know?"

Hailey motioned to the interim ME, although Hal had already forgotten his name. Or blocked it out. His Tyvek suit felt offensively bright and white, his presence wrong inside it. Hal wondered briefly if it was one of Anna's or if he had his own supply. But the fit implied the suit was his size and not Anna's.

"Victim is mid to late thirties," he went on. "Five foot eleven, approximately one sixty-five." The man paused.

"What else can you tell, Dr. Theobold?" Hailey asked, the sound of the man's name strange in his ear.

"Please," he said. "Call me Scott." Theobold pointed to the wound. "Assailant was likely right-handed. Wound direction is left to right and came from behind. Also likely that the assailant is at least six foot one. It would have been difficult to achieve that cut if the assailant were shorter than the victim." He put up a hand as caution. "But that's just a guess. I need to study the wounds more carefully before I can be certain that both victim and assailant were on their feet at the time of the attack."

Hal felt a hand on his back. For a moment, he thought it was Theobold's, and he resisted the instinct to shake it off.

"Hey," came a familiar voice. Roger Sampers stood above him, his gaze steady. Hal rose and drew a deep breath, gathering strength from the presence of Roger beside him. Roger, who had come to Anna's house after she'd been abducted. Roger, who'd found the pregnancy tests, who knew what was at stake.

"I'm going to take a walk over to Union Square," Hal said. "See who's sleeping down there."

Hailey rose. "I'll come with you."

"That's okay," Hal said. "You stay here, see what else we can learn about the attack. I'll see if I can't round up some folks and bring them to the station for questioning." He turned without waiting for her answer and walked away in long, purposeful strides. It seemed only in motion could he breathe.

And even then, the air burned in his lungs as though he had just walked through fire and inhaled hot black smoke.

26

"What the fuck are you playing at?"

Schwartzman woke to the sound of Roy's voice. There was no gentle stirring. Instead, she was thrown into full awareness, the edges of her mind as sharp as blades. Her pulse throbbed in her head and ears, the sound so loud, she imagined he could hear it. She kept her eyes closed, pressed her head to the pillow, and squeezed a fist beneath the sheets.

"I mean it," he said.

The voice was not in the room with her. She was still alone.

She drew a steady breath and shifted her head, opening one eye to look at the empty room.

"You stay the fuck out of here!" he shouted. The sound of skin on skin reached her, a hand striking, followed by a high-pitched cry. Another woman.

Schwartzman stared at the door. Had Roy Butler brought another woman here? She heard the soft sounds of crying; then a door slammed. She waited. Had Roy left? Was the woman in another room? Was she locked up also? She started to raise herself when she heard boots on the hardwood floor.

Growing closer.

She curled up on her side, face to the wall, and prayed he would go away. The hinge on the door creaked, and she squeezed her eyes closed. The smell of cigarettes assaulted her, and bile rose into her esophagus. She clenched her jaw to keep from being sick.

His fingers touched her chin, pulling her head to face him. She fought the panic as she pretended to be asleep. She let her neck hang loosely. Held her breath. After a moment, he let go. The boots retreated, and the front door slammed again. Afraid it was a trick, she kept her eyes closed and counted to one hundred once and then again. Finally, she rose and pulled the cord along the track. Hovering at the bedroom door, she stared at the hallway, scanning the floor for shadows. Then she made her way into the main room of the cabin. She was alone.

She turned on the small light over the stove and checked the room again. The kitchen faucet had been turned off, but otherwise, the room appeared unchanged. The cup of melted snow—the last of her water—was still hidden in the oven, and in the refrigerator, she found a handful of new yogurts but nothing else. Her stomach ached uncomfortably, and she sat at the table to eat one. As soon as it was gone, she longed for another. More than that, she longed for water. She filled her glass from the kitchen sink and stared at the clear liquid. The water had probably been running for an hour or two. Had Roy checked the drug when he was here?

Again she thought of the other woman. Perhaps someone who had come to help Schwartzman and Roy had caught her? It was more likely a wife or a sister. If Schwartzman had been awake, she might be free by now. If Roy hadn't come . . .

Maybe the woman would be back. If she had risked coming once . . .

Schwartzman closed her eyes and prayed that the woman—whoever she was—would be brave enough to come again. Then she tried to put it from her mind. Surely she wouldn't come back tonight, which meant Schwartzman had to keep herself alive by whatever means necessary.

She stared at the water, wondering if she'd managed to clear the drug from the pipes. There was only one way to find out. She lifted the cup to her lips and drank it down in long, satisfying gulps. Then she filled it twice more and drank again, stopping when the liquid filled her stomach.

She returned to the bedroom and sat on the bed, her back to the wall. Out the window, the sky was growing light. As she waited for the water to digest and the drugs—if there were any—to take effect, she thought about her work. Who was taking her place? Her last day in the office, she'd completed an autopsy on a victim of cardiac arrest, a thirty-eight-year-old man who had died in the shower. Thirty-eight. So young.

On January 18, she would turn thirty-eight. She counted back the days, trying to sort out how long she'd been in the cabin. Maybe she was already thirty-eight.

She pushed the thought from her head. She would celebrate her birthday when she was home. Soon. The woman would come back. Cut her loose. She would escape. The thoughts brought a wave of panic. Her heart racing, she felt the drug's fog settle over her. She shifted to lie on the bed, afraid if she fell asleep seated, she might slump down in a manner that might inadvertently cut off her own air supply.

To calm herself, she recounted her other active cases. She'd still been working on the autopsy report for a suspicious death of a man who'd died at a dinner party with his wife and three other couples. The other attendees had told the police they thought the man had choked on a piece of meat. Two people had tried to perform the Heimlich maneuver on him, without success. But she'd found no food in his trachea—nothing blocking his windpipe at all.

At the autopsy, Schwartzman had determined the cause of death was anaphylactic reaction—an extreme allergy that had closed off his windpipe. Unlike many victims of anaphylaxis, though, this victim presented with no signs of the most obvious indicators: mucous plugging, hyperinflated lungs, or petechial hemorrhaging. Nor did she find any signs of pharyngeal or laryngeal edema, which also pointed to this type of extreme reaction. It was a comment from Hal that had inspired her to run additional tests. The victim's wife and one of their friends, Hal had told her, mentioned that the man suffered from a narrow trachea that caused issues with food.

"Trachea?" she'd asked Hal, who had checked his notebook.

"That's what they said. That's the windpipe, right?"

"Yes," she had confirmed. Food would go down the esophagus not the trachea. In the autopsy, she'd confirmed the victim had some benign esophageal stricture, a tightening usually caused when stomach acids damaged its lining over time. But this condition did nothing to explain the choking. What's more, the piece of tenderloin the victim had supposedly choked on was in his esophagus not the trachea, which meant he should have been able to breathe.

Schwartzman had eventually discovered increased levels of mast cell tryptase, which suggested anaphylaxis. When asked about allergies, the wife confirmed that her husband had been allergic to bees. When Schwartzman ran a test for the presence of the antibody cells—IgE—specific for bee allergies, the results were positive. A closer look at the victim's stomach showed he had ingested a bee that had been ground up and added to the sauce on his meat.

Would Hal have seen those results? Had he made an arrest? Her thoughts settled on Hal as the drug pulled its thick blanket over her. *Hal.* If only she could get a message to him. *It's Roy Butler, Hal. Look at Roy Butler.*

She tried to whisper the words as she sank into the blackness.

27

Thursday, 6:30 a.m. PST

Hal woke to the smell of coffee and the soft purr of the Nespresso maker through the closed bedroom door. It smelled like Anna. The scent of rose on the sheets. He lifted his head and remembered, the moment of peace shattering.

He palmed his phone on the bedside table, hoping for something.

His three nephews and his niece grinned in the background picture he'd taken six or seven years ago. The youngest, just a few weeks old then, nestled in the arms of the oldest. He studied James's tiny infant face. "James reminds me of you as a baby," his mother had told him when they were alone. James's father, his brother-in-law, might not appreciate hearing his child looked more like his wife's brother than him. But his sister Becca had said it, too.

He stared at the tiny flat nose and the swollen pink lips. What would his baby look like? Would he or she look more like Anna? Or like him? How would their genes mix?

And what if he never got to see the baby? He felt as though someone were carving into his chest with a spoon.

Buster snored on the floor near the window.

Hal sat on the edge of the bed, willing himself to move. He held the phone tight in his fist and then threw it hard on the bed. How he would have loved to hear it explode against the wall. But he couldn't afford to break that phone. It had to be working when she called or when someone found her and called him.

From the bed, the phone rang. Hailey Wyatt.

"Hey," he said, struggling to keep his voice calm. Who would the call about Anna come from? Telly? Hailey? His captain? "What's up?"

"Theobold is in the morgue. Says we can come meet him in an hour."

She started to say something else, but the words became a blur. The results from last night's stabbing. The morgue. Anna's morgue. He shook his head, cleared his throat, and interrupted her. "I talked to a couple of the homeless who regularly sleep near Union Square. They were pretty drunk last night, so I wanted to go back and talk to them again this morning. And there are a few more I'd like to chase down before they pick up and move for the day." He tried to slow his speech, to disguise the obvious panic in his words. He could not go to the morgue. "Why don't you go see—" He couldn't remember the guy's name. The acting ME.

Her voice was pinched. "Hal."

"We'll catch up after. We've got three murders to work. We're behind the eight ball here. If we can clear these—" He shut his mouth. He was going to say that if they could clear these, then he could get back to looking for Anna.

Hailey's voice was soft. "We should meet up first. Roger's going to be in the lab in forty minutes. We'll go over the victims and the evidence, touch base on where we are. I think you'll be able to catch those guys sleeping for the next few hours. It's too cold to move now."

It was true. In the winter months, the homeless tended to sleep later, the harsh cold air keeping them bundled until the sun had risen in the sky. The other thing he heard in her voice was that she wanted to see him. She and Roger had already spoken.

"That work?" she pressed.

"Sure."

"Then I can go with you to Union Square."

Which meant he'd have to go to the morgue. "We need to divide and conquer. I'll start with the homeless. You can start with . . ."

"Theobold."

"Right."

There was a brief pause before she spoke again, as though she considered arguing. Then she said simply, "I'll see you in the lab later."

"See you there." He ended the call. It made sense to divide tasks. He didn't need to hear the cause of death. He could get the report from her and talk to the people who might have seen something.

And he wasn't prepared to go to the morgue. Not while the ME was someone other than Anna.

When Hal emerged from the shower, there was a text from Roger confirming their meeting at the lab. First Hailey, now Roger. Both of them checking on him. Only Roger and Hailey knew about him and Anna. He'd been so relieved that Roger knew, to have it out there in that moment, but now he wished it was still his secret. Then they wouldn't look at him with those expressions, the ones they didn't even know they were making. Their mouths partially open, as though they couldn't think about it without being winded. The sad-puppy eyes of pity. Hailey was especially bad. She knew his history with Sheila and had watched him like a sister, worried about him being alone.

I'll be there.

He made himself coffee, grateful that his mother wasn't in the kitchen when he entered. She'd set the table, and a bowl of hot oatmeal and blueberries was centered on a place mat, a folded napkin beside it.

As he was putting a top on the travel mug, his mother appeared. He leaned down to kiss her cheek and started for the door.

"Made you some breakfast," she said.

Steam rose from among the berries on the oatmeal, like little ghosts escaping. It turned his stomach. "Thanks. I'm not hungry," he said, avoiding her eyes.

"See you later," she responded. He could feel her gaze on him as he left the house. He was surprised she didn't argue. Eating a solid breakfast had always been one of her firm rules. That she didn't enforce it now made his fears about Anna worse.

When Hal arrived, the lab was hopping. A half dozen people—one tech trying to lift fingerprints off some tool with bright-orange rubber handles, one head down over a microscope, another working at a computer. But no sign of Hailey or Roger.

Hal crossed to the center of the room, where Naomi Muir was working at a light table, reconstructing a piece of shredded paper with a pair of tweezers.

"That ours?" he asked.

She looked up. "Nope. It's one of Kong's." Before he could ask, she nodded to the small break room at the rear of the lab. "They're in there." She lowered her head and returned to her work.

In the break room, Roger and Hailey were hunched over the table. A stack of files sat between them, but they didn't appear to be looking at anything in particular. Hal knew immediately they were talking about him.

"Coffee?" Hailey asked when she spotted him.

"I can get it."

She was already up, pulling a mug from one of the hooks under the cabinets. He couldn't remember the last time Hailey had willingly served him coffee unless she was up to get herself some first. And even then, she always did it with a kind of don't-get-used-to-this look.

Hal sank into the chair and opened his notebook. He was not going to talk about himself. Or Anna. He thanked Hailey for the coffee and nodded to Roger. "We have anything from the scenes that might help us find a suspect?"

Roger glanced at Hailey.

Hal's stomach tightened. "Do you know something?" he asked.

Hailey shook her head.

"About Anna?" Roger said. "No. Nothing yet."

The bridge of his nose ached, and tears burned his eyes. *Damn it.*

"We're still wa—"

Hal shook his head. "Tell me when you find something. For now, let's focus on these three murders. Close this case."

"Sure," Roger said.

Hal sat in front of his notebook, clicked open his pen, and drank from the coffee cup, letting the liquid burn his mouth until the pain distracted him from the fear. He wrote the date at the top of a clean page and nodded. "Okay then. What do we know?"

28

Georgia Schwartzman was not a woman who allowed herself to obsess about what others thought. If she had been, she would never have married Sam Schwartzman, not in a town like Greenville. And she had loved him. He had been the first man to hold her attention for any span of time. Their life together was good. She had loved him until the day he died.

But she had also enjoyed the fact that marrying him was viewed as a bit scandalous. Not by her family. Her parents had loved Sam, who'd worked for her father from the month he'd graduated from law school. That Sam was Jewish didn't bother them in the least. Her parents were progressive in that way. But among her decidedly prissy friends—both from high school and those from the small college she'd attended—many thought it shocking she would marry outside her Baptist upbringing.

After Georgia had skipped their weekly lunch on Wednesday, Patrice and Cheryl Ann had reached out to make sure she wasn't ill. She'd assured them she was not, lied that she had a couple of appointments that had gotten moved around, and promised to see them soon. This afternoon there was an event for the children's hospital, and she was beginning to waver on going. But what excuse could she make for yet another absence? Surely Patrice and Cheryl Ann would know something was wrong if she didn't attend.

And what *was* wrong?

She wasn't ill. She felt fine. She wasn't even particularly worried about Bella, but then how could she be? She had no idea what her daughter might be doing. And it felt so impossible to believe that someone had kidnapped her. She was a grown woman.

Her thoughts returned again to Spencer. If only she could sit down with him and have a conversation, clear up her doubts. But when she called his office, the receptionist informed her that he was still out. "I'm afraid I don't know when he is expected back," the woman said in a slightly bored tone.

Determined to take her mind off Spencer, Georgia strode into her closet and focused on what she might wear to the fund-raising event. She pulled down a blue sheath dress that set off her eyes. She hung it on a hook beside the mirror and then chose a deep-red one with a blouse top and tiny pleats around the skirt. Either would be fine. But looking back and forth between the two, she couldn't make up her mind.

There used to be a time when she could call Sam, and he would tell her what to wear. A silly thing, but she always appreciated his advice. And more than that, she appreciated that her husband took the time to give the question his attention. He didn't give her the pat answer that many of her friends got from their husbands—"Oh, dear, you'll look great in whatever you choose"—always delivered with a barely concealed roll of the eyes, as though a woman's attire were a trivial matter they were too important to address.

Spencer had been like Sam that way. And like him in other ways as well, or so she had thought. Staring between the two dresses, Georgia thought again of Spencer's assistant, Jenny Fontaine. Older than him, Jenny had added a layer of class to his office. She and the Fontaines used to exchange holiday cards, she remembered.

After leaving the closet, Georgia went to her desk and found her master card list. There on the third page was Jennifer Fontaine. Jennifer Fontaine and Lindsay and Valerie, her two girls. She was a single mother. Georgia studied the address, thinking. Ten years had passed since she'd sent Christmas cards, but the address on her list was the same one she'd seen the young receptionist write down.

Not that it meant Jenny Fontaine was still there. She might live anywhere now. But even as she calculated the odds that Jenny was still at that address, Georgia decided she would pay her a visit. She was at the front door before she realized she was still in her pajamas.

Changing quickly, she pulled her hair into a low ponytail rather than taking the time to style it, something she almost never did. In her car, she entered the Fontaines' address into the navigation system and saw the house was even closer than she'd expected. She could be there in ten or twelve minutes.

Suddenly she longed to go back into the house and crawl into her bed. She could spend the day sleeping and playing the silly movies Patrice was always watching with her daughter. Skip the fund-raiser and have a little dinner, a glass of wine, and more stupid television. She rarely watched TV, but there were surely a hundred things that she might get lost in.

Then she could shut out the doubts about Bella. That she'd been so wrong about her daughter's husband. That his adoration was actually something dark and sinister.

That Spencer had actually hurt Bella.

Which would mean that Georgia was the worst type of mother.

She followed the directions to the Fontaine house, which was clustered among a development built in the mideighties. The houses were almost mirror images of one another, their individuality expressed in the slightly varied front doors or color choices. Each had a small square front lawn on one side and a simple driveway and two-car garage on the other.

The awkward-sounding electronic navigator announced she'd reached her destination. Georgia parked on the curb and looked up at the house that belonged to Jenny Fontaine. A pink tricycle was on its side by the front door. *Perhaps grandkids,* she thought, trying not to lose her nerve.

Georgia walked up the front path and rang the doorbell. A dog barked from the inside, and tiny feet pounded across a hardwood floor. Then a woman's voice warned not to open the door, told the dog to hush.

The woman who answered was not Jenny Fontaine, though she looked a little like her. Her daughter, Georgia guessed. In one arm was a little girl, maybe three but maybe younger. Georgia had long since lost the ability to judge the age of children. In the other hand, the woman held on to the collar of a curly-haired dog with sandy fur.

"Can I help you?" she asked.

"I hope so," Georgia said, holding her hands together and trying to smile. Her lips quivered with the effort. "I was looking for Jennifer Fontaine."

The woman shook her head. "She's not here. Who are you?"

"I'm Georgia Schwartzman. I knew her a long time ago. Are you her daughter?"

The woman nodded. "I'm Valerie."

"I used to get your Christmas cards," Georgia added. "Is she still in the area?"

Valerie's mouth worked a moment before the words came out. "She passed away last year."

"I'm so sorry," Georgia said. Jenny's death hadn't occurred to her. She was younger than Georgia, but not by much.

"Is there something I can help you with?"

"I'm not sure," Georgia admitted. "I knew your mom when she worked for Spencer MacDonald. She was his assistant."

Valerie said nothing.

"When did she leave his office?"

"She quit last January," Valerie said.

"Because she was sick," Georgia probed, feeling her cheeks burn at the intrusion.

"She wasn't sick then. She just quit."

"Do you happen to know why?"

Valerie shifted her daughter onto the other hip, holding the dog between her legs as she did. She didn't ask her to come in, so Georgia stood on the front porch, unsure if there was something she ought to do to help.

"Why do you want to know?" Valerie asked.

Georgia searched her mind for a response that would make any sense. The police visit and then the things her friends had said. Her doubts. "My daughter is missing. She was married to him."

The little girl said something in her mother's ear, but Valerie hushed her. She leaned forward, interested now. "You think he had something to do with your daughter's disappearance?"

"I don't know," Georgia said quickly. "I have no reason to think that." She paused, longing to excuse herself, to tell Valerie she wasn't feeling well, that she wasn't making any sense. Return to her car and drive home. But the police had come to ask her about Spencer, and it had seeded this doubt. Wasn't that why she'd gone to his office? Why she had come here?

Valerie bounced the girl on her hip and scanned the empty street.

"Perhaps I'm not thinking clearly," Georgia admitted. "I came to see your mom, since she knew him well. I thought maybe . . ." But she couldn't articulate what she thought. Ideas spun around her like gnats, too fast and small to grasp.

"Mama worked for that man for fifteen years," Valerie told her. "And then she came home one day with one of those white boxes you take when you leave a job. One small box. Hardly had anything in it. Just pictures of us kids and the grandkids. She'd just up and quit."

"And she didn't say why?"

Valerie shook her head. "She couldn't work there anymore. Said she'd seen something she couldn't unsee."

Georgia felt her hand hover at her throat. Seen something. In his office.

"My sister, Lindsay, and I pressed her about it, but she wouldn't tell us. Said it wasn't illegal, but it changed everything for her."

Georgia felt light-headed and put a palm on the door trim to support herself. "She never went back in?"

Valerie shook her head. "And as far as I know, he never reached out. The company paid her accrued vacation leave, and that was it." She nodded to the little girl. "We took Madison out of day care the next day, and Mama helped watch her until she died."

The little girl—Madison—whispered again, and Valerie set her down. "Go on," she said. "I'll be there in a minute." Madison ran toward the back of the house, and Valerie took hold of the dog's collar. Her gaze remained on her child, and when she looked back, her expression had softened. "I've got to go help her."

"Of course," Georgia said, straightening her back. "Thank you. I appreciate your time."

Valerie reached out her hand and touched Georgia's arm. "I hope you find your daughter."

Georgia blinked hard and nodded. "Thank you." She turned toward the street and heard the door click closed behind her, the words echoing in her head. *I hope you find your daughter.*

Was Bella really missing? That was what the police had told her, and now Georgia believed it. The only question that remained was Spencer.

Jennifer Fontaine had seen something in his office that she could never unsee. She had left Spencer's employment that same day. Whatever she saw wasn't illegal, her daughter had said.

But somehow that knowledge did nothing to reassure Georgia Schwartzman. To the contrary, it left her with more questions than ever.

29

For Schwartzman, the goal of every waking hour was threefold. One, collect any new snow and melt it. Two, find a way to cut off the collar. Three, distract herself from the lack of food and water. With the last of the untainted water in a glass on the table, she turned her attention to the continued hunt for a cutting tool. She trolled through memories of her own cases, searching for ones in which a strange implement had been used. There would be no knives, no scissors in the cabin. She would have to invent something.

In one such case, a woman had killed her husband with the rack from an industrial oven. After months of fighting over the rising costs of the product for their small business, she'd heaved the fifteen-pound rack and swung it into the back of his head.

Pulling out as much cord as she could, Schwartzman tucked the slack under her arm. In the event that the cord started to retract again, at least she'd have a little notice. Then, on her knees, she opened the narrow oven, pulled the flimsy rack free, and checked for sharp edges. There were none. Setting the rack aside, she leaned into the oven, tugging on plates and levers, trying to free something she might use as a tool. Her fingers measured the thickness of the rubber collar. With the rack free, she yanked out the slim drawer at the base of the oven and searched its edges for one sharp enough to saw through rubber. Examining the underside of the oven yielded her nothing.

The refrigerator and freezer were the same. This was her third—or maybe her fourth—round of searching, and she'd found nothing rough-edged enough to act as a cutting tool. A useless waste of time, all of it. She sank into a chair and slowly released the extra slack in the cord, relieving the burn on the skin of her arm where it had been rubbing. On the table was the last of the snow water. She stared down at the liquid, guessed it was maybe 350 milliliters' worth.

She thought of the shooting victim she'd autopsied on the Friday before her abduction. There had been two bullet wounds. One had perforated the right fourth intercostal space and the middle and upper lobes of the right lung, leaving a hemorrhagic, pulpy wound track. She'd measured the liquid and clotted blood in the right pleural cavity. Fifteen hundred milliliters, about fifty ounces. She had a quarter of that now.

She drank the water slowly, letting it wash across her tongue and chill her teeth before swallowing it. She made the liquid last for five sips. Outside, snow was beginning to fall again, lightly. She closed her eyes, unsure what to do next.

As she rose from the table, a square of light appeared on the kitchen wall. She grabbed the table and stared at it, blinking to clear her vision, but it wasn't a hallucination. She took a step toward the wall as a fuzzy image covered the space.

Blinking, she thought at first it was a trick of her eyes. But it was still there—some sort of projection.

She stood three feet from the wall, her own shadow blocking the bottom of the image, and waited. A video began to play. A street. Cars passing. She looked around the room, searching for the source. A pinhole in the ceiling. A projector. Turning back to the projection, she clasped on to the cord from her collar. The camera panned the street in a jerky, mechanical movement, the world smeared across the lens.

And then it stopped. The film showed a wide view of the street, pedestrians walking. Holding her breath, she searched for something familiar.

The buildings were none she'd seen before, so they were not in San Francisco, not in Seattle, not in Charleston or Greenville. The scene zoomed in, and there was Hal. A strangled noise escaped her throat as he came into focus. She took note of Hal's light button-down and blazer. Khaki slacks, the casual suede oxfords he wore when they weren't working. A size thirteen—his clown feet, she would tease him. She blinked and swiped the tears from her face, not wanting to miss a moment of him.

The building behind him was a slate monolith. He carried a windbreaker in one hand but no jacket. January. No signs of snow. That eliminated the Northeast and the Midwest. The women on the street were fashionably dressed, slacks or dresses and light coats. Expensive handbags. A business city.

Nowhere near here, she thought.

Fear corked her throat.

He's looking for you.

Hal stared down at his phone, a frown on his face.

Only then did she notice the man who stood beside him. Small compared to Hal, he was probably five seven or eight and in his midtwenties. His features were Middle Eastern, and his navy suit made her think he was government. He talked to Hal as though to convince him of something. What were they talking about?

Hal's eyes lifted, and for a moment, it was as though he were looking directly at her. Those eyes. Her heart danced in her chest.

But then the eyes narrowed. The brow sank, and his mouth set in an angry line. He started into the street without looking.

She cried out at the car that drove straight toward him.

It halted only feet from Hal, who smacked the hood of the car as the driver waved through the windshield. Hal ignored him, his eyes still glued on her. Not her. The camera. Who was there?

It had to be Spencer.

The driver cracked his door and stood from the car, waving his arms in big, angry gestures and yelling. The phone in his hand was aimed at Hal.

Hal didn't look back.

The smaller man in the suit produced a badge and pointed it at the driver, waving him back into his car.

She froze, memorizing every detail, taking it all in. What did it mean? What was Spencer trying to tell her?

Hal continued in his path, straight toward her. She leaned forward in the chair as he grew close, her pulse thumping wildly in her throat. He was only feet away. She could smell the hint of clove and sandalwood in his cologne, feel the smoothness of the skin on the back of his neck, the rough texture of his unshaven beard.

He reached out, and she let out a gasp.

The film ended, Hal's face remained in the center of the screen. A sob broke free, and Schwartzman lunged forward, reaching for his image. Her fingers couldn't reach the wall. She stretched as far as she could. "It's okay. It's going to be okay," she said aloud.

She clung to the relief she'd felt at seeing his face. Whatever doubts she'd had about her abduction vanished. This was Spencer's work. Even if it was Roy Butler who held her here, Spencer was behind it. The projection was his doing.

This was Spencer's master plan. And there was Hal. Which meant when Spencer came for her, Hal would be there. He would come for her.

All she had to do was figure out how to avoid the drugs, stay sharp and focused.

And wait.

That was exactly what she would do.

She made a last stretch to touch the image of Hal's face. Her fingers grazed the wall when a reeling sound whirred from above. The cord yanked her back, and she let out a choking cough, gripping her neck.

The collar around her neck tightened, the cord shortening as it dragged her upward. She struggled to get hold of the cord and keep her feet on the floor. Scrambled for a chair and felt it slip out from under her feet.

Then she was off the ground. Hal's image stayed frozen on the wall. Black took over the corners of her vision. Her fingers gripped the cord, trying to pull it down, to create some slack. Her pulse throbbed in her eyes.

Her chest felt ready to explode.

From somewhere close by came the sound of a man's laugh.

She focused on Hal's face, tried to memorize his eyes, until everything went black.

30

Hal pulled up to the police department behind the patrol car that carried Billy Vandt. A twitchy homeless man who had been to the station more than a few times, Vandt was a victim of his own addiction. Unlike many of the homeless, he was not mentally ill, but the combination of an abusive father and bad luck had put Billy on the streets when he was only eleven. Aside from a few mostly harmless run-ins with the police, Vandt had remained out of trouble for the past three decades.

When he wasn't high or drunk, Billy had a keen eye and kept watch over his friends. Under different life circumstances, Vandt would have made a good cop. He was a reliable source of information when he wanted to be, and Hal suspected Billy knew more about the latest shooting than he was saying. Hal also suspected that a cup of coffee and the promise of a warm meal and a little cash would get him to disclose what he knew.

As he parked the car, Hal's stomach growled. He hadn't eaten all day. Locking the car, he headed across to the burrito place to pick up a couple of burritos and a Coke for himself and Vandt before their interview. Vandt needed a little time to sober up, and the patrol officers were going to try to get some coffee in him. Hal would give it a half hour or so before he headed upstairs.

He had managed to keep his head on the case for most of the day. Anna never far from his thoughts, he'd channeled his focus on solving this case so that he could get back to finding her. To that end, he had spoken to no fewer than twenty-five of the homeless population who lived on and around Union Square. Most of them had still been in their makeshift cardboard beds when he'd arrived, but a few had already moved. He'd traveled to three different areas of the city, all of which had become makeshift tent communities, before he'd tracked them all down. Normally, the inefficiency would have frustrated him. Right now he was just grateful for the motion.

Telly had yet to return his phone calls from the day before, but Hal had spoken to Harper briefly, and she was working to find some reliable PI help in Greenville to help him dig into Spencer MacDonald's friends and associates.

Hal ordered four burritos—two for Vandt, one for himself, and one extra before heading back to the station. Hailey was getting her daughters dinner and planned to meet him at the station. He was about to call her when a text from Telly filled the screen. **Denver freezing. Confirmed SM using burners.**

Hal read the words again, untangling the two sentences. Telly had sent an update on the weather first, then the information on MacDonald? Somehow the FBI had confirmed that Spencer MacDonald was buying burner phones, so MacDonald was talking to someone. Hal felt sure MacDonald would be contacting whoever held Anna.

The three dots ran across Hal's screen. Hal stopped on the sidewalk, eyes fixed on the dots. The breath he was holding burned in his lungs. Had the FBI been able to retrieve one of the phones? If MacDonald discarded it somewhere, they could take it. They couldn't remove it from him—not without a warrant, at least not legally, although Hal would have happily taken MacDonald's phone in the Dallas restaurant if he'd discovered an extra one during their encounter.

But if MacDonald threw one away . . .

The dots vanished. No message appeared. Hal resisted the urge to shake the phone as though it were a stuck vending machine. Nothing. Hal released the air from his lungs. "Come on, Telly."

The dots returned, cycled for several seconds, and disappeared again.

"Screw it," Hal whispered, dialing the agent.

"Azar," Telly answered.

"It's Hal."

"Yeah. I was just texting you."

"You were taking your time with it," Hal snapped. "Did you get his burner?"

"No," Telly said. "One of the Denver field agents followed MacDonald into a convenience store. MacDonald purchased a burner phone there. Removed it from its package and tossed his trash in the parking lot."

"The agent checked the trash."

"The contents of the trash can were brought in to evidence, searched thoroughly."

Hal exhaled.

"No phone," Telly said. "But it's—"

"Don't say it," Hal said at the same moment Telly said, "Progress."

Hal was ready to hang up when Telly called his name. "There's more," the agent said.

"What?"

"We're looking into the death of MacDonald's mother, Peggy MacDonald. She died right after—"

"Thanksgiving," Hal interrupted. "From heart disease. I remember."

"That was the coroner's findings, but we received a call from a friend of Mrs. MacDonald's, a man who had seen her the morning before she died. Name is Bryce Scala. Scala was adamant that Mrs. MacDonald was not ill when he saw her."

Hal crossed his arms. Peggy MacDonald was in her midseventies, not exactly a spring chicken. Why would Telly pay the Scala guy any attention?

"Scala was convincing enough that I sent a couple of local agents to Leisure Palms—that's the nursing home. Found out Mrs. MacDonald was visited by a man the day of her death."

The outside air felt suddenly stuffy.

"The man was older-looking," Telly continued. "But one of the nurses commented that there was something about him. His hair didn't look real, she said. And he seemed to be hiding his face behind the flowers he was holding."

Hal felt a pressure on the back of his neck, swiped at it uncomfortably. "What kind of flowers?"

"Just a bouquet."

"What kind of bouquet, Telly? Do you know?"

"Hang on," Telly said. "I'm reading the notes."

Hal pressed the fingers of his free hand into the hollow above his eyes. Even if the bouquet was what he thought, it might still be a coincidence. What kind of man would kill his own mother?

"The front desk staff and one of the nurses both described it as a big bouquet of mixed flowers—all yellow."

"Yellow," Hal repeated.

"Right," Telly said. "I read about the bouquet Anna Schwartzman got from MacDonald."

"It doesn't mean anything," Hal said, but the words echoed empty in the quiet car.

"We're working to get a better description of the man," Telly said. "We're also running a search on the flight manifests in and out of every airport within two hundred miles of Greenville or Tampa, Florida."

"And?"

"So far, no Spencer MacDonald."

Hal sat up in the car. If MacDonald planned to hold Anna, he would need a new identity. Did he have one? Had he used it on a trip to Florida? To kill his own mother? "He might have a new ID, too."

"Yes. We're working on the possibility that he was using another name. I've got a team compiling footage from the airports."

"Send me a link to the footage," Hal said. "I can help look."

"I've got eight people working it—dedicated tech people. And good facial recognition software. If he was on a plane, we'll find him . . ."

"Call me the minute you do."

"Promise."

"I'd like to talk to Bryce Scala," Hal said. "If he'd be willing to talk to me."

"Sure," Telly said. "I'll find out."

Hal ended the call and made his way to the station. As he crossed the street, a man handed him a flyer. Hal took it, too tired to argue. At the front of the station, he stopped to call Hailey. His eyes drifted to the flyer, which announced a meeting at a local church.

Is CHRIST GUIDING YOUR LIFE? WON'T YOU LET HIM? WE CAN SHOW YOU HOW.

The next words read, TONIGHT. JANUARY 18, 7:00 P.M.

He dropped the flyer, watched as the page floated in the air toward the street. He couldn't take his eyes off it. A man's voice snapped at him. "Watch it." The man veered around Hal to get into the building, but Hal didn't even glance up. Instead, he turned and strode down the street, drawing a trembling breath through parted lips.

January 18.

Today was Anna's birthday.

31

"Roy!" a woman's voice hissed.

Schwartzman squeezed her eyes closed against the drilling pain in her head. Fog pressed down on her. She struggled to break through its icy crust and emerge.

"Shh," a voice said. "Shh!" it came again, more emphatic. Moisture sprayed her face. He was close. She flinched, raising her hands to her face. Her eyes flew open.

She gasped.

The man above her jerked back, his hands bent at the wrists and tucked to his chest almost under his chin.

Schwartzman didn't move. Slowly, he edged close again.

Behind thick, smudged glasses, his eyes were a bright blue. The eyes were small, the lids above folded heavily over them. Small lines circled beneath them as well. He turned to look sideways. A blue elastic band, the kind she often saw on small children, attached his glasses to his head.

His mouth hung open, his tongue out over his bottom lip. He smelled of peanut butter. Bits of it had collected at the corners of his lips.

"Roy!" came the woman's voice. "Where you at?"

He covered his mouth with a child-like hand and giggled softly before pressing his finger to his lips again. His nose was small and rounded, his face full.

"Roy Butler!" the woman shouted.

Schwartzman stared at him. This man looked nothing like the Roy Butler who had worked in her morgue. Was it possible that they were both named Roy?

He smiled at her, like they were playing a game, but she had no idea what to do or say. He seemed gentle, kind. Her fingers found the collar around her neck, and she pulled, testing it. When the collar didn't give, tears welled in her eyes.

He touched her cheek, his finger dirty.

She tried not to flinch.

"Roy! Are you in here?" A woman's voice in the cabin. The sound of hard-soled shoes echoed on the wood floor.

Schwartzman closed her eyes and turned her head. Let her mouth drop open and tried to take deep, even breaths.

"Roy Butler. You are not supposed to be in here. This is Tyler's girl."

The man said something she couldn't understand.

"You get on out of here. Tyler catch you, he'll tan your hide."

He made a disappointed groan and stomped from the room, the soft rubber soles of his shoes nothing like the hard, heavy ones the woman wore.

Schwartzman fought not to open her eyes, sensing the woman watching her. She wanted to turn over and bury her head but dared not. The floor beside the bed creaked. Unable to remain on her back, her face and chest exposed, she made a throaty sound as though her sleep were disturbed and rolled over in the bed. The collar pulled and choked, the cord eventually releasing from the spool above to alleviate the tightness.

Her eyes still squeezed closed, she listened to the silence. The thud of footsteps still remained in the room. Something landed with a light tap on the table beside the door. A moment later, the woman's shoes clomped across the floor again. Muffled steps in the outer room gave way to the thwack of the screen door closing and the distant sounds of the woman's voice as she scolded the man.

Schwartzman pulled her hands to her chest, lifted her knees, and huddled into a tight ball. She touched her face, remembering the tears, but her face was dry. How terrified she'd been to feel that man so close.

He was a man named Roy Butler. But he certainly wasn't the Roy Butler she'd known from the morgue or the man who'd abducted her. This was a man with Down syndrome.

Schwartzman recalled a victim with Down syndrome who'd been killed behind a community college in San Francisco the year before. His wallet had been stolen, though his mother swore he'd had only a bus pass and ten dollars. His head bashed into the pavement, he'd been left to die. On internal examination of his head, Schwartzman had discovered a frontal subgaleal hematoma underlying the forehead contusion. There were similar temporoparietal subgaleal hemorrhages on both the left and right sides, as well as hemorrhage of the temporal muscles. A soft organ in a hard container, the brain has nowhere to go when the blood collects. When parts of the brain are squeezed, the result is herniation. In this case, the brain stem had been pressed farther down the foramen magnum, constricting the centers that control breathing.

His breathing had simply stopped.

It had been Hal's case. The thought of Hal made her heart ache. She pressed her hands to her belly, certain now that their child was growing there. They'd never caught the man's killer. Schwartzman recalled the roundness of the victim's face, the distinct features of his genetic anomaly. He had been in his early twenties, but everything about his face was boyish and kind.

The man who had been here, in this room, had seemed calm, too. Was it his mother who had called after him? Schwartzman replayed the voice in her head. The low tones of the woman's voice made Schwartzman think she was at least in her late forties, early fifties. A smoker, by the sounds of it, which made it harder to guess. If they smoked enough, a twenty-five-year-old could sound fifty.

Schwartzman wished she had gotten a look at the woman, but how could she have done that? She shifted her head on the pillow, the ache at her temples a reminder that she didn't have sufficient clean water. The snow had stopped, and without the metal slat, she had no way to reach the surrounding snow on the ground. She closed her eyes and studied the gentle pulsing in her temples. The pain could be from the drugs themselves, the dehydration, or perhaps caused by the near-strangulation she'd suffered more than once. The day before, she had eaten a yogurt and two peanut butter sandwiches. She was hungrier now, and the food only temporarily settled her stomach, which felt perpetually queasy, either from the drugs or the pregnancy.

But the more she ate of those foods, the more she would have to drink the drugged water. She was caught in a vicious cycle. At that thought, she had to fight the urge to scream and fight against the cable, the collar.

She forced herself to take slow, deep breaths. She would not break the collar. Certainly not on her own. Not without some tool.

She needed an ally.

She recalled the sound of a woman crying out when Roy—or the man she'd thought had been Roy—had struck her. But maybe it wasn't a woman. Maybe the person who was struck had been the man with Down syndrome.

She thought about the man who'd hovered over, pressing his finger to his lips as he'd evaded his mother or sister. Pairing that man with the child-like writing of the Holocaust tattoo on her arm, she was suddenly relieved. Likely, he had written those numbers. As hateful as they were,

172

they might have seemed like a game to him. Something he'd seen his family do. She thought again about Roy Butler. Roy. The boy's name was Roy. "Tyler's girl," the woman had said. But the man in her morgue was Roy Butler. Or maybe he wasn't. Maybe the Roy Butler who had worked in the morgue wasn't actually Roy. He might have used his brother's identity to get the job. And there was only one reason for Tyler Butler to steal his disabled brother's identity—Tyler already had a record.

She opened her eyes and stared at the track on the ceiling. For the first time, she really studied its finish, the screws that held it to the ceiling. Was it new? She'd assumed this had been installed for her, but what if it wasn't? What if she was wrong about the projection? What if Spencer wasn't behind this? Or what if Spencer had decided to let someone else have her, torture her?

The woman had called her Tyler's girl.

What if he regularly brought women here? Perhaps he'd been close to capture, so he'd changed his name and taken his brother's. It would work once. But that meant another woman had lived in these walls, been drugged . . . and then what?

What had happened to her when Tyler Butler was done?

32

Hal was at his desk when the internal call came in. If he'd been paying attention, he would have hesitated to answer. But now it was too late. The voice on the line was Scott Theobold.

"I called Hailey first," he said. He must have heard the dread in Hal's silence. "But she wasn't answering, so I thought I'd try you."

Hal shifted in his chair. "Sure."

"I'm finishing the autopsy on our first gunshot victim, and I've found something I think you should see."

"What is it?"

"Can you come down? It's in several places, and I could photograph it, but I think it might be clearer in person. I'm also collecting it to send to Roger, so I could get it to him first, if that's the process. I was under the impression that Dr. Schwartzman did her best to show you her findings before she separated the evidence from the victim."

The rushed sound of Theobold's voice, the long explanation, exposed the man's nervousness.

"I'll come now," Hal said and hung up the desk phone. He stared at Hailey's empty chair and wondered how soon she would be back. He sighed. *Get up and go, Harris.* He rose from his chair and went.

On his way down the department stairs, the tightness that had lived in his chest since last Saturday clamped down. He came through the lobby doors hardly able to breathe, almost stumbling out onto the department's steps. *Breathe. Breathe.* He hurried down the stairs and around the side of the building, stopping before he reached the morgue building to force air into his lungs.

Six days she'd been gone. Almost a week. He thought about the statistics on missing persons. The chances of finding someone alive halved after twenty-four hours. Then it halved again sometime in the next thirty-six. He pushed the number from his head. The needle would remain at 100 percent until he had her in his arms.

Within a few strides, his lungs expanded, and he drew air to fill them. He would work this case and find Anna. Things would go back to normal. No, they would be better. She was pregnant. Everything would change. It would be a new normal. He glanced back up at the department building and wondered again if he should have waited for Hailey to return to the station. But having Hailey at his side as he walked into the morgue would not have made this easier.

Nothing would, short of Anna herself.

He squeezed his fists against the pain in his chest. *Where are you?* He wanted to scream. His heart thumped like a caged rabbit beneath his ribs.

Pull it together, Harris.

The sooner you catch this son of a bitch, the sooner you get back to finding Anna.

Inside the building, Hal refused to see the worry in anyone's faces or feel their eyes dissecting his own expression. Instead, he strode down the hall to the morgue's door. Through the small window, he could see Dr. Theobold at work.

Gripping the handle hard, Hal almost barreled into the door when it didn't open. It took him a minute to realize it was locked.

Anna never locked the door when she was inside working.

He rapped on the window, and Theobold looked up, raised a blue-gloved hand.

The acting medical examiner removed his gloves and disposed of them before opening the door for Hal. Theobold then returned to the sink, washed his hands, and put on a fresh pair of gloves before returning to the body. That explained why Anna never locked the damn door. It was a waste of time.

Theobold returned to the body and adjusted the sheet to cover the victim's face. Clasping his hands together, he turned to Hal and offered a tentative smile. In it was a flash of fear.

Hal pulled on a pair of gloves as well and turned to the table.

"My sister died when she was nineteen," Theobold said.

Hal turned to the medical examiner. "How?"

"Car accident," he said, as though apologizing that it wasn't something more dramatic.

"I'm sorry," Hal said.

Theobold looked up, surprised. "I was twenty-two, just finishing at Berkeley. I had planned to go into research medicine . . ." He let the words trail off. Her death had changed his plans. It was understood. What was unclear was why Theobold had shared this. Perhaps he thought Hal could relate.

But there were no similarities. Anna was not dead. And she was not his sister.

Theobold lifted a notebook and started reading. His voice held a nervous tremor as though he were a high schooler giving a presentation. "Male victim, five eleven, one hundred and eighty pounds. Aged thirty—"

"I don't think I need his age," Hal said. "Unless it's relevant to what you wanted to show me." He tried to keep his voice calm, soothing. Theobold was being thorough, but Hal didn't need thorough. He needed efficient. He needed answers, and then he needed to move on.

Removing his gloves, Theobold opened his laptop and unlocked the screen, double clicking on a file. "A gunshot entrance wound to the right side of the chest is centered eighteen inches below the top of the head and three inches right of midline. It is a five-sixteenths-inch round defect with a circumferential margin of abrasion measuring up to one-eighth inch in maximum span. The wound has no associated soot or stippling."

It was too much detail, much more than Hal needed, but he caught the gist. Gunshot to the chest. No soot or stippling meant the shooter was at least eighteen inches from the victim.

"A gunshot exit wound of the right side of the back is centered nineteen inches below the top of the head and four inches right of midline. It is a half-inch, curvilinear, slit-like defect with no margin of abrasion." Theobold pushed his glasses up the bridge of his nose.

"Through and through," Hal said.

Theobold looked up. "Yes."

"Any fragments recovered?"

Theobold consulted his notes. "Not in conjunction with this wound, no."

"And the other bullet?"

Theobold cleared his throat. "The second bullet perforated the anterolateral right fifth intercostal space—"

"What did the bullet hit? What killed him?"

Theobold set down his laptop and removed his glasses. "I'm not used to homicide. I usually just submit my reports in writing."

"You're doing a great job," Hal said. "This is just—" He closed his mouth. What could he say? It was awkward? Impossible? Torture?

Theobold nodded. "Let me back up. I called you down for this." He double clicked on a close-up of the victim's shirt, a collared light-blue golf shirt that looked new. On its right side was the hole from the first bullet. Theobold zoomed in on the image. As he did, a tiny spot of gold appeared on one edge of the hole.

"What is that?"

"At first, I thought it was something on the shirt." Theobold switched to another image, this one taken through a microscope. "But now I think it's paint."

"Gold paint?"

Theobold nodded. "It looks like it may have come off the projectile."

"You think the paint was on the bullet?"

"It's a theory," Theobold said carefully. "Roger agreed it was possible. I sent an image to him. There's probably not enough residue to perform tests on chemical makeup, but he's going to try."

Testing would take days, maybe longer, depending on how backed up the lab was.

"I thought seeing it might help," Theobold added.

Hal nodded, trying to place the gold paint in the puzzle of this case. "I appreciate it. Was there paint on the other shooting victim?"

"Not that I've found so far, but I'm planning to go back for another look next."

"Let me know if you find anything."

"I will," Theobold promised. "And I'll get the rest of my report to you tonight."

Hal walked to the door, removing the gloves as he did. At the door, he took a last look back. "Thanks, Doc."

Theobold nodded, his expression unreadable.

Hal made his way back out of the morgue building, happy to be in the open air again. Gold paint ought to have been a helpful clue, but without the bullet or cartridges, there was no way to confirm it was transferred from the bullet itself. Hal walked toward his car, thinking about taking another look around Union Square with an eye out for gold paint. As he reached his car, his phone rang. Telly.

"Azar," he said, his voice breaking on the word.

"I don't have any news," Telly said quickly. Like ripping off a Band-Aid so that Hal didn't hope for too many seconds.

"Okay," Hal said.

There was a pause on Telly's end.

Something was wrong. "What is it?"

"I'm getting pulled," Telly said after a moment.

"What do you mean? You're supposed to stay with him. Every step." Hal was shouting, his voice bouncing across the parking lot. "They promised," he added, lowering his voice.

"I've got two more days—today and tomorrow."

"Today's almost over," Hal said. "You can't count today." Even to his own ears, he sounded petulant, but he couldn't help himself.

"After tomorrow, I'll make sure someone keeps an eye on him, but it won't be full-time." There was a brief pause before the agent started talking again. "And we're flagging all his credit cards for purchases. There's nothing out of the ordinary. We don't have anything on him."

"No," Hal said, a forceful bark. "He's waiting for us to give up, to stop tracking him." Hal heard the desperation in his own voice. "What about his mother's death? You said the Tampa police were working that angle?"

"They are, but there's no clear footage of the man who visited Mrs. MacDonald the day she died. And they haven't been able to locate MacDonald on the flights around the time of her death."

He didn't want MacDonald in prison in Florida, but having him free without a tail was worse. Much worse. His gaze on the building where Anna worked, Hal leaned across his car, laying his free hand on the roof, slick from the moisture in the air. "You can't give up."

"I'm not giving up," Telly said.

But the tone of his voice said exactly the opposite. The door to the morgue building opened, and a dark-haired woman emerged, pulling her coat tight across her as the wind tried to blow it open. Anna, for a moment. But not Anna.

Hal ended the call without saying good-bye.

33

Schwartzman woke to breath on her face. Her eyes sprang open, and she wriggled to the corner of the bed where she pressed herself against the wall. The collar jerked her back. She tucked her fingers beneath the band, trying to draw breath.

"You're scared," came the voice. A child's voice. It was Roy.

Slowly, the outline of his face emerged in the dark. His chin rested on one hand, his head barely higher than the bed. He was kneeling on the floor, breathing noisily through his nose.

"Roy?" she whispered.

He nodded, his tongue filling the gap between his lips.

"Are you alone?"

He shook his head.

She stared past him at the bedroom door. "Who's here?"

He smiled, pointing at her. "You."

She smiled back, the sensation stretching uncomfortably on her lips. "Right. But no one else?"

He shook his head again.

She tugged the covers up and tucked them under her arms, putting another layer between them. "Do you think you could help me, Roy?"

His eyes widened in interest. "I left you a key."

"I got it," she whispered. "Is it a key for the door?"

He nodded again.

She turned the collar until the clasp faced Roy. "I need a key to this so I can take it off."

He shook his head, eyes wide. "You have to keep that on," he said. "Mammy said so. Keep it on all the time."

"Because of Mammy."

He nodded.

"Or because of Tyler?"

"Because of Mammy and Tyler."

Not Dad, she thought. Tyler. Perhaps brothers, as she had suspected earlier. "I don't have to keep it on because of Spencer?"

He tilted his head. "Is Spencer in my school?"

She shook her head. "No. Spencer is a grown-up, like me."

"Does he work at Walmart?"

"No. Not at Walmart."

"Where, then?"

"Spencer is just visiting. He doesn't live here all the time."

"Like you?"

"Like me," she agreed. "How long am I visiting?"

"Probably a long time. As long as Tyler wants." His gaze floated up toward the ceiling and then back down to her. "Tyler doesn't have rules. Roy has rules," he added, pointing to himself. "But not Tyler."

She swallowed, fighting back tears.

"You don't want to stay here?" he asked.

"I miss my home."

He nodded slowly.

Somewhere outside, a car door slammed. Roy jumped to his feet, frantic.

"Roy!" a voice called from outside.

Schwartzman fisted the covers, freezing. Roy Butler's voice. No, *Tyler* Butler's voice.

"Oh no. Tyler. I have to go."

He scurried from the room, gone too quickly for her to reinforce the need for a key or to ask for something to cut with.

The slap of skin on skin rang out, followed by Roy's shriek. A sob. Then a squeak of a metal spring stretching. A screen door. He was coming in. She lowered herself in the bed, turned her back to the door, and held her breath.

Boots made their way across the wood floor, the sounds growing as they approached. Did he have a weapon? Could she launch herself at him and take him unaware? And then what? What if he wasn't carrying the key? What if there was someone else with him? What if she couldn't overpower him?

The bedroom door opened, and his boots came heel-toe into the room. She sensed him looking down at her. She squeezed her eyes shut, gripping her arms to her chest. She was too rigid to be sleeping. He would know she was awake.

His fingers brushed the hair off her forehead. Her pulse hammered against her ribs, throbbing in her head, in her arms and fingers.

"Dr. Schwartzman," he whispered, leaning close to her ear and drawing out her name like something bitter in his mouth.

She fought to relax her whole body, to act as though the drugs had knocked her out. The smell of him invaded her nose—sweat and dirt and pine and alcohol reeking from his pores. She struggled not to flinch or turn away.

"You're quite a prize," he whispered again. "I look forward to trying you out. Not long now." He spoke the words slowly, pleasure in his voice.

His lips touched her cheek. The feel of his tongue on her skin. "Think my little brother wants some sweet Bella, too. What do you say?" He let out a low chuckle that made her flinch. "You want to pop little Roy's cherry?"

Her head throbbed, the blood coursing through a loud rhythm in her ears. Issuing what she hoped sounded like a little sleep sound, she shifted onto her belly, lying flat. Let her hair fall across her face. Willed him to go away.

"Just a few more days together, but I'm going to enjoy them." She felt the covers shift off her legs, his fingers on the skin of her calf.

Her eyes filled. She bunched her fists in preparation to fight. She would not let him touch her. He would not touch her.

His hand groped through the cotton of her sweatpants.

She swallowed a gasp.

Prodding fingers cupped under her buttocks, probing at her.

She held her breath, tried to shift again. But he had placed a palm on her back, pressing her down with one hand while the other dug between her legs through her clothes.

What was she going to do? How could she fight him in this collar? But she could not let him touch her. She would not be raped. She thought of the baby. Her baby.

Tyler froze.

The screen door hissed open. The hinge squealed as it closed.

Tyler let go of her. "Roy? That you?"

A moment later came the long squawk of the screen door opening again.

"Goddamn it, Roy!"

Tyler removed his hands.

Schwartzman took small, stilted breaths.

His boots crossed the bedroom floor.

She remained frozen, praying he would leave.

And then his boot steps faded across the living room, followed by the slow squawk of the screen door.

"Get over here," Tyler shouted. A beat passed, followed by a high-pitched cry. Roy.

Then the voices were gone. A car door opened, then closed.

An engine and tires whispered in the snow. They were gone. Or Tyler was.

Once the engine noise had receded into the distance, Schwartzman sat up slowly. Her muscles ached from the clenching, lactic acid saturating their fibers. He was gone for now.

But he was coming back. There were no rules for Tyler. And there was no one here to stop him. Today, she had Roy to thank for the distraction.

She wouldn't get lucky twice.

She needed a way out. And she needed it now.

34

Sitting up in the hotel room bed, Spencer stared at the ringing phone. As he stared at the number, there was a slight tremor in his hand.

201-2777.

How a phone number could bring it all back, like being a child again. He hadn't called that number since high school. Hadn't let it enter his consciousness since the first year of college. How was the phone number for his father's church office still even in his head?

But there it was.

And someone was calling him from it.

The phone whistled its trill little sound, his mother's voice echoing in his head. Every day as he'd entered the house from school. "Call your father."

He imagined the black phone on the wall, its twisted cord short and tight beneath it. In his mind, he touched the tight coils, tried to thread his pinkie finger through them without pulling them loose. They had always seemed normal until that time he'd gone to Sadie Duncan's house. After that, nothing about his house was ever normal again.

Sadie Duncan's was the one party he'd ever been invited to, in the first grade. Her family had the same black phone, but its cord stretched out so long that it almost touched the ground. He had wondered how his own family could get a long, stretchy cord like that. He would wind himself up inside it and spin across the kitchen.

He had come into the kitchen for a glass of water in the middle of the party when the phone rang. Sadie's mother put a finger up to him and answered the phone. Smiling and talking rapidly to whomever was on the other line, Mrs. Duncan had tucked the phone beneath her chin and moved across the kitchen, darting here and there like a hummingbird. She got a glass from the cupboard and crossed to the sink to fill it, returned to the doorway to hand it to him. Spencer watched, mesmerized as the cord stretched easily from one end of the room to the other as she worked.

He had never seen his own mother talk on the phone. He had witnessed her answering the telephone, of course. When it rang, she gave it a menacing glance as though it threatened to ruin her day. Then she crossed to the wall to lift the shiny black receiver off the base. Ramrod straight and thin-lipped, she spoke in short, clipped sentences as though she had something much more pressing to attend to. When the call was done, she went back to one of her boring tasks—mending, cooking, polishing, or cleaning. Occasionally, he saw her at the kitchen table with a cup of steaming tea, reading. But the only book she read was the Bible.

Spencer stood from the hotel bed and crossed the room. His phone had stopped ringing. He set the phone down on the dresser and watched it, wondering if the caller would leave a voicemail. Imagining his father's voice made it difficult to shake off the overwhelming sense of dread.

Why would his father's church be contacting him? There would be some mundane reason, he told himself. He'd been in the church on Monday. Had it only been five days earlier? He stared around the generic Detroit hotel room. That was all it was. Someone in the church had gotten his cell number, probably one of the old ladies who worked in the office, the same ones who'd been there when his father was alive.

Perhaps he'd left something there at his mother's service. But he knew he had not. He waited for the bell announcing a voicemail, but none came. He drew slow, even breaths, but the dread sat like acid in his stomach. No amount of breathing could dispel it. He crossed to the closet.

There, he opened the hotel safe and removed the thin plastic sack that contained two prepaid phones. He unwrapped one, powered it up, and dialed the number he knew by heart.

"Yeah," came the answer.

"I'm checking in," Spencer said, walking purposefully across the room. It helped to move. Plus, hearing the solid sound of his own voice settled the discomfort in his stomach.

"You don't need to check in on me," the man said with his hillbilly accent. Spencer had found the twang humorous at first, but not now. "We're all fine here," he added with a little hiss on the *H*. "Just fine."

Spencer felt a twitching in his jaw. The man was a Neanderthal, so he let it go. "How did she respond to the video?"

"Just about passed out," he said. "Guess your girl's got a crush on that n—"

"Watch it," Spencer interrupted, talking over the last word.

The man laughed his barking laugh. Spencer had known the man was a redneck idiot from the moment they'd first corresponded. Living in his hick town, working as an orderly across four counties, Tyler Butler had been barely surviving. With Caleb's assistance, Spencer had gotten him a job with the San Francisco ME's office, set him up in a little apartment, and paid him on top of his meager salary. Tyler was to keep track of Bella's every move, as much as he could. He was never to go to her house or put himself in her life outside work, but while they were working together, Tyler was instructed to make Bella's life uncomfortable, make her nervous. Scare her, even. But he had to do it without getting caught.

But Tyler had fucked that up—lost his temper and threatened her, called her a kike. There was no going back to his job at the morgue after that. Tyler had begged for another chance. Begged like a child. Spencer was not one for second chances, but Tyler's location in northern Idaho fit well into this part of his plan.

But now the man had chewed through Spencer's remarkable patience. Spencer calmed himself by imagining how satisfying it would be to wring the man's neck. The job could have been the easiest $50,000 this guy ever earned—or would ever earn. But each conversation made Spencer all the more certain that Tyler Butler wouldn't live to collect his money.

"You know our agreement," Spencer said. "I'll call in and check on things when and as often as I see fit."

"Yeah, well, you checked in, so we're done. I got things to tend to here," Butler said. "Got to make sure your girl's in good hands, you know."

"Be careful, Mr. Butler," Spencer warned. "We have a very specific deal, if you remember."

"Yeah, I remember. Seems like there ought to be a bonus in it. A little incentive not to taste the cake. I got a look at the frosting, and man, it ain't easy. You get what I'm saying?"

"You ought to watch yourself, Mr. Butler."

"Yeah? And what're you going to do about it?"

"There is the matter of your compensation."

"Oh, you'll pay me, all right," Butler said. "I'm the one in charge here. I've got the goods. Don't go threatening me." With that, Butler ended the call.

The rage settled into his limbs as Spencer sank onto the edge of the hotel bed and stared at the ugly maroon carpeting. He was still due in Cleveland and Richmond and had four more investors to meet. He had the Scala business to finish. But suddenly, none of that mattered. He could not leave Bella with that man. Spencer had thought Tyler would be satisfied with money, but men like Butler weren't smart enough to know what was good for them.

Tyler Butler thought he had five days left with Bella. In fact, he didn't even have forty-eight hours. Again Spencer chastised himself for forgetting to empty the final safety deposit box. He could have been on his way to her by now.

But it had to be done. He considered Bryce Scala. That, too, was a loose end that needed tying. Scala would be back in Florida now, so Spencer would have to rely on Caleb's help.

Caleb. Spencer tucked the burner phone into his laptop bag to dispose of later and thought about how he would break the news to Caleb. One way or another, he would, because if something happened to Bella, everything he'd gone through was for nothing. He wasn't Tyler Butler. He couldn't just pick up any woman and be satisfied. It was only Bella. It had always been only her. He would go back to Greenville, collect the contents of the safety deposit box, and call Caleb from there. Get his help with Scala. Make it up to him another way. Caleb knew he was good for it.

Then he would go to Bella.

His phone buzzed from the dresser. A voicemail from his father's church. Spencer deleted it without listening. He didn't need another omen. It was crystal clear what he needed to do.

35

Hal woke with two thoughts in his head. One, that a week had passed since Anna had been taken, and two, that he remembered where he'd seen gold paint. When he'd been walking around Union Square after the stabbing, he had noticed a series of flyers announcing an upcoming art show for next weekend. The posters were black with gold foil letters, but across the bottom of each was a slash of gold paint. That night, he had watched a couple pull one down and carry it away after the woman recognized the artist's name. Only in the hours of sleep did he recognize that the gold strip on each flyer was slightly different, longer or shorter, the brushstrokes bolder or less noticeable. It occurred to him that it might have been the artist who had added the paint to each one.

Out of bed, Hal got a cup of coffee and shared his theory with Hailey over the phone. After that, he'd gone to Union Square to collect a flyer that Roger could compare to the paint found on the victim's shirt. With the flyer dropped at the lab, he and Hailey planned to go to the gallery and speak to the artist.

Hopefully, it wouldn't take Roger much time to provide a reasonable guess about whether the paint was a match. Hal longed to jump on this one lead and force it into whatever hole it had to fit to close this case. He knew that wasn't how it worked, but his patience had worn thin.

He slid into the department car with Hailey and buckled his seat belt. She had offered to drive, and he had agreed. His nerves didn't need the added irritation of San Francisco traffic. They drove in silence, the soft rock on the stereo the only noise in the car. Hal knew she had plenty of questions, and he was grateful he didn't have to answer any. She was turning onto Montgomery Street in the financial district when his phone rang.

Telly's name appeared on the screen. He wondered if the agent had found something definitive on the death of Spencer MacDonald's mother. Or if he was calling to remind Hal that today was his last day on the job. That the bureau would be pulling him after today. "What's going on, Telly?"

"Did I catch you at a bad time?"

"Yes, but tell me what's going on." The fear constricted his throat, corking his voice, which came out tight and strange.

"Two things."

"Tell me."

"First, MacDonald is leaving Detroit early, and he's skipping the rest of his stops. He's changed his flight to return directly to Greenville."

Hal froze against his seat. "Why?"

Hailey glanced over at him, her expression questioning.

"No idea," Telly admitted. "We had his itinerary flagged, so we got an automatic notification from the airline."

Hailey turned west on Pine Street and started up the hill. They were getting close to the gallery. He leaned forward and read the street signs, trying to focus on both her and Telly. "But you're still on him? You'll go, too." It was not a question.

"I think the gallery is here somewhere," Hailey said as they reached Quincy. "Can you check the address?"

"Uh," Telly stuttered across the line.

"Telly," Hal repeated. "You are going to Greenville."

"Today was my last day. I told you that. I've been called back to Dallas right away."

"You're on this case until we find her," Hal said, his voice rising. "That was the deal."

"We've got a situation in Dallas—a serial bomber. Haven't you read the news?"

Hal tried to remember the last time he'd seen a paper or checked the news on his phone. Before Anna was taken.

"I'm sorry, Hal," Telly said.

Hailey pulled to the curb and checked her phone before driving half a block more. The gallery was just ahead. On the front window in black script were the words *Right Wrong*, the name the artist went by. The familiar swath of gold paint underscored the words.

Hailey put the car in park and looked over at him.

"That wasn't the deal, Telly. I'm dealing with a double homicide. I need you to go there." He nodded to Hailey, who shut off the engine and cracked her door.

"Three bombs, six injured, and one dead. In the past two days," Telly said. "I'm needed in Dallas."

"I got a promise that you'd stay on him," Hal said, his voice thinning, desperate even as anger filled his chest and burned his throat. He knew he should stop, but he couldn't. The FBI had to follow MacDonald. Someone had to watch him. "They gave me the agent just out of high school, but that was okay because there was a promise that you'd be there. That you'd follow him."

Hailey rounded the car and pulled open his door.

He wished the fear in her eyes was for their suspects in the gallery, but he knew it wasn't.

"I'll call you later, but you've got to fix this," Hal said.

"I don't think I—"

"You have to." Hal ended the call and stood from the car. Hailey was still watching him. As he closed the door and started for the gallery, he avoided looking at her face. His own fear was enough to make it feel as though he were drowning. If he added hers, he would never surface.

36

Georgia woke feeling guilty Saturday morning. She'd let the week get away from her, and now she was woefully behind. The weekend would have to be productive. Already, she'd planned an afternoon luncheon. Patrice had called to tell her that something was going on with Evelyn's husband, Dell, so a few of them were going over there today. Dell had always had a wandering eye, but Evelyn had done her best to ignore his trysts. Patrice said maybe Dell had found more than a tryst this time. Poor Evelyn. No wonder she was drinking so much more these days. Tonight she'd go to a show at the Centre Stage with a few friends. She was grateful to be busy, but already this morning had flown by. How had it gotten so late?

Whatever was happening with her, she needed to snap out of it. Her plan had been to wake up early this morning and go to the bank before it closed—she'd forgotten to get cash to pay the gardeners, who came on Monday. The staff was preparing lunch, but she needed to be home in plenty of time to make sure everything was set. It gave her only an hour or so.

Tomorrow, she would attend church and take a long walk. Getting her heart rate up a bit would be good, too. Traffic was light this morning, increasingly rare now in Greenville, and the block before the bank, she decided to stop at Starbucks for a soy latte. She'd read that some ingredient in soy milk ate away at the lining of the stomach, so she didn't let herself have it very often. She did love the slightly sweet vanilla flavor, and today felt like a day for a treat.

As she was pulling out of the Starbucks on Pleasantburg, a gold Lexus almost clipped the front of her car. She raised a hand as the driver swerved around her, but he didn't even notice her. The profile of his face was instantly familiar. The sight of Spencer MacDonald elicited a small shriek in the back of her throat. The Lexus sped away, and before she knew where she was going, Georgia had raced onto the street behind him.

She passed the Wells Fargo bank where she had intended to stop and glanced at the clock. 11:20 a.m. She did need cash. She could get it tomorrow, if only she could remember the damn code for her ATM card. She kept meaning to get that thing reset. Ahead, Spencer had stopped at the red light. She gripped the wheel and considered turning back.

The light turned green, and she moved forward, following behind a Volkswagen between her car and Spencer's. When the Volkswagen turned right, she was directly behind him. He turned on to Furman Hall Road toward the highway. She left some space between them and followed. Highway 276 went into downtown Greenville. He might have been heading to his office. She might catch him there, and they could talk. But what would she tell him when he asked why she'd come to his office on a Saturday? She could say she was in the neighborhood and saw his car.

No. That would sound strange. She'd have to think of another excuse.

She lifted her phone and dialed his number. If he answered, she could ask to meet him. The call rang over her car speaker. Ahead, his profile appeared as Spencer glanced at something. The phone, surely. He would see it was her. He would answer.

"You have reached the voicemail of Spencer MacDonald . . ."

She stabbed the "End Call" button on the dash screen. He'd seen it was her and ignored her. Her mouth felt suddenly dry, her heart pounding. What was wrong with her?

What was wrong with him?

As she expected, Spencer turned on to 276, heading downtown. She followed. He sped up so rapidly that for a moment, she thought he must have spotted her. He changed into the fast lane and passed several slower-moving cars before swerving back, his driving suddenly erratic. She remained in the slow lane, pulse pounding. A black Mercedes SUV passed her, and the gold Lexus grew smaller in the distance. *You have to catch up.* Drawing a deep breath and checking over her shoulder, Georgia changed into the fast lane and followed behind the Mercedes. The odometer approached seventy-five, and she checked her rearview mirror. She'd never had a speeding ticket. She didn't like driving this fast. But she was closing in on the Lexus, so she kept going.

Where the highway became Buncombe Street, Spencer turned left. He *was* heading to his office. Well, she would follow. She shifted her shoulders back as she steeled her nerves. At least they were going the speed limit again. At Academy Street, she kept a few cars between them, waiting for Spencer to get in the left lane. His office was only a few blocks from here.

But he didn't turn left. Instead, he went right. She missed the light and watched with growing panic as the Lexus got farther ahead. There was a short break in oncoming traffic, and she drove out between two cars to follow. The driver behind her blared his horn, and she waved a hand as a belated thank-you, ignoring the gestures he made through his windshield. From there, Spencer turned onto Washington and then Main, in the heart of the downtown business district. Spencer drove into the parking lot adjacent to Wells Fargo. She drove past, pulling to the curb across the street.

When Spencer emerged from the car, she hardly recognized him. He wore a pair of sweatpants with slim legs, the kind tennis pros wore when the weather got cold. On top he had a crewneck sweatshirt, black with no logo. She'd never seen him in anything like this. He was always so dapper. Even when he worked at home, he always wore a collared shirt. What was this?

As he jogged toward the bank, she had the ridiculous notion that he might be robbing it. She grabbed her phone and stared at it. But who could she call? She set the phone back on the passenger seat and then picked it up again to dial Bella's number from her list of contacts.

The call went straight to voicemail. An electronic voice told her to leave a message. She wished it were Bella's voice.

Lowering the phone, she thought of the detective's business card that sat on the table by the front door. But what could she possibly report? That Spencer was in town and walking into the bank? In strange clothes?

She stared at his car, sitting in the lot. Why would he come to this branch when there was a Wells Fargo just two blocks from where he'd first passed her? That was where she'd been headed herself. As she stared at the building, she realized she could casually run into him inside and say she'd been doing something downtown. She could confront him right here. She gathered her purse off the floor on the passenger side of the car, tucked her phone inside it, and reached for the door.

But he was already walking back to the car.

He held a large manila envelope tucked under his arm in a way that reminded her of a quarterback running with a football. He glanced around as though expecting he might be followed. She froze as his gaze scanned past her car, but he didn't seem to see her.

Spencer acted nervous, twitchy. Why did he look so guilty? The parking lot remained quiet. There was no rush of bank employees or police running after him, so it was unlikely that he'd robbed the bank. No, he'd gone inside and picked up something. Was it valuable? Was that why he held it that way?

She didn't have time to think.

He was in his car. She tossed her purse back on the passenger seat and slammed her door closed again. The Lexus pulled out of the lot, and she hesitated. He was a free man. He had the right to go wherever he wanted.

And yet, she wanted to know where he was going. She felt she deserved to know. She promised herself that she would never admit what she was doing to another human being.

Then she started her engine and followed her daughter's ex-husband.

37

Schwartzman's arms ached as she held the house key Roy had brought her loosely between two fingers. Some hours earlier, her right hand had lost the strength to grip it with enough tension to saw away at the thick rubber of her collar. Even after working at it for the past twenty-four hours, the metal edge had made only a tiny divot. Afterward, she'd been unable to sleep. The house was silent, the air outside still, but her mind managed to conjure noises. Every time she almost dropped off, she was jolted awake by some imaginary sound, sure it was Tyler Butler coming for her. The night sky was pitch, the moon nowhere in sight, the clouds like ash smeared across a dark page.

Her head raged. She lay on the bed and watched the snow fall through the window. She should have been elated. Snow meant water, but it felt like too little too late. She recognized the signs of her own dehydration and knew she needed more water than the snow could provide. To conserve energy, she had spent the majority of the last day in bed, trying to rest. Yesterday, she ate two yogurts from the refrigerator and several handfuls of cereal to try to quell her hunger, but the food made the thirst so much worse. Every couple of hours, she got out of the bed and switched the cup on the windowsill for an empty one, letting the water melt beside her bed while the snow filled the other one.

What had begun as a rabbit-like fear had slowed into something deeper, more insipid. Lethargy. Dread. And she was helpless to prevent it. Hal would not find her, and Tyler would hurt her, and then Spencer would come. Whatever her ex-husband had in store for her, he would not let her get away again. Would he kill her? It seemed likely, but she also knew he would not do it right away.

He would want her to suffer.

The torture she had endured these last days was nothing compared to what Spencer would do to her. This she knew for certain. With some difficulty, she sat upright in the bed and drained the water from the cup on the table. The snow fell more lightly now, though the sky remained a solid bank of gray. She glanced at the spot on the wall where she'd used the key to keep track of time—six fine lines scratched into the drywall. The count was probably off by a day or two, but it was close enough.

She'd been here almost a week.

Exhausted, she stood from the bed and padded into the bathroom. The cord stuck along the track, and she had to stop several times to yank it along, her face hot from the effort. She was not sweating. Her body lacked the necessary hydration for sweat production. She hadn't peed in almost a day and a half. She ran the water in the sink and splashed her face with the cool liquid, pressing her lips tight against the water. She yearned to drink. Her thirst was overwhelming. But so was her fear that Tyler Butler would be back, and that if she were unconscious, he would assault her.

She would have to drink soon. The baby needed the water. She needed it. She set the empty cup on the back of the toilet, hoping that placing it an arm's distance away would dampen the desire to fill it to the brim with water from the sink and drink. As the hard plastic clanked against the white porcelain, an idea floated into her head.

Setting the cup aside, she pulled the cover off the toilet tank. Water. At the bottom of the tank, beneath the flapper, was a thin layer of silt, but the water in the back of the tank should be clean. Bacteria could make its way from the bowl to the tank. It was a possibility. But it was certainly cleaner than the water in the bowl. What she didn't know was whether it was drug-free. But she felt desperate now.

It was worth a try.

She dipped her cup into the water, lifted it to her mouth, and took a swallow. As the drug was tasteless, there was no way of knowing whether the water was drugged. It tasted of dirt and rust. It was as wonderful as any water she'd ever had. She took another small sample, maybe four ounces in total, and swallowed it down.

Leaving the bathroom, she made her way into the kitchen to distract herself. She opened the refrigerator, expecting to find the same contents from the day before. But tucked into the butter dish was a folded piece of paper. She glanced over her shoulder and retrieved the paper. As she unfolded the page, something fell to the floor with a little clink.

She looked down and saw a small black key like the kind that fit a luggage lock. On the paper, written in red crayon, was the word *key* in large, child-like handwriting. A crooked red heart was drawn beside it. She created slack in the cord running to her collar and slowly lowered herself until she could reach the key with her fingertips. She gripped it in her hand and folded the note into her pocket.

In the bathroom, she twisted the collar around her neck until the clasp was at the front. Then, working by feel, she tried to find a way to fit the key into the collar. The cord pressed uncomfortably across her face, and no matter how she turned the key in her fingers, she could find no place where it should go. Frustrated, she paused to draw three deep breaths and tried again. She was reminded of her time in surgical rotation in medical school. Procedures often lasted six or eight hours while the surgeon worked in fine, tiny movements to remove a tumor near vital organs or repair a blood vessel only two millimeters across. She closed her eyes and focused as though she, too, were performing some lifesaving surgery, letting her shoulders relax as her hands manipulated the small key.

After some time, her legs began to shake, and her hands cramped. This required endurance, and she had none. She lowered the key and opened her eyes, sitting on the toilet seat to rest. Her body ached from going so long with so little movement, and she knew she ought to be stretching and trying to exercise. She would need her strength to fight whoever came for her. As she studied the walls around her, she realized she felt no effects from the drugs.

Was it possible the toilet water wasn't drugged?

Lifting the porcelain lid off the back of the toilet again, she filled the cup and drank it, then a second. If she was right, she had a clean source of water. Why hadn't she thought of the water inside the toilet tank sooner? Would they drug it now that she'd started drinking it? She scanned the ceiling, but she found no sign of any recording device in the bathroom.

She replaced the toilet lid and lifted the key off the countertop. For the first time, she noticed the tiny print on one side of the key's hard metal head. It read *Samsonite*.

38

Hal stepped out of the interview room with Hailey on his heels. The artist had confessed to shooting the two men in Union Square—one who'd been sleeping with his wife and the second who had been in the wrong place at the wrong time. Roger's team had collected the gun and was running ballistics. Police had found a box of bullets in the artist's studio, and several were marked with the same gold paint they'd found at the scene. The artist admitted that he'd been working with the paint just before he'd loaded the gun; the paint had been transferred. It would be an easy case to try, and the DA would be pleased.

Marshall was in the hall to greet them. "Nice work, team." Their captain shook hands and clapped backs. "Press conference at four. Mayor will be here."

"Yes, sir," Hailey said.

Hal said nothing but made his way to his desk where he sorted through messages on his phone. Three from Roger. Two from Naomi in the lab. Two from his mother. His sisters. How he longed to see Anna's name on his phone. He still had her listed under "Schwartzman." He vowed he would change it. As soon as she was home.

Out of the corner of his eye, he watched Captain Marshall return to his office and close the door. It was unusual to see the captain in the department on a Saturday, but a double homicide at one of the most popular tourist spots in the city had had everyone working overtime. The shooting in Union Square was solved now; there was only the man who'd been stabbed on Stockton.

Hal turned to Hailey and leaned on his desk. "Roger's got a print off the knife found in the trash can at Post and Grant. He's running it now. With any luck, it'll give you a suspect."

Hailey looked up, her gaze narrowed. "Give *me* a suspect?"

"You don't have to cover for me."

"What are you doing?" she asked, her voice quiet, though they were alone.

"The FBI is dropping their tail on MacDonald. He's heading back to Greenville. I've got to go."

She said nothing, and he appreciated that she didn't try to stop him. "What should I tell Marshall?"

"Nothing. I'll deal with it when I find her."

Hailey watched him.

The words remained unspoken between them. *If* he found her. But he couldn't think that way. He had to believe he would. And if he had Anna, nothing else mattered. He'd happily give up this job. There were other jobs. But Anna, his baby . . .

Hailey stepped forward and gave him a short, tight hug. "Be careful, and call if we can do anything."

"You'll—"

"I'll follow up on the case."

He didn't thank her. That was the kind of relationship they had. He thought of all they'd been through, and then he turned his attention to getting to Greenville.

On the drive home, he booked a flight and called Telly twice.

He was almost at Anna's when Telly called him back.

"Hi, Hal."

Hal knew immediately that Telly wasn't going to South Carolina. He was going back to Dallas. "You have information on MacDonald's itinerary?"

"Yeah, but I can't—"

"I know. You're going to Dallas. I need you to send me the itinerary. I need to know when he arrived in Greenville. Can you do that?"

"Of course. But what are you going to do?"

"What choice do I have, Telly? The FBI is quitting the case."

"Hal, we're not quitting. We just have to shift priorities. We're out of leads—"

"I don't care, Telly. Just send the itinerary."

"I'll send it now."

"Thanks."

"There's something else, Hal."

Hal gripped the wheel. "What is it?"

"The guy who called us about Peggy MacDonald's death . . ."

"Yeah," Hal said, remembering. "Scala. You were going to get me his number."

"Bryce Scala's dead."

Hal froze. "Dead. How?"

"A holdup in a grocery store parking lot, a mile from his house in Malabar."

"When?"

"This morning—about three hours ago. Local police called me, since he was tagged in our system for this case. Shooter asked for his wallet and, when he handed it over, shot him twice in the chest and took off. Scala was still wearing his five-thousand-dollar watch. Police found the wallet in a trash can a few blocks away. Cash was gone, but everything else was still there. Scala's wife thinks he had maybe fifty or sixty bucks in his wallet."

"MacDonald was behind that," Hal said. "I'd put money on it."

"Police are talking to witnesses and canvassing the area, but you know . . ."

"Yeah," Hal said. He knew. They'd never find the shooter. This news made his arrival in Greenville all the more urgent.

"I'll send that itinerary," Telly said.

Hal ended the call as he pulled to the curb in front of Anna's house. As he was getting out of the car, his mother and Buster walked down the street. "You're home early," she called out.

"I've got to pack."

"Pack?"

He nodded. "I'm going to South Carolina."

"Okay," she said. "I'll help." She let Buster off his leash and followed the dog into the house.

Standing on the sidewalk, Hal glanced at the itinerary Telly had sent. MacDonald would have beat him to Greenville by now. Without hesitating, Hal thumbed through his recent calls until he found Detective Leighton's number. He would need her help in South Carolina.

Harper answered on the first ring. "Hal?"

"Remember when you called me and asked if there was anything you could do to help?"

"I remember."

"Well, now there is."

"Name it."

Hal explained what he needed, and Harper said it was no problem. Thanking her again, Hal ended the call and started for the house. In the bedroom, his mother already had a suitcase laid out on the bed.

"You okay to stay here with Buster?" he asked.

"You don't worry about us," she said, the dog pressed to her side. "You go out there and find your girl."

Hal didn't answer, afraid to jinx it. He knew that he wasn't coming back until he had exhausted every lead. Not until Spencer MacDonald was either dead or in prison. Not until he had Anna.

39

Though no closer to escape, Schwartzman was at least more physically comfortable. The toilet water, although a little rust-flavored, appeared to be drug-free. In less than twenty-four hours, her headache was gone, and her mind felt sharper. To ensure proper rehydration, she drank every two hours, taking in all she could until the quantity of liquid in her stomach made her nauseated. With the freedom to drink as much water as she wanted came the freedom to eat the high-sodium foods stocked in the kitchen. She made peanut butter sandwiches whenever she felt the least bit hungry. The diet wasn't ideal, but it was far superior to starving. Healthy babies had been born under much worse circumstances. Concentration camps, for instance.

Between eating and drinking, she had gone back to moving from room to room, staring at every corner, wall, and piece of furniture in an attempt to find something to cut the collar. She considered again if Tyler Butler had kept other women here. If so, had they discovered any methods of escape? She had noticed, for instance, that the toilet tank's innards were made of hard plastic rather than metal, so there was nothing there to break and use as a saw. The freezer had no ice maker, which surely would have had some sort of metal piece that might have been sharp enough. The cover on the oven clock was plastic. Even the stovetop heating coils, normally attached to the appliance by a thin metal piece, were simply lying on top of their respective insets, which explained why the stovetop didn't work. The drip trays had been removed as well.

She returned to the bathroom to drink and was replacing the porcelain lid when she heard shuffling in the outer room. She froze behind the closed door, her fingers reaching instinctively for the lock, though there wasn't one.

The footsteps were short, uncertain. The shoes squeaked occasionally like sneakers. It made her think of a child.

There was a knock on the door. "Hello? Hello?"

Roy.

She cracked the door and peered out at the young man in the hallway. He wore a wide smile and a pair of SpongeBob pajamas. "Are you alone?"

He grinned and pointed to her.

"Are we alone?"

He nodded. "I came as soon as Mammy left for church. I told her I was too sick to go because I didn't want to, and she made me promise I would stay in my pajamas and rest." He smoothed the button-down top. "See? I'm doing just like Mammy said. I'm staying in my pajamas, and I'm resting here with you."

"What about your brother?"

He shook his head with a serious face. "No. It's the weekend. Tyler does all his driving on the weekends."

"Driving? What kind of driving?"

"The big truck. He goes all over in it, and he sleeps in the back. It has a bed and a refrigerator, and sometimes he lets me have a Coke from there but not very often. He says Cokes cost money."

Tyler was a truck driver, which explained how she had gotten here. Her brain was turning. "I'd love to buy you a Coke."

"You would?"

"Absolutely."

His smile turned into a frown. "But you can't buy me a Coke."

"Not right now," she said, trying to come up with a plan. "Your brother only does driving on the weekends?"

"From late Friday till late-late on Sundays. Today is Sunday."

Sunday. She'd been here eight days. So he was back tonight.

"I wish you could buy me a Coke," he said.

She studied the disappointment on his face. He'd come over here in his pajamas, but for what? Surely his mother wouldn't approve of him being there. But his mother was gone. And Tyler was gone.

"Maybe we could do a project," she suggested.

A smile lifted his high cheekbones and narrowed his eyes into a squint. "What kind of project?"

She furrowed her brow, pretending to be lost in thought. Her heart was racing. This might work. How she needed this to work. It could be her last chance. She fought to be calm, concocting a lie. "Actually, I don't think we can do it."

His lips turned into a frown. "Why not? I want to."

"But we need crayons," she said, disappointed.

Roy jumped up and down. "I have crayons."

"You do?"

"Yes. I have lots and lots of crayons."

"Okay." She paused and shook her head again. "But we need other stuff, too."

"What? What other stuff do we need?"

"Do you have paper?"

He clapped his hands together. "Yes."

"Wow. You have everything."

He patted his chest. "I have everything."

Her heart throbbed in her throat. "But we also need scissors."

He paused a second and then pointed to himself. "I have scissors, too. I have crayons and paper and scissors. We can do our project. We can do it!"

"We can," she agreed, clapping her hands together. "As long as your scissors are sharp. We need sharp scissors."

His hands fell to his sides, and his shoulders dropped. "My scissors are not sharp. They are not sharp at all."

"Oh no," she said, fighting against the tears in her eyes. Of course he didn't have sharp scissors. "Shoot." Several seconds passed before she said, "I wonder if your mama has scissors you could borrow this one time."

He shook his head firmly. "Oh, no. I'm not allowed to go in Mammy's sewing room. Not ever. I cannot go in there. Never go in the sewing room," he went on. "Never ever because Mammy's machine is very expensive, and if you accidentally move it, you can break it. It breaks very easy. Very easy." He continued to shake his head, as though it was programmed into him and beyond his control.

"I understand," she said, interrupting. The fear was so clear in his voice. He didn't want to get his mother's scissors, but she needed them. He wasn't going to bring her a knife—too obvious. The water she'd just ingested seemed to rise into her throat. She didn't want to lie to him. She longed to find another way. But how? This man might be her last chance at freedom. Swallowing her nausea, she turned toward the bedroom.

"It's okay," she said. "We can't do the project today, but maybe another time." She started walking, praying the bait would work. He would get in trouble. He'd probably be beaten. But she could be killed. Her eyes squeezed closed, the panic threatening to shut off her airway. *Please don't leave.*

The seconds stretched out long and silent as she ushered the cleat along the track above her head.

"But I want to do the project," he said, his voice thin and pleading.

She turned back. "I do, too."

"Can we do it, then?"

"Can you find us some scissors? Maybe in the kitchen?" She drew in a slow breath. "A knife could work, too."

His eyes went wide, his head shaking again.

"No knife," she said, hurrying back to him. The cleat caught on the track, and the collar stopped her, cutting into her throat. She gasped and coughed, tears running down her face. When she looked back up, Roy was staring at the cord. His eyes narrowed, and then he turned his gaze on her.

"Roy," she said softly.

"You're trying to trick me," he said, aiming a finger at her.

"No," she said. "I would never—"

"You don't need scissors to do a project. I never use scissors."

"We were going to make paper dolls. We need scissors to cut the paper."

"I don't want to make dolls. I'm a boy, not a girl." He began to slowly back away from her.

"They don't have to be girl dolls. You could make boys . . . and we could color them."

He shook his head as he spun on his heel. "No!" he shouted as he raced down the hall.

"Okay, then," she called after him, her voice cracking so that she was nearly shrieking. "We'll do something else. Whatever project you want." She was trying to follow him, but the cleat moved rigidly along the track, the cord refusing to yield from above. "Roy!"

The screen door squealed and then slammed shut. As she reached the end of the hall, she caught sight of Roy racing across the snow in his pajamas. He didn't look back. Soon, he was out of her narrow view.

Tyler would be home late tonight. Would Roy tell his brother what she had done? Even if he didn't, Roy was not coming back.

If she had any chance of getting out of here, she had to do it on her own.

40

Hal stepped through the automated doors of the Greenville airport into cold, wet morning air. He was supposed to have been here hours earlier, and the delays had left him edgy and impatient. Some mechanical issue on the connecting flight through Charlotte. The wind cut through his jacket. Frost dusted the bushes across the street, and he thought of the snow on Thanksgiving, walking with Anna on the streets, buzzed and happy. He was half-asleep, feeling the effects of the red-eye flight and the long layover. It was afternoon, but it felt like the middle of the night.

A horn jolted him. Harper waved from a Subaru parked at the curb. He put his duffel in the backseat and climbed in beside her, reaching immediately to move the seat back as far as it would go.

"Hi."

"Thanks for coming."

"Of course." She shifted into first gear and pulled away from the curb, the car rattling beneath them. She wore jeans and a dark gray sweatshirt with a UNC logo. Her hair in a ponytail, she looked like a mom in a mom car. He wondered if it was smart to involve her. The South felt like a foreign country to him, and he'd wanted an ally down here. She'd left her husband and daughter in Charleston and driven three and a half hours to be here. And for what? To get closure to her case. And to help a friend. She'd said as much on the phone. He had to take her at her word. And he was grateful. "We know what he's up to?"

"He's at home now. Came home from the airport and hasn't been back out," she said, checking her phone. "My guy was able to drum up a couple of retired cops to take shifts, sitting on the house. They've been there since he got home."

"Thanks for doing that. I'll pay whatever the costs."

"For now, it's a fun distraction from retirement." She shifted the car into second with another rattle and followed the signs toward downtown.

Hal thought about MacDonald inside the house. "He came straight from the airport?"

"We weren't at the airport when he arrived, so we're not positive, but the timing seems right. Pulled into the garage and took in his suitcase."

"Nothing else? No grocery bags or anything?"

"No."

That was worrisome. It meant he wasn't staying at home for long. Even if he didn't eat at home often, everyone needed something from the store after a big trip. "If your guys are okay, we'll let them keep an eye on MacDonald for now."

"They're good," she said. "Where are we headed?"

"I thought we'd go see Georgia Schwartzman."

Harper's gaze slid to meet his. "Her mother."

Hal nodded.

She glanced down at her own sweatshirt and seemed to consider her attire. "You have the address?"

Following the directions on Google Maps, Hal directed Harper north of downtown, through several upscale commercial areas and winding streets. The farther they drove, the bigger the houses got. When they turned into Greenville Gates, it looked like a country club. A strip of unnaturally green grass separated the road from a walking path, along which dogwood trees had been planted at perfectly spaced intervals. They made several more turns, the houses still expanding in size as they navigated the streets. As the houses ballooned, so did the lots, until each mansion sat in the center of a San Francisco–size city block.

Harper slowed in front of a mailbox, and Hal double-checked the address. "This is it."

"Wow," Harper said.

Wow was right. The house was something out of *Gone with the Wind.* Set back from the road by a curved driveway, the large colonial rose from a lush green lawn the size of a football field. As they approached, Hal saw that a porch encircled the entire main floor, wide enough for a full-size table on one side and two couches and three chairs around a large, square coffee table on the other. All the furniture had been done in the same fancy rattan outdoor furniture that he saw only in the catalogs that sometimes ended up in his mailbox by mistake.

The porch was empty, but three cars were parked in front of the house—a Lexus convertible, a Mercedes SUV, and a navy-blue hard-topped Porsche.

"I'll just park here on the end," Harper said with a little laugh.

"You'll blend right in." As he started to crack his door, she reached behind him and pulled a pink sweater from her bag. She took the sweatshirt off and replaced it with the sweater.

He got out of the car and waited for her as she pulled the rubber band from her hair. "My mama would die if I showed up to a house like this in a sweatshirt."

"I have a feeling they'll be paying more attention to me than to you," Hal said.

She didn't argue as they approached the walkway to the front door. Doors, actually—two of them, side by side and tall enough to make him feel short at six foot four. They mounted the steps, and he felt Harper slow beside him. He had a sense of foreboding that was at odds with the huge house and its meticulous grounds.

Hal rang the bell. Only moments later, a black woman in a uniform with a white apron opened it, like she'd been standing right behind the door. Looking at her, Hal felt as though he'd been tipped back a hundred years.

"Can I help you?"

"We're looking for Georgia Schwartzman," Harper said when it became apparent that Hal was speechless. She wasn't a slave, he reminded himself. But the uniform, the apron . . . It felt too close to some historical line.

"Mrs. Schwartzman is entertaining."

"Tell her we're friends of Anna's."

"Anna," she repeated.

"Mrs. Schwartzman's daughter," Hal said.

"Oh, you mean Bella."

"Yes," Harper said as Hal cringed. He imagined Anna's response to hearing that nickname from her mother. Had Anna told her what that name represented? Didn't Anna's mother know what MacDonald had done to her?

"Please. Come in." The woman excused herself and returned a moment later. "Mrs. Schwartzman said you can join her and her guests on the veranda," she said with a wave toward the back of the house.

He and Harper exchanged a look.

"It's very cozy," she assured them, as though heat had been the concern.

The veranda was actually an outdoor space, accessed through a long glassed-in hallway. The full-height glass windows were sliding doors that could be opened in the summer months. At the far end was a mammoth fireplace, where logs crackled and snapped. Along the window to the east was a large trellis covered in a green vine that would undoubtedly bloom in the spring and be gorgeous. A line of rosebushes awaited their own blossoms beside it.

Hal stepped around the doorway and felt the collective hush of the room. He hadn't realized he'd been out of view until then, but the reaction made it clear.

One woman let out a sharp gasp.

Georgia Schwartzman motioned from the table. The woman bore a striking resemblance to her daughter, though only in the eyes and lips. She had a small, pert nose and straight blonde hair that had been curled at the bottom. Nothing like Anna's dark, untamed curls.

"You're friends of Bella's?" one of the women asked, the titter in her voice divulging the fact that she'd been drinking.

"Could we speak with you alone?" Hal asked Georgia Schwartzman. "Just for a moment."

"Of course. Excuse me, ladies." Georgia rose quickly and went around the table the long way. She wore a wool skirt that covered her knees and a sweater with a wide belt that accentuated her narrow waist. Her black flats had bows on the toes and little gold plaques with something etched on them. A designer's name, no doubt.

She passed by them without stopping and waved toward the house. "I'll be right back, ladies. Patrice, don't you dare tell that story until I'm back!" She paused next to the maid. "Maya, will you bring out another bottle of the rosé?"

"Yes, ma'am."

"I'll have another vodka soda," the drunk woman announced a little loudly.

Harper and Hal followed Georgia Schwartzman down the hall and into a den. It smelled of books and dust and remnants of cigars, decades old. He guessed that it had belonged to Anna's father.

She motioned them to sit on the couch and took a place in the chair. The veneer of elegance and control wavered. Her eyes suddenly looked slightly puffy, swollen as she alternated her gaze between Hal and Harper. Smoothing her hands along her skirt, she spoke with a crack in her voice. "Is there news?"

"Then you know Anna is missing?"

She nodded. "The police were here. They asked if I had spoken to her. But I hadn't—" She swallowed as though something large and uncomfortable had stuck in her throat. "I haven't."

"And you don't have any idea about who—" Hal stopped himself. He wasn't ready to mention MacDonald. He wanted it to come from Georgia. Surely she'd thought about the possibility. He knew the police had mentioned Anna's ex-husband. "Do you have any idea where she might be?"

Georgia shook her head. "Bella has always been quite independent."

"Independent," he repeated. "You think maybe she's run away?"

Georgia picked at invisible lint on her skirt. He saw some shift in her, some softening. As though there were a war going on inside her, long-held beliefs battling a reality that was just becoming clear to her. "I guess I didn't think of it as running away if you're an adult."

Hal clenched his teeth. So denial was going to win out. He leaned forward, feeling his voice harden. "She hasn't been seen at her home. She hasn't come to work or called in. She left without her keys or her purse or her phone. Does that sound like Anna?" Hal thrust each word like a blade, trying to puncture Georgia Schwartzman's perfect posture and her clothes and her makeup and the whole damn place and bring her down, make her crash and break apart. Make her feel like he did.

Harper sat straighter on the couch. "Your daughter had felt threatened by her ex-husband, Spencer MacDonald."

Georgia looked up, her gaze holding his only momentarily before skittering away.

"Anna is pregnant," Hal said, the words a whisper. Coming out of his throat, they felt like a scream.

Harper stiffened beside him.

Georgia's eyes went wide, and her fingers pressed to her throat. She sank momentarily against the chair. "Pregnant."

"Yes," Hal said. "There were two pregnancy tests found in her home when she went missing. Both were positive."

Georgia's gaze flicked across the room as though making a list of things she needed to do with this new information.

"I assume you didn't know," Hal said.

"No."

"Is there anything you can tell us that might help us find your daughter?" Harper asked.

Georgia nodded slowly. "I really shouldn't—"

Hal felt his anger rise with every word.

A sudden racket in the hallway—breaking glass and the sound of someone tripping—was followed by a woman's gasp.

Georgia Schwartzman jumped from her chair and hurried into the hall. "Evelyn, are you all right?"

Hal rose, too, and walked into the hallway, where the drunk woman leaned against a doorjamb, hand to her mouth. Tears filled her eyes.

"Maya," Georgia Schwartzman called. "Can you help me, please?"

The drunk woman was whispering, shaking her head. "I can't believe it. I can't believe Dell's going to leave. What am I going to do, Georgia?"

The maid in the uniform returned. "Help me get her to the guest room," Georgia said.

"Can I help?" Hal asked, approaching, but Mrs. Schwartzman put a hand up and shook her head. "No. Please."

Hal stopped and glanced back at Harper. Then the two of them watched as Georgia and the maid half led, half carried the drunk woman away. One of her shoes—a sandal covered in small gold spikes—remained on the floor of the hall.

"Maybe we should come back?" Harper said.

But Hal couldn't wait. If Georgia Schwartzman knew something, he had to know now. Every minute counted.

Sounds filtered down the hall from the back bedroom, and a few minutes later, Georgia emerged. "I'm afraid now isn't a good time."

"We need answers." Hal struggled to sound calm.

She smoothed her skirt again and touched her hair with the palms of her hands as though making sure it was still there. "Perhaps we could—"

But Hal didn't let her finish the sentence. "Have you kept in touch with your daughter's ex-husband?"

Her gaze darted down the hall, then back at him. There was a subtle shift in her posture, a reinforcement, as though she were afraid of being knocked down. "Last summer when he was in jail, I visited. I felt a responsibility. He was married to Bella, and his own mother was down in Florida. His father gone."

Hal fought to keep a steady gaze. She felt a responsibility to her son-in-law, but she'd left her own daughter to fend for herself in Charleston with that man on the loose.

"And since he was released from prison?" Harper pursued the line of questioning.

Georgia Schwartzman shook her head. "Once or twice at the club, but that's it."

"Did something change?" Harper asked.

Georgia Schwartzman let the question hang in the air, wrapping her arms across her chest and rubbing her shoulders softly. Her gaze floated toward the front hall table where a picture of her and a man who must have been Anna's father sat in a gilded frame. Hal wondered if she was channeling Anna's father. If she heard him urging her to help or telling her that she needed to pay attention to their daughter's life, to be there for her. Or maybe she'd noticed the way the dust swirled in the air and thought the room was due for a cleaning.

"Mrs. Schwartzman," Hal said to pull her from her reverie.

The drunk woman called her name and let out a single sob. Georgia Schwartzman stepped toward the back bedroom, pausing to place one hand on the wall. Her veiny hand with nails tipped with the color of red wine appeared to grip the wall as though she were pulled between two places. "I'm sorry," she whispered. "I have to attend to my guest."

"Of course," Harper said, holding out a business card. "If you think of anything that might help us find your daughter and your grandbaby . . ."

Georgia Schwartzman's eyes looked momentarily wet, but she blinked quickly, and any emotion vanished.

"We need your help," Hal said. "I don't think she ran away on her own."

Georgia nodded and took the card, walking from the room without another word.

A moment later, Maya reappeared in her black uniform and those black nursing shoes and ushered them to the door.

When the door had closed behind them, Hal marched toward the car in long, angry strides. His mother had come to be with him, to stay and care for him so that he could focus on Anna, on finding her. Anna's own mother could hardly be bothered to interrupt a luncheon to talk to them.

Harper ran up alongside him. "Slow down."

He reached the car and kicked at the air, holding back the anger that corked in his throat.

Over the top of the car, Harper called his name.

He turned to look at her.

"A baby?" she said. "For real?"

He nodded. "For real. Nobody knows . . . Only a few people, I mean."

"But it's yours."

It wasn't a question, so he didn't answer. Instead, he opened the door and sank into the passenger's seat.

Harper didn't press him as she started the engine. She backed out of the line of luxury automobiles, the Subaru clunking inauspiciously, and started back toward the road. "Where to now?"

"His house." There was nothing left to do but watch him . . . and wait.

41

Hal and Harper arrived at MacDonald's house around 2:00 p.m. and parked across the street. They spoke briefly with the retired officer who'd been watching the house long enough for an arc of sunflower seed shells to form on the street outside his car window. According to him, MacDonald had not left home, though he'd brought the trash can to the curb and pulled his car out to sweep the garage. It seemed cool weather for a spring-cleaning, but it went with the theory that he wasn't staying long. The retired officer left about ten minutes later, saying he was planning to be back to relieve the night shift at 5:00 a.m. Someone else would come tonight at 10:00 p.m. There were others they could call if Hal and Harper needed a break.

Hal didn't want a break.

Harper positioned the Subaru where the retired officer's Chevy Impala had been, at the corner of the street to the east of MacDonald's house. The slight curve in the road gave them an almost dead-on view of his place even from fifty or sixty yards away. Hal recognized the location immediately, remembering the view from the traffic images that had come up in the investigation of MacDonald's crimes. The camera above that same stoplight had caught Anna emerging from her car with a bag from a hardware store, where she'd bought items intended to frame MacDonald so that he would go to prison for the crimes he had committed.

Hal had barely known Anna then, but he could not imagine what had been going through her mind. How desperate she must have been, how out of her mind with fear and grief to think that she could create her own justice.

But who was he to talk? Sitting on the street, he was prepared to create his own justice, too. He wanted only a chance to face MacDonald alone. But he knew the camera was watching them. Not to mention Harper beside him.

They passed the time mostly in silence. The radio would drain the car battery, and Hal lacked the ability to make small talk.

It was growing dark when MacDonald came out of his front door. He wore khakis, a T-shirt, and tennis shoes. Hal had seen MacDonald only in a suit and button-down. The casual attire looked unnatural on him, but it also highlighted how thin and strong he was. His pants hung loose from his hips, his bare arms ropy and lithe. MacDonald walked across his driveway slowly, scanning his surroundings as he approached the mailbox. His gaze caught on the Subaru, hovering for a moment on the car before he ducked down to look in the box. It must have been empty because he turned, empty-handed, and proceeded back to the house without a backward glance.

"No mail," Harper said.

"No mail, no groceries," Hal confirmed.

"I'll call tomorrow and find out if he's got a forwarding on the mail."

"Either way, he's not here for long."

She nodded. "I agree."

A while later, Harper turned in the seat and pulled a cooler from the back. Inside was a Tupperware filled with pieces of fried chicken and biscuits wrapped in aluminum foil. Though they were cold, he could imagine how good they would taste warm. They ate in silence, drinking coffee from a thermos in two small tin camping cups.

MacDonald's house went dark a little past eight. The street was dead soon after. Hardly a car passed over the next hour. At ten, another officer came to relieve them. He was spritely and alert while Hal felt groggy and tired. Hal hated to leave, but he needed the rest. He hadn't slept at all on the flight.

"Promise to call if so much as a light goes on."

Harper didn't plan on going home to Charleston until they found Anna or she had to go back to work, so she'd made arrangements for her and Hal to stay at the home of a friend who was out of town. At the house, Hal followed Harper down the hallway to a small guest room. "I can sleep on the couch," he offered.

"It's fine. I'm set up in their daughter's room already. Get some sleep, and we'll head back in the morning." She turned to leave him, and he called after her.

"Thank you."

"You don't have to thank me, Hal. I want to see her home safely." She took a step and stopped. "Her and the baby." She paused as though wanting to say something else. Finally, she whispered, "And I want to see that bastard burn for what he's done." There was an extra layer of heat in her voice.

"Me, too."

When she was gone, Hal took off his shoes and lay down on the bed. His eyes burned with exhaustion. His phone rested in his hand. He didn't have the energy to return the missed calls from Roger and Hailey. He needed to focus on Anna. If he lost Anna, he would never forgive himself for not quitting his job and directing every effort on finding her instead of the San Francisco cases.

His thoughts drifted back to what he'd found in Anna's house the day she vanished. Was she still pregnant? What kind of stress did it take to cause a miscarriage? He turned on his side, refusing to let the thoughts sit in his brain. Instead, he stared at the wall beside the door, studying the way the moonlight cut through the blinds and projected stripes on the blank wall. He recalled Anna's description of the room in MacDonald's house, the projection of herself tied up in Ava's garage on the wall. How terrified she had been. At the time, Hal had been 2,600 miles away. That wasn't going to happen again. The police had never found any evidence of that projection, likely a computer file MacDonald had deleted. In this town, Hal doubted there had been much police effort to gather evidence against Spencer MacDonald.

He closed his eyes and focused, willing his mind to sense her, wherever she was.

He woke in the dark, a single blade of moonlight streaked on the wall. For a moment, he was confused, out of sorts. The moonlight didn't come through the bedroom window on that side of his bed. He sat and blinked in the dark until he remembered where he was.

He turned and checked the time on his phone: 2:50 a.m. He'd slept for four hours, maybe a little longer. He set his feet on the floor and stood, smoothing the comforter on the bed. He used the bathroom, rinsing his mouth with water and swallowing several long drinks before heading down the hallway to the kitchen. A small light shone above the stove. The room was tidy, the house silent.

He could go back to bed but doubted he would sleep. He was here, in MacDonald's backyard.

He stared at Harper's keys on the kitchen table and knew what he was going to do.

42

Sunday, 11:15 p.m. MST

Without the drugs weighing her down, time passed excruciatingly slowly. Over the course of the long day, Schwartzman found herself missing the draw toward sleep, the ability to wake up having passed hours without awareness of this place and her situation. When she lay on the bed and tried to rest, she couldn't. The synapses in her brain fired rapidly, ideas and questions making it impossible to shut down her mind. Movement would have helped as a distraction, but the collar made it awkward. Not to mention the terror she felt at the thought she could be yanked off her feet and strangled at any moment.

For several hours after Roy had left that morning, she'd listened for him to return, praying that his curiosity and boredom would lure him back, despite his suspicion of her. Once it was close to noon, Anna gave up hope of seeing Roy again, since his mother had probably come back from church. Schwartzman went through the conversation again and again, trying to calculate how she might have gotten him to bring her what she needed without arousing his suspicion. Eventually, she had to compel the thoughts away.

She made it a point to drink as much water as she could stand and made herself three peanut butter sandwiches, which she kept in the bedroom and nibbled. For the bulk of the day, she sat up in bed with the two keys Roy had given her—the one that looked like a house key and the Samsonite luggage key. Alternating them back and forth, she sawed at the collar and tried to wedge them into the place where the two sides of the collar came together. But even with all the time in the world, she wasn't going to free herself with those keys.

In the afternoon, she rose from the bed and spent several hours inspecting the bedroom one foot at a time, imagining the room as a corpse that had to be inspected. As she went, she tested every piece of trim, the doorknob, and the window handles, running her fingers along each surface in search of something rough enough to cut. She returned to the baseboard heater, trying again to find a way to get the collar against its thin metal edge. Then she tried other things—the bed frame, the unfinished edge of door trim where a piece was missing or had never been completed. The rails that supported the two dresser drawers.

Nothing worked.

As the sky darkened, her panic crested. It was now Sunday night, and Tyler would be home soon. Would he come to her tonight? After seeing the projection of Hal on the kitchen wall, she had kept to the bedroom. Desperate to see Hal, she didn't think she could stand seeing him projected on the wall. Her mind was playing too many tricks on her already. Watching him cross the street with that car coming at him, she'd been so terrified that he would be injured or worse. Spencer would love that. He would love to hurt her that way.

If something did happen to Hal . . . if something had . . . she wasn't sure she could muster the strength to fight.

In the darkness, she gathered her nerve and rose from the bed, holding tight to the cord above her. She left the lights out in the bedroom and made her way into the similarly dark kitchen. As her eyes adjusted, she studied the walls and ceiling. The two times she'd felt like someone had purposefully strangled her had happened in this room, which made her think Tyler had some way of watching her in here, perhaps from the same place where the video of Hal had been projected. She wanted to locate the camera and block its view. Assuming there was only the one camera.

The table slowly took shape in the dark, along with the edges of the counters, the square of the kitchen sink. She opened the cupboard beside the refrigerator and pulled out the jar of peanut butter. Holding on to the cord, she moved across the room, wishing for a way to silence the clank and whir of the cleat along the track.

Nearing the oven, she searched for the telltale red light of a camera. Surely there would have to be a power source, but she could see no sign of electricity at all. The tiny hole in the ceiling, no bigger than a dime, had to be the projector, but was it recording, too? Setting the peanut butter down, she took a moment to study the small indentation in the ceiling drywall.

Feeling confident something was there, she dragged a chair from the table to the oven and, feet still on the ground, opened the jar of peanut butter. Taking the cord in her left hand, she wrapped it around her palm about a foot above her collar. Then she dipped her right hand in the peanut butter and stood on the chair. Squinting in the dark, she located the small hole in the ceiling and smeared peanut butter across it.

She stepped down and waited for a reaction. If her being near the ceiling triggered the cord, it should have retracted and strangled her.

Nothing happened.

After several minutes, she crossed to the sink to retrieve the roll of paper towels. As she was turning, the tiny red light on the smoke detector caught her eye. She stared up at the white disk shape on the ceiling, noticing for the first time that it looked brand-new.

She shifted the chair and stood on it, her left hand still wrapped in the cord. The middle and ring fingers of her right hand were covered in peanut butter. The first thing she noticed was an oblong hole on the side of the disk that faced the kitchen. Where she expected to see the inside of the smoke detector, she found dark glass, like the lens of a camera. Using the thumb and index finger of her right hand, she twisted the cover until it released. Attached to a regular smoke detector with its nine-volt battery was a device with a long, narrow glass piece.

A camera.

43

Hal shifted his knees, which were pinned under the hard plastic of the Subaru's dashboard. Even with the seat all the way back, he could barely wedge himself inside. He was edgy—too much coffee, no sleep. He'd been strung out on jobs dozens of times before. When he was sure of a suspect's guilt, Hal found himself driving by a suspect's haunts, looking for him, waiting for a screwup, for that last piece to fall into place so that they could arrest the son of a bitch.

There were times when the buzz was electric and exciting, despite the days or weeks of exhaustion.

This was nothing like that.

He'd never felt so empty, so maxed. It was as though he'd been beaten—inside and out—and left to die. When he showered, he'd taken to turning the water to scalding temperatures as he scrubbed soap into his skin. These were the rare moments when the pain in his chest felt manageable. The harder he scratched, the hotter the water, the easier it was to breathe.

But only for those moments.

Once the water was off and the steam had dissipated, his skin no longer held the pain. And it was his heart that ached again.

He looked down at his cell phone, thought of Harper. Had she seen the note he'd left on the kitchen counter and realized he was gone? Surely she was sleeping.

He started composing a text to her. But what would he say? That he'd gone out for a drive? That he'd decided to sit in front of Spencer MacDonald's house all night?

That he didn't give a rat's ass about whether the South Carolina police called it harassment, he was going to sit here until MacDonald led him to Anna.

And he would.

Maybe an hour later, Hal jolted upright in his seat as MacDonald's garage door opened. He checked the clock, wondering if he'd fallen asleep. It was 4:10 a.m.

Hal watched MacDonald get into the car. The gold Lexus pulled out of the garage and turned toward him. Hal lowered himself in the seat, hunching down as much as he could, given the size of the car, and waited as MacDonald drove past him and turned left at the light. When the Lexus was out of view, Hal started the Subaru, cringing at the god-awful sputtering sounds. The damn lights went on automatically, and he shut them off as quickly as he could, waiting an extra beat before following in MacDonald's path.

Hal trailed at a distance. He had memorized the shape of the Lexus's taillights and knew their unique lines well enough to hang back without losing him. MacDonald made a few turns, winding out of his neighborhood in the direction of his country club. Hard to imagine the country club was open for business. Or maybe they held their local Klan meetings there.

The South made Hal nervous. Or maybe it was just the part of the South that was Spencer MacDonald—white sociopaths who beat and then hunted their wives. Hal would bet there was more than one of them at MacDonald's fancy country club.

Hal had seen some heinous crimes perpetrated in the name of love and jealousy and stupid, careless ones executed without thought or regard for the value of human life. But the cruelest slayings he'd worked in his career were ones committed by men of MacDonald's demographic—rich white ones without morals who believed their power made them exempt from the laws that governed other men.

Wherever he was going, MacDonald seemed in no hurry, and Hal had to concentrate on maintaining sufficient space between them. He followed as MacDonald drove farther out of town, from one abandoned road to another. When MacDonald took another turn, Hal drove past, waiting a full minute before making a U-turn and following again. He kept his lights off and followed the distant taillights, excitement stirring. This had to be it. Why else leave his house at this hour? MacDonald was going to Anna.

Hal gripped the steering wheel and drove. MacDonald remained on the long country road for several miles without turning. Roger had searched properties in MacDonald's name and come up empty, but he had to have something out here. No one took this kind of drive in the middle of the night without a good reason. In the darkness, horses looked like ghostly shadows in the fields along the road.

MacDonald's brake lights glowed momentarily in the darkness and then went off again. As he passed that section of road a minute later, Hal scanned for wildlife that might have caused MacDonald to slow but saw none.

They drove on for another two or three miles, passing an occasional small, squat house but otherwise seeing almost nothing.

Hal was shocked when the blur of blue and red erupted from the blackness. He blinked several times before the apparition of lights felt real. A police car. MacDonald had been speeding. Hal had accelerated to follow, not wanting to lose him in the winding country roads.

He watched the patrol car fill his rearview mirror, slowing his speed and hoping that the officer would speed around him. How fast had he been going? What was the last posted speed sign? He wiped his face with his hand, turned on his indicator, and pulled slowly to the shoulder.

The police car pulled in behind him. He rolled down the window and fought the urge to get out of the car.

He couldn't stop here. He needed to follow MacDonald. This would lead him to Anna.

Ahead, the taillights of MacDonald's Lexus disappeared.

His pulse thundered in his ears. She was here. He grabbed his cell phone and found Harper's number. Pushed the "Call" button as a thin white man with a narrow mustache emerged from the patrol car. Dread pooled in Hal's gut.

As the officer's shoes crunched in the gravel, Harper's voicemail invited him to leave a message.

Hal whispered into his phone. "I had a tail on MacDonald. Need backup ASAP. Pulled over here. Anna may be close." He left the call live and set his phone on the passenger seat, screen down.

"Raise your hands where I can see them," came a voice.

Hal lifted his hands.

"Keep them where I can see them."

Hal held them still, sensing the officer approaching the window. As he turned his head, he caught sight of the gun in his peripheral vision.

The sound of chatter bled through the microphone. Suspicious character.

"Officer, my name is Hal Harris."

"Did I ask for your name?" the officer snapped.

Hal flinched. The barrel of the gun hovered just inches from the car window, almost pressed to his face. "I'm a detective."

The flashlight shone in Hal's eyes. "I never seen you before."

"I'm a detective from—"

"I didn't ask." The officer cut him off.

Hal closed his mouth. His phone buzzed on the seat beside him. He couldn't see the screen. Harper calling? He considered reaching for the phone but knew it would be a mistake.

"I want you to get out of the car, real slow."

"Of course," Hal said, lowering his voice, trying to seem small, an impossible feat shoved behind the steering wheel of the tiny car. "I realized my lights were off," Hal said. "It's a friend's car."

"You gonna get smart with me, boy?" The drawl on his words reminded Hal where he was.

You're not in San Francisco. You're in South Carolina. The South. He felt the cold rush of sweat as the fingers of his left hand felt for the door handle. Statistics ran through his head—the number of routine traffic stops that ended in an officer discharging his weapon, the proportion of those that involved a white officer and a black suspect.

The latch clicked, and the door opened with a screech.

He felt the officer jump. His own pulse trumpeted.

On the passenger seat, the phone went quiet and then began to buzz again.

Hal made no move for it, planting both hands firmly in the air as he eased open the car door with his hip.

He started to turn to face the officer but decided against it. Harder to shoot a man in the back. Or harder to justify the shooting with Internal Affairs. Sweat dripped down Hal's shoulder blades. He moved his hands to the back of his head, one at a time, turned his head so the officer could hear him. "Sir, I'm a police—"

"I warned you about talking," the officer said, the pitch of his voice cresting to a new high.

"My badge is in my left rear pocket," Hal said, shifting his body sideways. He aimed his right side toward the officer. Harder to hit a sideways target. Better to be shot on the right side than the left, where the heart was.

Just then the hum of a car came from the opposite direction, farther in the woods. Hal squeezed his eyes closed, praying for help. Another officer. Something.

The car slowed, and Hal heard the whir of a window coming down.

"Thank God you have this man in custody."

Hal swung toward the voice. Losing himself in fury, he took two steps toward the car where Spencer MacDonald sat, wearing a smug smile.

"You," Hal seethed.

"Stop it right there," the officer warned.

"Officer Potter, I'm so glad you're here."

Hal froze, sweat dripping off his face.

"Evening, Mr. MacDonald," the officer said.

"Call me Spencer, please, Dan. I so appreciate your coming out. I know you were on your way home, but I didn't know who else to call."

"It's no problem, Mr.—uh, Spencer."

Hal edged back toward the Subaru.

"Hold up there," the officer said. "You stay right where you are. No funny business."

"Please be careful, Dan. I've seen this man be very violent."

Hal felt the officer's gaze on him. The man was maybe five foot eight. Hal would seem like a giant to him. He had an inclination to get down on his knees, but he imagined the gun at the back of his head. No way to run. He stood in place.

"I left my house and realized within a few minutes that I was being followed."

"Why were you following Mr. MacDonald?"

"I am a detective," Hal said carefully, keeping his voice soft and low. "From the San Francisco Police Department. I'm—"

"He's delusional," MacDonald interrupted. "A crazy man."

There was a moment of quiet, and Hal wondered what the officer was thinking.

Hal started talking again. "I have my badge, Officer. I have my badge in my pocket. You can call my department."

"How many years have I been taking care of your mother's portfolio?" MacDonald asked. "He's been stalking my wife twice that long, out in California. When she tried to get away from him, he came here to harass her."

Did that mean Anna was here? "His ex-wife was abducted from San Francisco," Hal said, the words spewing from him as he struggled to keep them slow and controlled. "If this man knows where she is, he needs to tell you right now."

"Dan, he's a total nutter."

"This man was arrested for the murder of two women," Hal countered. "Call your department and ask them."

"Sure, cast the blame at the innocent man," MacDonald said. "Watch it, Dan. He probably hit his head running from the police."

"I *am* the police," Hal went on. "Call the San Francisco Police Department. I can give you their number. They'll confirm what I'm saying."

"Shut up!" the cop shouted. Too close. The barrel of the gun was inches from Hal.

Hal was breathing heavily, winded as though he'd been running. The air that had felt cool at the airport was now humid and thick. Sweat pooled along his waistband.

"Be careful, Dan," MacDonald warned. "He's very dangerous."

The officer tucked the barrel between Hal's shoulder blades. Hal considered how quickly he could act. Would he be fast enough to disarm the officer? It wasn't smart to touch a suspect with your gun. It put the weapon in jeopardy. One quick move, and the gun could be in the hands of the suspect. But if Hal didn't take the gun quickly enough . . . If he didn't get the gun, he'd have a bullet in his back.

"My wife has disappeared, Dan," MacDonald said. "She's gone missing, and he was the last one to see her. This man."

"Down on the ground," the officer said.

"Officer Potter, Spencer MacDonald is lying to you. He's trying to manipulate you."

"I said, get down!"

Hal lowered himself to his knees, one at a time, gripping his hands on his head. He watched MacDonald, who leaned out of the car like he was at a drive-thru. Every time the officer looked away, MacDonald gave Hal a shit-eating grin.

"All the way down," the officer said.

His hands on his head, Hal bent over and tried to figure out how to get down without using his hands. "Officer . . ."

"Keep your hands where I can see them!" the officer barked, and Hal could hear the frenzy in his tone.

"Okay. I'm moving, nice and slow." Hal dropped to his elbows.

"He's making a move!" MacDonald yelled.

The officer's shoes shifted in the gravel. A grunt emerged from his lips.

Hal rolled to his side, forearms over his face, trying to keep his hands in the air. "Don't shoot. Do not shoot."

Even as he spoke, his entire body tensed like a coil, anticipating the explosion of gunfire.

44

Schwartzman stared up at the red flashing light. It had to be a camera. She waited for the cord to snap her up again, but nothing happened. Did the cord's retraction work via a button Tyler pushed? Did he watch and laugh while she almost choked to death? Could he work it remotely? She looked at the lens and at the peanut butter still on her fingers. Then she smeared the oily spread across the glass, creating a layer that would certainly distort any image and would likely also block most of the light. Finally, she screwed on the smoke detector's cover.

For the next few minutes, she kept the cord twisted around her left hand, waiting for someone to realize what had happened. As the minutes ticked by, she felt awake and clearheaded. When five or ten minutes had passed, she washed the peanut butter from her hand and turned on the kitchen lights.

Sure that her movements wouldn't be recorded, she started another search of the kitchen. She had to be more aggressive, pull things apart. If she couldn't find a tool, she would have to make one. With the door propped open, she worked her way through the refrigerator, pulling at the shelves. Plastic, most of it too thick. She pulled a shelf from the refrigerator and tried to break it over her knee. It didn't break. She slammed it to the floor. No luck. She shoved it back into the refrigerator. Even if she managed to break the plastic, it would not give her the rough edge she needed to cut through the rubber.

She considered the inside of the freezer the same way. The icicle, which had seemed like such a win at the time, now looked thin and wimpy in light of what she needed.

She closed the refrigerator door and leaned across the counter, staring at the electrical socket. Would there be something inside the outlet? Fooling with electricity seemed like a risk.

But so did waiting for Tyler Butler to come back.

As she pushed herself up, she glanced behind the refrigerator and saw something shiny on the floor. Bracing herself on the counter, she wedged her leg between the cupboards and the refrigerator, pushing the old machine aside until she could fit sideways in the gap.

She slid in and looked down at the floor, praying for a knife, a blade. Instead, she found a small scrap of foil, the inside of some discarded packaging only an inch or two in diameter.

As she moved back out of the gap, she caught sight of a metal plate on the backside of the refrigerator, one corner bent. An empty screw hole gaped in the corner of the resulting triangle, maybe three inches at its base. She ran her finger along the plate's edge, applying pressure until the metal cut her skin. Sharp.

Sharp enough.

Heart racing, she shut off the kitchen light so the cabin would look dark. From the bedroom, she retrieved a flannel pajama top from the stack of clothes and returned to the kitchen. Moving by feel, she found her way back to the refrigerator and wedged herself into the narrow gap between the counter and the machine. With her hand wrapped in the flannel pajamas, she bent the corner back farther, pressing it until it almost folded back on itself. Then she opened it out flat again and folded it back.

Bent and flat, bent and flat. Over and over.

When her arm ached, she paused, stretching it out behind her for several moments before starting again. Soon, the piece bent more easily, then as smoothly as slicing through warm butter, until she began to feel the bottom end loosen.

She kept working it—bending and then straightening, each time giving the triangle a little twist to try to break it free. Tired from the repetitive motion, she distracted her mind by recounting the experience of anatomy class in med school. Seven, eight, or even nine hours spent on her feet, dissecting the vascular system or the respiratory system.

Still working her left hand, she rested her forehead against the side of the refrigerator and felt the vibration of the machine against her skull.

She didn't know how long had passed when, finally, she heard the crack of the metal breaking. She stood up, breathless, and moved the metal more quickly. Bent, straight. Bent, straight.

And finally, the triangular piece released into her fingers.

She let out a cry of relief and then cupped her hand over her mouth. Silence.

Moving quickly, she returned the refrigerator to its place and carefully hid the metal triangle inside her bra. Leaving the flannel pajamas over the kitchen chair, she used a paper towel to wipe the peanut butter off the camera and the projector. She threw away the paper towel, returned the chair to the table, and retrieved the pajama top before making her way back to the bedroom. Under her bra, the metal dug into her skin as she dragged the cord along the track into the bedroom.

There, she slipped back into bed with the small triangle of metal and the flannel pajamas. With the covers over her head, she began to saw at the collar around her neck.

45

Hal tasted dust on his tongue and felt the grit of it between his teeth. "Officer, I am not armed," he said, clearing the fear from his throat. "I have no weapon. My wallet's in my back pocket. You'll find my badge there, too."

The pulsing of his heart roared in his ears, deafening and amplifying sounds in alternating beats. In the down moments, Hal felt certain he could hear the officer's heavy breathing, the low chuckle of Spencer MacDonald's enjoyment as he watched from his car.

"I am an officer of the law," Hal said, cheek still pressed to the ground. He moved his tongue over the roof of his mouth to remove the dirt, but his mouth was a desert. "I am a detective. Spencer MacDonald was charged with killing two women. He has kidnapped a third. Please don't shoot me. I'm on your side. We are the same. Please. Please see me." His voice cracked. Tears tracked over his cheeks, the salty taste mixing with the chalky flavor of dust.

"What's your name?" the officer asked.

Hal sensed the gun still on him and raised his head only a couple of inches. "My name is Hal Harris. Harold Clint Harris. I'm a detective with the San Francisco Police Department. I work in Homicide."

He felt Potter's hand on his backside and his wallet slipped from his pocket. Shame burned his face.

"You stay right there," the officer said.

"Yes, sir. I won't move. I'll stay right here." Hal felt a lump of relief in his throat, as though Officer Potter had saved him from some other crazy person, and it was not Potter himself who'd been holding a gun to Hal's head.

"I'm telling you, Potter," MacDonald called across the street. "He's dangerous, this one."

"You probably best be going, Mr. MacDonald," Potter said, his footsteps moving away from Hal.

Hal let out the breath he'd been holding and turned his face to wipe the tears on his shirtsleeve. He didn't move his arms. Didn't shift. The adrenaline burned in his gut. Sweat slid across his back.

"But I want to press charges," MacDonald called out, his voice taking on the tone of a petulant child. "I want him in jail."

"Press charges for what?" Potter asked, his voice now some distance away.

Hal remained frozen in place, face in the dirt. Breathing. Still breathing.

"For following me," MacDonald called out.

"Following you along a public road doesn't constitute a crime."

"He was sitting outside my home."

"Afraid that's not a crime either," Potter said. "You want, you can stop by and speak to someone at the department in the morning."

"Oh, for God's sake. What good is the police if they don't do their job?"

Potter didn't answer. Hal could hear the sound of a voice over a radio. MacDonald's car revved as he started to make a U-turn, nosing his car to within inches of Harper's Subaru. The Lexus's tires closed in on his fingers, and Hal prepared to roll out of MacDonald's path.

MacDonald seemed to change his mind and stopped. Maybe he realized he'd accomplished the goal of terrifying Hal, so instead he backed the Lexus into the middle of the road, facing the same direction he'd been headed before. "Fuck you, Harris," he hissed and was gone.

Hal still didn't move. His hamstrings and quads stiffened. Potter talked into his radio. A door opened, and footsteps approached. Hal wanted to look backward—it felt impossible not to check and see if Potter still had his service weapon drawn.

But he didn't dare.

Suddenly, the sound of another engine filled the night air, nothing like the expensive purr of MacDonald's Lexus. Instead, it was low and guttural, like an ancient truck. The sound steadily increased, the headlights adding a glow to the darkness, along with Potter's own headlights and the blue and red strobe.

The sound of honking followed, loud and cranky like an old man shouting. Over and over. Hal imagined a truck full of Klansmen. And Potter would be his only witness.

How long would it take him to get into the Subaru? Could he outrun them? He'd have to go straight, continuing along the quiet country road. The word *lynch* rose in his mind, bringing with it the sour taste of stomach acid.

The sound of brakes. A woman's voice. "Hal! Are you okay? Officer, do not shoot that man. He's an officer. A police officer."

Harper.

He turned his head, unable to make out her face beyond the headlights. His eyes teared at the sound of her voice, momentarily reminded of that first time he'd talked to Harper, over the phone, when Anna had run off to South Carolina. Before . . . before all of it.

Harper was talking rapidly. Her voice rose and fell as she told him that she, too, was an officer. Charleston. MacDonald. An old case. Missing. Words were audible, but sentences were lost to the roar of the truck's engine.

"I know who he is," Potter said finally.

"You have to let him go," she said.

"I am letting him go." Potter's voice sounded exasperated.

Shoes—soft-soled now—ran toward him, and Harper was on her knees beside him, holding his arm, helping him up.

"Harper."

"Oh my God. You scared the devil out of me."

"I'm okay." The words were as much for himself as for her.

"Let's get you out of here."

He rose, dusted himself off, and took a step. His hips and legs were stiff, frozen. "How did you find me?"

"Lucy."

Hal shook his head at the reference to her daughter. "What? How?"

"I'll explain later."

When Hal turned, Potter stood a few feet away. He held out Hal's wallet. "Sorry for the confusion."

Hal wasn't sure what confusion he was referring to. Confusion that a black man might not be a killer? That a rich white man could be the guilty one? He took the wallet and returned it to his pocket. "Where did he go?"

"Not sure," Potter said, jerking a thumb over his shoulder. "Headed back into town, I think."

Hal looked down at the front of his clothes. To Harper, he said, "We've got to find him."

"You want, I can put a call in, send a car by his house," Potter said, all graciousness now that Harper was there.

"No, but thanks," Hal said, the sarcasm thick on his tongue.

"I'll follow you back to MacDonald's," Harper said quietly.

Hal nodded.

It was still dark when they arrived back at MacDonald's house. No lights. No sign of life inside. Harper got out of the truck and met him in the street. Together, they stared at the house.

"What now?" he asked.

"We knock on the door." She took a step toward the house. "Or I do."

Hal nodded, stepping back to the Subaru to wait. His phone buzzed in his pocket. A text from Telly. He checked the time: 6:00 here, which meant 5:00 a.m. in Dallas.

Got a potential lead.

Hal dialed.

"Hey," Telly answered. "You're up early."

"I'm in Greenville," Hal said, and not particularly kindly. "What's the lead?"

"Our Atlanta office arrested a guy last week for passport forgery. We think MacDonald might have been a client."

A passport. He planned to leave the country. Hal looked up at MacDonald's house, where Harper still stood at the closed front door.

"Based on some financial documents, it looks like MacDonald may have bought two passports."

Hal felt steam build in his lungs. "That means he's got Anna. He's going to try to get her out of the country."

"Or he bought two passports for himself. Two different identities."

"Well, find out," Hal barked. "We need to know his alias before he leaves the country."

"The forger managed to erase his hard drive before his arrest. Our Atlanta tech team is working to retrieve the lost data. As soon as I have any details, I'll call you."

"He's gone," Hal whispered. "I followed him this morning, but—" He halted, not wanting to explain the whole story. "But I lost him. What if he's going to get her and leave now? Today. We need to stop him, Telly."

"How do you know he didn't go to the office?"

"At four in the morning?"

"Okay," Telly said. "I'll call the field office down there and get someone on him."

"I want to know where he is. As soon as you hear anything—"

"I'll call," Telly promised.

Across the street, Harper knocked on the door again, shaking her head. MacDonald wasn't opening it.

Hal crossed the street and met Harper in the driveway.

"I'm guessing he's not home." She frowned and held up a finger. "Stay here." Harper left him in the driveway and rounded the far side of the house.

Hal took a few steps so that he could see her. On her tiptoes, she was trying to look through a small window set high in the wall.

"This is the garage," she said, jumping up. "But I can't see inside."

Hal approached and looked in the window, confirming what he already knew. "Car's not there."

A car drove by on the street, and both of them froze. "Let's get out of here," Harper said, hurrying back to the street. "I'll leave the truck here for now."

Hal handed her the keys to the Subaru, and they climbed in as though they knew where they were going. But they didn't.

Hal stared down the block in both directions. "Where was he going at four in the morning?"

"There's nothing farther out that road. Potter confirmed it."

"He was leading me on a goose chase."

"Because he had the police coming."

"That must have been the plan," Hal said. "Get me arrested so that he could lose the tail." Hal touched his head and felt the dust still stuck to his scalp. "Or get me shot."

Harper exhaled, shaking her head.

"How did you find me?"

"Jed put a GPS tracker in the Subaru. It technically belongs to the lab, but they're down a van right now, so he keeps it in the car. It allows him to track mileage for work."

Hal shook his head. "You said Lucy."

Harper smiled. "It also allows him to track Lucy when she has the car so he can make sure she's where she says she is."

"So Jed tracked me?"

"I've got the software. When I woke up and your bedroom door was open, I figured you'd gone back to MacDonald's. Then I got your voicemail, and I got nervous. When you didn't answer your phone, I knew something was wrong."

Hal leaned his head back against the headrest and closed his eyes. Exhaustion settled in his bones, braiding itself with fear and desperation, leaving him feeling both wired and totally fried. He had lost his only lead to Anna. Spencer MacDonald had set a trap for him.

He had walked right into it.

And now MacDonald was in the wind.

46

Leaving the truck behind, Hal and Harper took the Subaru to look for MacDonald's Lexus. They started at his office and then went to the club and the gym. They drove to the airport and went down the lanes of parked cars, one by one. They contacted the local police and asked for assistance—an APB, calls to every airport within a three-hour drive, and a subpoena for his cell phone records. They weren't likely to get it—especially not at this hour—but they asked anyway. Starving, they stopped for doughnuts and coffee and kept looking. Hal offered to take Harper back to her friend's house and let her rest, but she refused.

"Two heads are better than one," she said.

And time is of the essence, he thought. Because every minute that passed was a minute that MacDonald had a head start.

After the search, they picked up the truck Harper had borrowed and went back to the house. Harper took a quick shower, and Hal stretched out on the living room floor. The sound of Harper making a fresh pot of coffee roused him. Twenty minutes after that, they were on the road again. At MacDonald's office a second time, they spoke with one of the partners, who got in touch with MacDonald's assistant to confirm his calendar for the morning. It was empty for the rest of the week, which made sense. He was supposed to go from Detroit to Cleveland and then to Richmond, Virginia. He was not supposed to be home.

With nowhere left to go, they were heading back to the house when Hal's phone rang with an unfamiliar number: 864, South Carolina's area code; and 244, a Greenville prefix. He expected MacDonald's voice— some kind of taunt. Instead, it was Georgia Schwartzman.

He put the call on speaker. "I'm here with Detective Leighton. How can we help you?"

"I'm sorry I didn't call earlier. I'm afraid I've been caring for my friend. She's . . ." Georgia Schwartzman stopped talking.

The drunk friend, Hal thought. How long ago that seemed now.

She began again. "I'm wondering if you might drop by the house." Her voice cracked as she added, "Please."

Hal and Harper exchanged a glance. The last thing he wanted was to go back to that house, but she had been acting strangely when they were there before, like she had been holding something back.

"I won't take much of your time," she promised.

"We can come now."

"Yes," she said in a breathy rush. "That would be great."

Harper made a U-turn, and they navigated back to the house where Anna grew up.

Hal had no idea what to expect, only that the place brought out mixed emotions in him—anger and sadness and discomfort. He didn't imagine Georgia Schwartzman hosted a lot of black people. He wondered what she would think of him and Anna. On second thought, he didn't give a damn.

She opened the door as though she'd been waiting at the window. No sign of the maid in her uniform. Or of the drunk woman.

Georgia took one look at Hal's clothes, still covered in dust, and let out a gasp.

The fury built in his chest. "Spencer MacDonald almost got me shot," he said. "You want me to spray off somewhere? Sit outside?"

"Oh, no," Georgia said quickly, flushing a bright red. "Of course not. Come on in, please." As though that wasn't convincing enough, she gave a little wave.

Harper stepped into the house, and Hal followed.

Her hand floated to her throat. "I could make some coffee. Would you like some? Or tea?"

Hal stopped walking. He didn't want coffee or tea. He didn't want a nice chat. He wanted to scream and rant.

"That's not necessary," Harper said, her tone diplomatic.

Hal held back his remarks.

"Why don't we sit in here?" Georgia said, motioning to the living room. Hal eyed the white sofa, the expensive-looking Persian rug.

"To be honest, Mrs. Schwartzman," Hal said, "I'm not much in the mood for sitting. I'm trying to find your daughter and save her from that man."

Georgia Schwartzman flinched but, to her credit, did not step away. He noticed then that she was dressed casually in jeans and a long-sleeve T-shirt. Her feet were bare. She wore no makeup. She looked more like Anna this way, but seeing Anna in her did not make him less angry.

He was at his wits' end. He had South Carolina dirt in his teeth and ears, down his shirt, and in his pants. He felt the dull nausea that always followed an adrenaline rush. He hadn't slept. He hadn't eaten. He needed a shower, but what he needed most was to find Anna. And he wasn't convinced Georgia Schwartzman would help him.

"Why don't we go into the kitchen?" she said, as though that were a compromise to his wanting to leave.

"Why don't you tell us why we're here," Hal said, crossing his arms.

Georgia smoothed her hands over the sides of her jeans. "I'd like to help you find my daughter."

"Now you'd like to help?"

Georgia's mouth opened and closed.

"Not when we were here last time?" He waved toward the back of the house. "When you were entertaining your friends?"

"Hal," Harper said.

But Hal didn't stop. The anger had built like steam in a compartment that was increasingly too small. "It's a fair question," he said, half to Harper. "Because, Mrs. Schwartzman, you didn't seem to want to help when she was trying to get away from him, when you told her that she should stay married to a monster."

Georgia sucked in air, pressing her hand to the base of her throat as though Hal were coming for her neck.

"Hal," Harper whispered again.

But Hal shook his head. "You were supposed to protect her. That's a mother's job. Or if you couldn't protect her, at least believe her. When she told you that her husband hit her, at least give your own child the benefit of the doubt."

Tears welled in Georgia's bright-blue eyes, spilling over and trailing down her cheeks. "I thought I was protecting her. I believed Spencer was a good man."

"You believed it after he threw her across the room? After she lost her daughter? Your granddaughter."

"That's enough, Hal," Harper said, but Georgia put a hand on Harper's arm and shook her head.

"He's right," she whispered. "I was blind."

"How did you not see what he was?" Hal couldn't help but ask. Maybe he did want to understand her. Maybe he needed to know why she'd let Anna down.

"I was alone and afraid. Sam had died." She swept her arm into the air. "He was everything—for both of us—and then he died." Her mouth twisted in grief. "I had no idea how to go on—how to do . . . any of it. Spencer seemed so competent, so—" She cut herself off, holding a hand over her mouth as she started to cry in earnest.

But he didn't feel sorry for her. Losing a husband and a father was bad enough, but Georgia had made that loss so much worse. "To help your daughter with her grief, you saddled her with an abusive husband? To help *you*?"

"God, no. Of course not." Sobs shook her shoulders. "I just didn't want her to be alone. She was an only child, like me. I was afraid for her. I didn't want her to feel how I did. She and Sam had been so close, and without him, I didn't know . . ."

"Anna doesn't need taking care of. She can take care of herself. Don't you realize how strong she is?"

She cupped her face in her hands, her shoulders shaking. "Please. I don't know what to do. You have to find her. You have to make sure she's all right."

"So now you want to protect her? It's a little late." He spun and began to pace.

Harper didn't move. "Mrs. Schwartzman, what did you want to tell us? Why did you ask us to come here?"

Hal rubbed his head, making another loop of the room. This was a waste of time.

"Mrs. Schwartzman, please," Harper said.

"Please," Hal growled. "Is there anything you know that can help us find Anna?" He thought of the baby. Her grandbaby. Who was going to bully her into telling them something he could use? Only him. And he'd do it gladly.

"I followed him," Georgia Schwartzman said. "Saturday."

Hal froze. "What?" Why hadn't she told them this when they were there yesterday? He clenched his fists. "Where did he go?"

"He went to the bank downtown. The Wells Fargo, and then he drove out toward Judson."

"I don't know Judson," Harper said, her pen poised on her notebook.

Georgia Schwartzman waved her hand as though it were irrelevant. "It's a poorer neighborhood. I was surprised he went out there."

"And you followed?" Hal pressed.

She nodded, averting her gaze as she spoke. "He stopped at a convenience store and came out with a plastic bag. I couldn't tell what was in it at first, but he didn't get in his car. Instead, he walked into a playground—it was empty. He sat on a bench and pulled something from the bag. It was difficult to see what it was. Something in packaging, which he unwrapped."

God, don't let it be his lunch.

"Then he put it to his ear. Like it was a phone."

A noise came from Harper.

A burner phone.

Hal moved beside her. "What then?"

"He sat on the bench for about ten minutes and made phone calls."

He opened his notebook. "When was this?"

She pointed to the kitchen. "I wrote it down in my planner. I have the address of the convenience store, too."

He nodded. "Could you get that?"

"It's in the kitchen." She waved, and they followed. She opened one drawer and then another.

Hal felt the tension mount in his gut. She couldn't find the planner. But when she turned to face him and Harper, she held a small book in one hand and a plastic bag in the other.

Hal stared at the bag. "What is that?"

"It's the phone."

Hal reached for the bag. "The phone he was talking on?"

She nodded, letting him have it. "After he left the playground, he dumped the bag in a trash can and got back into his car. I waited until he was gone and went to the trash can to retrieve it. I don't know why, but something made me think it might be useful."

Hal took her shoulders and kissed her cheek.

She let out a little squeak.

"Will it help you find her?" Georgia asked, her eyes wide and afraid.

For the first time, she looked like a mother.

"It might," Hal said with a rush of genuine hope.

Please, God. Please give us a lead to follow.

47

The air under the sheet was stuffy and the metal awkward in Schwartzman's hand as she worked through the last millimeters of the thick rubber collar. Her arm ached, and her fingers were tight, stiffened in the position of gripping the thin metal triangle. Her cutting hand was wrapped in a flannel pajama top for protection. Even then, the cotton sheet was spotted with blood from where the metal had nicked her neck and stabbed into her left hand, which held the collar steady. Every so often, she had to stop the process.

Twice, she'd gotten up and gone to the bathroom to drink clean water from the toilet tank. At some point, she rose and made her way to the kitchen, ate something, and stretched her fingers, bending them backward on the countertop.

Tears filled her eyes at the pain, and as a distraction, she stared at the spot on the wall where she'd last seen Hal's face. Then she returned to the bedroom to hide herself back under the sheet. She'd been at it all night, working as consistently as her fingers would allow, listening for the sounds of someone coming.

Outside, the black sky lightened to a deep purple and then magenta. She set the metal down and pulled the collar from opposite ends, twisting it to try to broaden the cut. She had been sure the rubber would eventually tear. But it didn't give. Not a millimeter. Her stomach growled again, the effort burning through calories her body didn't have stored. But she refused to stop. Not until she was free.

To keep herself awake, she'd taken to biting into her lower lip as she worked, creating small cuts that bled. The pain kept her alert, even as exhaustion overwhelmed her. She stretched out her arm and closed her eyes. Just for a minute.

She was so close. She would be free so soon . . .

48

Not surprisingly, the burner phone Georgia Schwartzman had retrieved from the park trash can was dead. Luckily, the charging port was common enough, and the cord for Georgia's Kindle fit it perfectly. While they waited for the phone to come to life, Georgia made breakfast.

Hal spent the passing minutes staring at the phone and willing it to come to life. Twice, the screen brightened, but when he went to make a selection on the screen, it went dead again.

"You've got to let it charge awhile," Harper told him, not for the first time.

Hal texted Telly asking for updates, even though Telly had promised to be in touch the minute he heard anything. When two minutes passed without word from Telly, Hal's chest began to tighten again, so he texted Roger and then Hailey to keep himself busy. Asked if they'd linked the knife the San Francisco police had found in the trash can to a suspect in the Stockton Street stabbing.

Neither responded. Not that he could blame them. It was 4:00 a.m. in San Francisco.

Georgia served breakfast at the kitchen island, biscuits still steaming and hot with a thick meat gravy. Hal was ravenous, fighting not to eat too quickly. His plate was almost empty and Georgia was offering seconds when the phone finally came alive for real. The breath hitched in Hal's throat as he took the phone into his hands, as though it were a tiny, broken bird he had to save.

The phone was flip style, as basic as they came, the screen pixelated and gray. When the display came to life, the battery showed two bars. Pushing his plate aside, Hal drew a breath and navigated directly to the call history.

There were only two calls on the phone's history—the same number twice. Area code 208.

"Area code 208," Hal said.

Harper was on her phone. She looked up a moment later. "Idaho."

Hal hit redial and listened to the phone ringing on the other end. Once, twice, then a voice. "You know it's five a.m. out here."

Hal punched up the volume as Harper leaned in. Hal tried to think of something to say.

"Thought you weren't in until later. You already landed?"

Hal's heart trumpeted in his throat. With a glance at Harper, he tried to raise his voice to a higher decibel, fisted his hand, and muffled his response. "No. Not yet."

There was a long pause on the other end. "Who is this?"

"Who is *this*?" Hal asked without disguising his voice.

"Shit," came the response, and the line went dead.

"Do you recognize the voice?" Harper asked.

"I don't know." Hal's mind raced, the few words playing in his head over and over. There was something about that voice. The slight twang of country that gave it a nasal quality. *Idaho. Idaho.* "We need to track the number."

Hal dialed Telly. After four rings, the call went to voicemail. He didn't have time to leave a message. Ending the call, he redialed immediately. Once, and then another time when he got voicemail again. Finally, Telly answered.

Talking as fast as his lips would move, Hal told Telly about the burner phone and explained that he needed to trace the number's owner.

Telly didn't miss a beat. "Give me the number."

Hal read it out loud and then repeated it to be certain he had it right. "I need the information, Telly. I need it now. This guy—he's got her. I know he does."

"I'll get it. Give me five minutes."

Hal ended the call and clutched the phone in his fist. For a moment, he was at a loss. He should be moving. Going to Idaho? But the area code didn't mean that was where the phone was. It could be anywhere. He needed to know who owned the phone.

Unable to sit still, Hal dialed the Idaho number again, turning the phone to speaker. It rang only once before a voice said, "You've reached Tyler. Leave a message, and I'll get back to you."

Tyler. Tyler . . . He couldn't think of anyone named Tyler, but the voice was familiar. *Tyler. Idaho.*

"Who is it?" Georgia asked. "Do you know him?"

Harper was watching him, too. But he didn't answer them. He was thinking.

Hal dialed the number again, closed his eyes, and listened to the voice. And then he realized why the voice was familiar.

It belonged to the morgue assistant who had attacked Anna more than a year before. Not Tyler, though. The guy's name was Roy. Roy Butler.

Hal's phone rang. Telly. He answered it, breathless and pacing the room, although he didn't remember standing from the kitchen island.

"I've got him," Telly reported. "I just sent you an image. Name is Tyler—"

"Butler?" Hal asked.

"Yes. How did you—never mind," Telly said. "We're getting the cell records, narrowing down the cell towers, but the cell phone company has some initial reporting. The phone's somewhere in northern Idaho, near the Washington-Idaho border. It's an active spot for us—Hayden, Idaho, is a headquarters for the Aryan Nation."

Idaho. Anna was in Idaho. With the Aryan Nation.

He was going to Idaho.

"As soon as we narrow on his location, I'll get a team out there."

"Keep me posted." Hal ended the call and turned to Harper and Georgia. "I need to get to Idaho. I've got to call the airlines." Already, his mind was spinning over the details. How fast could he get there? What airline might get him closest? Hands trembling, he pulled up a map on his phone. From Greenville, there wouldn't be anything direct. Damn it.

"I can take you to the airport now," Harper said.

Frantic and desperate, Hal turned toward the door. Idaho was a day's travel. It was too far.

"I think I can help," Georgia said, busy typing on her phone.

"You did help," Hal told her. "The phone was a huge help."

"Wait just one minute," Georgia said, still typing. Her nails clicked on the screen.

Hal glanced at Harper. He needed to call the airlines. If there was a morning flight, he wanted to be on it. "Thank you, Georgia, but we really need to go now."

"Oh, but just one minute—"

Hal tensed his muscles as though ready to launch himself toward the door. "How far is the airport?"

"About thirty minutes, I'd say," Harper said.

He glanced at Georgia, who was still staring at her phone. A moment later, it dinged, and she smiled. She looked up at him. "I got you a ride to Idaho."

"A ride?" There was no time to drive to Idaho. "I think I'll fly."

Georgia smiled. "Of course. My friend Patrice's husband has a jet. A very nice jet."

At the word *jet*, his mouth fell open.

"Patrice was one of the ladies here yesterday. Her husband, Bill, is on his way to Seattle today, but he's willing to make a stop in Idaho. And his pilot can be ready to leave at 8:15 a.m." She glanced at her watch. "That gives you just enough time to get to the private airfield."

Hal was speechless.

"Private airfield," Harper said.

"It's right at the small downtown airport. Do you know where that is?"

Harper glanced at Hal and shook her head.

"It's just inside the 385 loop," Georgia said. "Write your number down here, and I'll text you the directions."

Hal wrote his number on the pad of paper.

"I'll send you Bill's contact information, too. Call me if you have any problems, but he'll be there."

Tears welled in Hal's eyes. How long would it take to jet to Idaho? He would be there today. Would he see Anna today? Was it possible? He blinked back the emotion and took Georgia's hand in both of his, enveloping her tiny palm and her wrist like they were a couple of playing cards. "Thank you."

"You go get my girl, Detective."

"You've got my word." Hal gave her hands a final squeeze and started for the door.

"And if I can ask for one more thing?" Georgia called out to him, her voice cracking.

"Yes, ma'am."

"You'll come back with Anna and the baby," she said, searching his face.

She knew it was his baby. Of course she did. "You better believe it," Hal said.

Georgia smiled a shy smile and then waved them off. "Go on now. Hurry up."

Hal couldn't help but run for Harper's car. Forty minutes until the jet left. Four, maybe five hours to Idaho.

He reached the car, laid his palm on the warm roof, and closed his eyes. *I'm coming, Anna. Hang on.*

49

The sound of a car engine jolted Schwartzman awake. Heart pounding, she sat upright in the bed. Her fingers found the sharp metal triangle sitting atop the sheets. The light had shifted in the room, and the soft gray of dawn outside the window had given way to a bright midmorning.

She had fallen asleep.

The engine outside grew louder, closer. She felt for the collar, praying that she'd managed to free herself, but it was still there, split but not broken.

She pushed the sheet off her head and studied the bed. There was blood everywhere. Heart drumming, she listened for the car while she yanked and twisted on the collar, the last millimeter of rubber still holding it on her neck.

Her pulse throbbed. She had maybe three minutes until the car arrived at the house. If she couldn't get the collar off, she had to hide the blood. Moving frantically, she rose from the bed, fumbled to take off the hoodie, and buttoned her own shirt over her bra. She balled the bloodied hoodie and shoved it in a bottom drawer.

Then she picked up the metal with the sleeve of her flannel button-down and began to carve into the rubber with fury. She let out a cry as she caught the skin on her neck but did not stop. The car grew closer, her motions more frantic. She jabbed her neck again and again. Sawed, pulled at the rubber, chafing the back of her neck as she struggled to free herself.

Gravel crunched under the tires of the approaching car. Tears streamed down her face as she dug the metal slowly through the rubber. She pressed the metal hard and made a final cut.

The collar broke free.

She gasped as the cord retracted, the collar flying up to the ceiling. As it passed her face, the end of the collar snapped her in the eye. She blinked white spots and dropped the metal. Rubbed her neck as she listened to the car.

The engine seemed close now. Every pop and clink of gravel against the tires and undercarriage grew louder. She glanced around the room and realized she was still a sitting duck. She needed a weapon. If he was coming here to hurt her . . .

Dropping to the floor, she scanned the floor for the little triangle. She couldn't see it. Where had it gone? She thought about gripping the tiny piece of metal. How would she hold it? It was too small. She would have to be too close.

The galloping of her heart in her throat, she stared at the collar hanging on the ceiling track. Then she scrambled to her feet and ran from the room. In the kitchen, she grabbed the single cast-iron fry pan with its wooden handle from under the counter, pushing the cabinet shut before she bolted back to the bedroom.

Her legs were weak, her knees threatening to buckle as she stumbled through the cabin, her muscles unaccustomed to fast motion. She reached the bedroom and closed the door. Outside, the car engine shut off.

She would crawl back into the bed with the collar and make it look like she was still wearing it. Stepping up on the bed, she grabbed hold of the collar and yanked. The collar came down several inches before the cleat caught in the track and jammed. She pulled harder, jerking it, but it didn't release. The collar was pinned six or eight inches from the ceiling. She let it go, and the cord retracted to the ceiling, the rubber collar swinging back up with it. She grabbed for it again, trying to pull it loose.

A car door slammed. Boots on gravel. Then on the wooden front steps.

She pulled and tugged, but the cord did not yield. The collar hung from the track in the middle of the room. There was no way to hide the fact that she was free.

Palming the fry pan, she crossed the room and pulled the shades closed, trying to darken the room. There was still too much light. The collar hanging from the track was too obvious. She tried to think of a way to conceal it when she heard his voice.

"Everything is good," Tyler said. "Ready. Just like I promised. I'm here now. You're probably about ten, fifteen minutes out. You want me to put her in anything special? Make her take a shower or get her cleaned up?"

Ten or fifteen minutes out. That had to be Spencer. Spencer was coming, and then there would be two of them.

Schwartzman shifted toward the door, adjusting the fry pan in her grip. He was coming in. She eyed the collar again, figured she had only a second or two to take him down before he saw it.

"Okay. Take it easy," Tyler said. "I know the deal. Cash for her untouched. Better bring the cash, though. We don't take kindly out here to being fucked with." A low growl. "You're not in a position to threaten." A pause. "Not out here you're not." A pause, and Tyler mumbled something under his breath. His footsteps grew closer, more rapid. He was angry.

Her pulse drilling painfully into the wounds on her neck, Schwartzman pressed herself into the space behind the bedroom door, between it and the small bureau. She gripped the pan handle in both hands, held her breath, and counted. One, two. The bedroom door burst open. Tyler Butler walked in. His eyes were on the bed, the lump of the pillow where he thought she would be.

It took a moment before they tracked to the collar, hanging from the ceiling.

Schwartzman was already swinging. The flat bottom of the fry pan struck him in the face, the cast iron connecting with his nose with a loud pop. Tyler howled, cradling his face in both hands. Blood streamed down his face and dripped between his fingers. Schwartzman lifted the pan as he blinked in an effort to clear his vision. A moment later, he wheeled around, swinging a fist blindly for her. Schwartzman ducked and swung the pan back in the other direction.

The edge of the cast-iron pan struck his skull above the occipital lobe. He flew forward into the bed. She raised the pan and struck again, this time connecting with the parietal lobe. The head of the pan flew across the room, leaving her holding the short wooden handle. Tyler rolled off the bed, arms splayed to his sides. Blood flowed from his nose. He was unconscious but likely not dead. She wanted to tie him up, but there wasn't time.

Spencer would arrive soon, and she needed another weapon.

She palmed Butler's pants, hoping to find a gun. All she found was his phone. She shoved it in the pocket of her sweatpants and nudged him with her foot, still holding the handle of the fry pan. He didn't move.

She checked his pockets again. No keys. They had to be in the car. She looked again at Tyler, lying unconscious on the floor. He could be out for hours, or he might wake in a few minutes. If Spencer arrived in the meantime, it would be two on one. She reached for the collar and yanked again, seeing if the cleat would unjam from the track. Maybe she could tie him with the cord. But it remained stubbornly stuck.

She had to get in the car and get out.

She left the bedroom door and noticed the lock on the outside. Punched it in and tested the knob. Locked. It wouldn't stop him, but it might slow him down.

Running across the cabin floor, she stared down at her bare feet. She should have taken his shoes. And she had no weapon. She stopped, considered going back into the bedroom for the head of the pan. It was not an effective weapon, and she couldn't make herself return to that room.

The sound of another car engine reached her ears. Unlike the first one, this one sounded close. Too close.

She glanced out the window in the front door. A dark sedan bumped along the dirt road, slush spinning off the tires.

Spencer.

50

Frozen in the front room of the cabin, Schwartzman had only a few seconds to think as the car made its final approach up the road. Even from twenty yards away, she knew it was Spencer. Knew from the knuckles that gripped the steering wheel, caught in the light. Knew from the way he spun the car out before wheeling it around to park facing the house. Knew from the first glimmer of his carefully gelled blond hair and the way he cocked his head as he leaned forward to look through the windshield.

Her fingers found Tyler's phone in her pocket. Fumbling, she tried to find a way to dial. The screen was locked. She pressed the button to make an emergency call, watching as Spencer cracked the car door and stood, tall and lean and confident. Ugly and cruel. Here to take her.

"Nine-one-one. What is your emergency?"

"My name is Anna Schwartzman. I'm being held in a cabin. In the woods. I don't know where I am. The man who has me is Tyler Butler. And there's another man coming. He's going to hurt me."

"Ma'am, okay. Slow down."

"He's here. Spencer MacDonald is here. Please. Call Hal Harris at the San Francisco Police Department. Send the police. Please. Please."

Spencer stretched his arms as though he were on his way to a picnic, and she hissed into the phone. "He's here now. My name is Anna Schwartzman. I'm the medical examiner for San Francisco. Please help me."

Then she turned and ran for the freezer. She set the phone on the counter, leaving the call live as she opened the door and reached for the icicle at the back.

The ice was cold in her palm, a salve on the wounds she'd incurred carving off the collar. The emergency responder's voice bled faintly from the phone as she crept toward the door. She peered out at Spencer as he made his way toward the porch.

She crouched behind the door, breathing heavily. Glancing in the direction of the bedroom, she wished she had the fry pan, even without its handle. Spencer's foot mounted the first stair. It was too late. The icicle would have to do. *Stab and run. Get to Tyler's car.* The keys had to be inside.

Get in and lock the doors.

Drive away.

Tears filled her eyes. The icicle burned in her palm. She drew raspy, shallow breaths. Spencer stepped up the second stair, then the third. She raised the icicle above her head as he reached the porch.

His hand in a fist, he rapped on the door. His face was hidden from her. When no one answered, he would sense something was wrong. She drew another breath, tensed, and waited as he knocked again.

Then the door cracked open. His foot crossed the threshold. Schwartzman counted to three and pounced.

She slammed the door hard on his foot. Opened it and slammed it again.

Spencer howled, and she opened the door and charged at him, stabbing at his eye with the icicle.

Spencer turned his head, and the icicle caught his temple, carving a deep scratch in the skin above his ear. The momentum drove her forward. The icicle slipped from her fist and shattered against the porch. She gasped and cried out. A sob popped like a balloon in her chest. Stunned, Spencer stepped back, and she used both hands to shove his chest hard.

He fell backward, slipping on a patch of ice and landing with a thump in the snow. His eyes were wide, his body still. Blood dripped from the side of his face.

She jumped off the stairs, tripped, and scrambled up again, running for Tyler's car. The snow burned her feet. She fell again, scraping her palms on the hard, icy ground as she tried to propel herself.

The shock worn off, Spencer let out a sharp laugh, like a bark. "Bella," he howled, the teeth of the word biting her as his hand caught her ankle. His fingers were like metal, unyielding and cold.

She tried to kick free, reaching for the root of a tree just showing itself above the snow.

With a yank, Spencer tore away her chances to grab the tree root. He jerked again. Then he was cackling. He laughed so hard that the pulsing sound vibrated in her lungs. His fingers gripped her anklebone like a metal vise. She kicked and twisted, clawing at the ground to get away.

But he held too tight.

The loose sweatpants rode down, the rough ice shredding the skin of her thighs. He swung his other hand up and caught the inside of her leg, grasping her skin and dragging her toward him in angry jerks.

She raised her free foot and kicked out, catching his shoulder. His grip loosened momentarily, and she darted from him. She'd reached the porch steps when he caught her again, his fist descending on her back like an anvil.

She collapsed, striking her chin on the stair. The taste of blood filled her mouth. Wrapping her hands around the first rung, she fought him as he yanked her backward.

There was nowhere to go. No weapons inside. Nowhere to run. She wasn't fast enough. She wasn't strong enough. Tears burned her eyes. She'd thought she was smart enough, that she could create a weapon and wield it effectively. But she couldn't. And there was no backup plan. No one to save her.

Only herself.

Spencer took hold of her hair and yanked, the strands ripping from her scalp like the heat of an open flame. Her hand came free to reach behind her and grab his hand, wrench it free.

He let go to grab her shoulders. His weight pinned her down, pressing her abdomen into the hard edge of the stair. Her baby. He was going to kill her baby.

Again.

Something tiny caught her eye from beneath the stair, a silver object in the half-melted snow. A key.

Her eyes filled with tears. If only she'd found the right key. If she'd gotten free just an hour sooner. How far could she have gotten? She reached through the slats. Her fingers gripped the key, and she rolled it into her fist as Spencer wrenched her off the steps. He grabbed her right arm and hoisted her up. The key slipped in her opposite fist, and she clenched it more tightly, clinging to the idea that she'd been so close.

He would win. Spencer would win.

Would Hal find her? Would he even know what had happened?

Spencer wrenched her to her feet, and she stumbled toward him. He struck her face with the flat of his palm. Stars danced across her vision.

The sound of an engine in the distance.

Someone was coming.

Spencer gripped her arm at the shoulder, drawing her closer.

She clenched the key in her fist, the long, sharp end jutting out between her thumb and forefinger. She dipped her head down, and when he reached to yank her up again, she swung the hand behind her, circling it in a wide arc. He gripped her chin and pulled her face up.

"You are mine."

She spit in his face.

He stumbled back, still gripping her arm as she brought her fist to his temple. Leveraging the strength of his grip, she drove the short metal end into the bone shielding his temporal lobe.

He spun and stumbled back toward the house, stunned.

His fingers reached for the key in his temple. It had barely entered the skin at all. The key wasn't sharp enough. She wasn't strong enough. She scanned the ground and saw a metal shovel leaning against the house. She ran, slipping on the frozen ground, her feet raw and bloody. As she gasped for breath, blood sprayed from her mouth.

She grabbed the worn wooden handle of the shovel. Splinters slid into her skin as she whirled around.

Spencer stood with the bloody key in his hand. Partially hunched over, he watched her with hooded eyes.

She raised the shovel and moved it slowly in circles, like a batter getting ready for the pitch. One shot. She would have only one chance.

His lips curled into a smile as he took a slow, unsteady step forward. "Bella, Bella." Blood tracked down his face, dripping off his chin.

She blinked quickly, her pulse throbbing, her muscles tight and quick.

He lunged, roaring as he came at her.

She swung the shovel, striking his shoulder as he drove at her. He rammed her into the house, the shovel between them. She tried to wrench it free, to take another swing, but he held the metal spade under his arm. She twisted away from the house, clinging to the wooden handle.

A terrible crack split the air, and she stumbled. In her hands was the shovel's handle. At the end was a sharp, splintered point.

She spun around.

Spencer stood against the house, the metal shovel raised in his hands like a trophy, his eyes closed, a huge, ugly grin on his lips.

Without hesitation, she lowered the handle like a dagger and ran toward him. She pressed her feet into the hard, frozen ground, dropped her shoulder, and came at him full force, aiming right beneath his ribs.

There was a low, soft thump, almost like music, as the wood entered below his sternum at the xiphoid process.

Spencer's eyes popped open, as though his lids were connected to the pressure in his abdomen. He made a sound, barely a groan.

His smile was gone.

The shovel dropped with a clank to the ground.

She gripped the handle, partially embedded in Spencer, with both hands. Tucking it under her arm for leverage, she twisted and turned it upward.

He reached for the stick and tried to pull it free. She leaned in and pushed. Her feet numb, she felt only her toenails digging into the snow. Everything she had—everything she'd saved up—drove that stake into him.

His hands dropped to his sides, and his mouth fell open. Blood saturated his shirt and dripped down the front of the handle. Her hands were slick with it.

She gave the handle one last hard push and stepped back.

Spencer stared down at the handle but didn't touch it. She should yank it out. If it was puncturing his abdominal aorta, he would bleed out faster if she removed it.

But she couldn't.

What if she pulled it out and there was no wound? What if it was all a joke? He would open his eyes and laugh. Stand up and come after her again.

Slowly, Spencer slid down, his back pressed to the outside of the house, until he was sitting on the ground. His fingers made their way to the handle. He hesitated to touch it, as though it were something strange and foreign.

As he went to reach for it, she cried out.

He looked at her, eyes wide, as though she, too, were something foreign. Then his gaze returned to the handle.

She scrambled away before he could pull the handle free. She grabbed the head of the shovel and lifted it in the air.

The sound of an engine floated over the snow somewhere behind her.

Her eyes felt the pull of the road, but she didn't let herself look away. She would not be fooled.

Spencer closed his eyes, and she held her breath.

"Bella."

"No." She held the shovel high, unsteady on her feet.

His left hand dropped to his side, and she started to step away. It was over. It had to be over.

His fingers caught the bottom of her shirt, and he pulled her toward him.

She stumbled.

His left hand darted out, and he caught her leg, jerked her close.

She toppled into him, the two of them falling against the house. The handle still jutted from the soft tissue below his ribs as he curled his lips into a gruesome smile.

"Mine," he hissed.

She arched her back, lifting the metal spade over her head, and brought it down on the front of his skull. A hard crunch of bone snapped in the air.

He had her—her shirt and her leg—but she raised the shovel up and brought it down again. And again. Over and over until the face of her monster was gone.

The car noise grew louder until the engine was inside her skull, like a thousand bees. Fat white flakes began to fall around her.

Still clutching the shovel, she pulled her shirt from his grip. Tears streamed down her face as she batted his arm away from her skin. Moving slowly, she crawled backward.

She wiped the blood from her face and rose. The shovel in her hand, she turned, ready to fight.

In the dull gray light, the man who ran toward her looked like Hal—his broad shoulders, the fists of his hands pumping as he ran. And then he was there. He lifted her up, and he smelled like dirt and sandalwood and home.

And she realized that she must have died.

51

Hal jumped from the FBI Suburban before it had come to a complete stop. He had the door open as soon as he'd seen Anna in front of the tiny log cabin, standing in the snow, the spade of a shovel in her raised arms. A lifeless, almost faceless body lay slumped against the house beside her.

"Anna!" He ran, his shoes slipping on the ice, righting himself, then sprinting the distance to where she stood. "Anna!"

At the sound of her name, she swung toward him, her motion off-kilter as though she were drunk. The spade fell from her hands, and it was only then that he saw she was barefoot, the skin on her feet scarlet red and bleeding. Blood splattered across her hands and face and dripped from wounds on her neck.

He took her in his arms, sweeping her up so her feet were off the cold ground. She put her arms around his neck and let herself be held. Her eyes searched his, but there seemed to be no recognition. A moment later, she collapsed.

He carried her back to the Suburban, shouting at the agents to get her to a hospital. Sitting in the back, he put his forehead to hers and touched his hand to her neck so he could feel the comforting thrum of her pulse. And he talked to her. Whispered how much he loved her. How scared she'd made him. How he didn't want to wait to tell people they were together. That he didn't want to be friends. That he would be anything she needed. And everything.

He talked and talked. When he looked up, it was because someone had opened the car door. They had stopped in a large field, a chopper in its center, the propellers kicking ice in a sweeping circle. Two paramedics stood at the door, motioning for him to bring Anna. He helped them get her on the gurney and carry her to the helicopter, feeling the power of the propellers on the bare skin of his head.

"I'm afraid you can't—" one of the paramedics told him.

"No," Hal said, and climbed in beside her.

The two paramedics stepped away and spoke to one of the FBI agents. Only one returned, climbing into the helicopter on the other side of Anna. Soon, they were in the air. Hal watched the monitor as the paramedic attached an IV and checked her vitals. He followed the directions the paramedic gave him, keeping one hand on her arm, feeling her skin against his. He would not let go. Not ever again.

When they landed in Boise, they took her away from him. He called his mother, then Roger and Harper, and finally Georgia Schwartzman. Short calls. She was alive. They were at a hospital in Idaho. He would call later. He had hours to kill, but he couldn't kill them on the phone. He couldn't talk. Couldn't form sentences. He spent every second on his feet, pacing the family waiting area and praying. *I can't live without her. Please, God. I cannot live without that woman.* Over and over and over.

And then the doctor came out. Smiling. "Dr. Schwartzman is very dehydrated, but otherwise, she's okay."

"Is she talking?"

"She is. A bit. She told me to tell you she was all right."

Hal almost fell to his knees. She was all right. That was all he'd asked. Then he thought about the pregnancy. The baby. He'd only asked

God for Anna, afraid that asking for the baby was too much. Now he felt like he'd failed her. "She's—she was pregnant."

The doctor nodded. "Blood test confirms high levels of HCG, so everything looks good there, too. There's no way to know much more at this point." The doctor nodded toward the door behind him. "You want to come see her? She might be asleep, but—"

"Yes. Yes, please."

Over the next twelve hours in Boise, Hal watched Anna. Mostly, he watched her sleep. He couldn't take his eyes off her. He remembered when she was in the hospital almost two years earlier. Anna had woken in her apartment to find Ken Macy—a colleague she'd been out with a single time—unconscious in her bed. Macy had been stabbed eighteen times. Anna had been brought to the hospital, and Hal had spent that night sleeping in the chair beside her. He'd woken the next morning to discover the hospital bed empty. Fearful of being blamed for the attack on Ken Macy and driven by the need to try to stop Spencer MacDonald on her own, Anna had flown to Charleston. Hal recalled the fear he'd felt when he'd woken and she was gone. The frustration.

Now he slept with his head on her bed, his hand resting on her shin or one arm draped protectively across her. She moved, and he woke. He didn't get much sleep, but every time he opened his eyes to the sight of her, it was like waking to a dream. She was safe. She was there. He could touch her and prove it to himself. So he did. Again and again.

———

The next day, with the help of a call from the governor of California, Hal got Anna flown home to San Francisco, where she would return to Zuckerberg San Francisco General Hospital. Like the doctors in Boise, the ones at General assured him that she was a little dehydrated but otherwise fine.

As she regained her strength, Roger and Hailey visited. His mother came. Anna was in good spirits, alert and with increased energy each day. The only thing she didn't want to talk about was the pregnancy. The doctors had opinions about what type of screening she should do—based on the trauma she'd been through, based on her age, based on the "miscarriage" of her first pregnancy. Anna refused them all.

Each time a doctor brought it up, she cut them off. "I don't want to hear anything about it," she said. "There's no reason to believe anything is wrong with the baby. No tests, please." The yearning in her voice had brought him to tears.

Some of the doctors were more reasonable than others. One simply reminded her to eat well and take her vitamins.

"Of course," Anna had said. "I'll do everything to keep him healthy."

Him.

But it was more complicated than that. She'd been drugged. There was no way to know what kind or how much of an impact the drugs had had on the baby. They might see the adverse effects of the drug during the midpregnancy ultrasound. The baby might measure small because of delayed growth, or there could be more serious birth defects.

Other issues could arise once the baby was born. Still others would be unknown until the baby was a toddler . . . or later. Anna didn't want to know if there was something wrong with the baby because she would raise him despite complications.

And Hal would be there.

"Everything's okay," one doctor whispered to Hal in the hallway after Anna had told her to stop talking about the pregnancy. Hal wanted to scream at the doctor. What right did she have to tell him everything was all right?

He'd almost lost Anna.

The baby was all right—that was what the doctor was saying, he was certain. But he didn't want to hear that either. He wanted to respect Anna's request. And he wanted her home as soon as possible.

In the quiet hours when he couldn't sleep, he reminded himself that it was over. Tyler Butler, who they'd known at the morgue by his brother's name, Roy, had been arrested.

Butler had been MacDonald's cellmate during the short time MacDonald was in prison after his initial arrest. Butler had been serving time for setting fire to a synagogue filled with worshippers during a white supremacist rally. Thankfully, no one had been harmed, though the building was a total loss. MacDonald had kept in touch with Butler, who'd worked for a coroner before his arrest. MacDonald figured he might be useful if he could get a job in Anna's morgue. When the time came, he had helped Butler get a job with the SFPD, using Roy's name, since Tyler Butler had a record. With Tyler inside the morgue, MacDonald had eyes on Anna.

MacDonald.

There was no more MacDonald.

Spencer MacDonald is dead.

And for the first time in many years, Anna was safe.

52

After two days of observation and IV fluids, Anna was released by the doctors at Zuckerberg San Francisco General with a clean bill of health. Hal's mother had spent much of that time tidying Anna's house and filling the refrigerator and freezer with meals to last a month. For his part, Hal spoke daily to the Idaho FBI office handling the case against Tyler Butler. Butler's mother had been arrested and charged as an accessory to Anna's kidnapping. The real Roy Butler was in the custody of social workers who understood his needs. Anna had been relieved to hear that the young man with Down syndrome was being cared for.

While the FBI sent Hal a steady stream of reports, it was Spencer MacDonald's autopsy that provided the biggest relief. Hal had witnessed the dead Spencer MacDonald with his own two eyes, but the fact that MacDonald's dental records and fingerprints had been matched to the body was a welcome confirmation.

Spencer MacDonald was really dead.

Hal and Telly kept in regular contact, too. Between other cases, Telly was working to identify Bryce Scala's shooter. It seemed likely that MacDonald was involved, and Telly hoped MacDonald's computer and phone would provide a suspect. Along with a couple of agents who specialized in financial crimes, Telly was also digging into MacDonald's computer to locate the hacker, Caleb, who had made millions for himself and MacDonald through insider trading.

Telly was also working to identify the potential investors MacDonald had met with in Dallas, Denver, and Detroit on the chance that their identities could help the authorities locate Caleb. Penny Moore, the octogenarian widow MacDonald had dined with at Sapphire in Dallas, told authorities that MacDonald had been recommended by an old work contact of her husband's, but she'd been unable to provide the FBI with any helpful information, like a name. Telly had his work cut out for him.

But Hal had to hand it to the young agent. He did really good work with his nose in those damn reports. Anna had insisted on sending him something for his help. After some back-and-forth, they'd decided on a generous gift certificate to Sapphire. Hal had signed the card, *Now you can eat truffle fries every night for a month . . . Yuck.* And then Anna had added, *Love and gratitude, Hal and Anna.* Hal wasn't much for mushy sentiment, but he didn't argue.

Now that all the pieces of the case were in the right hands, Hal could slow down enough to think about moving on with their lives. The drive from the hospital to Anna's house felt unreal, like moments of a dream. He found himself brushing a hand against her leg or shoulder, unable or unwilling to let physical space come between them. They parked at the curb, and Hal helped her out of the car. Together, they walked toward the house, and he found himself wondering what would happen from here. How would they be now?

Hal unlocked the front door, and Anna stopped on the threshold, hesitant. Buster greeted her, his tail wagging. Anna rubbed his head distractedly.

"What is it?" Hal asked. More than ever, he was tuned to her every expression and word, as though all the days of being without her had left him starved of some vital nutrient.

She scanned the front room. "I don't want to live here . . ."

Hal surveyed her house from the door. He was afraid to ask where their relationship stood, afraid to mention making a change to be together, to live together. They had yet to discuss it, and the fear that being with him wasn't what she wanted overshadowed everything. He'd promised himself that he would give her space and time. She might not be ready, after all that had happened. "If you don't want to live here, we can find you somewhere else. Or . . ."

She shook her head. "That's not what I mean." She turned to him slowly, and he set her duffel down, taking her hands and searching her face.

"What is it, Anna?"

"I don't want to live here alone," she said.

Hal met her gaze. The seriousness in her eyes broke momentarily, and he caught a flash of her playful self. "Anna?"

"Will you move in?" she asked.

His heart dropped. He wanted to pick her up and spin her around, but he was terrified of hurting her. "Move in?"

She started to turn away from him, but he caught her hand.

"Yes. God, yes. I'd love to move in. I want to marry you, Anna. I want you to be my wife." He felt a rush of pure joy and started to bend to one knee.

She pulled away. "No!"

He got back to his feet, flustered. "What? What is it?"

"I don't want that." She pulled her arms across her body. "I don't know if I'll ever want it."

His fingers touched the place where his chest felt blown open. The room was suddenly too quiet and too loud, as though both were possible at once. He couldn't breathe. He was sweating and chilled, and he thought he might be sick.

MacDonald had ruined her.

Hal froze in place. Tears filled his eyes. He shook his head, and they fell onto his cheeks. "I don't know what you're telling me."

She stepped toward him, and he held a palm out, unsure if he could remain standing if she touched him.

"These past days have been—" He shook his head. "I don't have a word for them, Anna. I wanted to die. I thought I would. And now you're here. And—" He motioned to the baby that she wouldn't let the doctors talk about. "And we might be having a child. And I love you. I love you more than I've ever loved anyone. I understand you may not feel the same way. You've been through a lot. Maybe you need time and space. But I don't." He felt the tears slide into his mouth. "I don't need time. I know what I want."

With the words out, he turned to leave.

"Before you go," she said, "can I talk?"

He swallowed hard, nodded.

Her lips curved into a smile as she got closer.

It might have been a cruel joke on her part, but he reached for her anyway. He was too far gone. If she let him go, if she pushed him away, he would not go easily. He would fight. Nothing she could do would be worse than what he'd already suffered.

Her hand gripped his, and his breath was whisked from his lungs.

"I don't want to get married," she said, moving close to him. "I don't want to be married again. I don't want to be a wife. I felt pressured into marrying Spencer. By the situation—my father's death, my mother's loneliness, her fear of being alone . . ."

She closed her eyes, and he thought of the rape she'd endured at MacDonald's hands. On their first date. The anger flowed through him again. How she'd ended up married to him. What that must have been like.

If he could go back and kill MacDonald himself, he would.

She opened her eyes and stood on tiptoes to kiss his cheek. "I want to be your partner," she whispered, then kissed the other cheek. The smell of her was overwhelming, and he wrapped his arms around her, unable to hold himself back.

"And I want to be your lover," she said, kissing his lips and drawing away before he could kiss her back. "And your colleague and your best friend and your coparent . . . and everything else."

"Except my wife."

She grinned and pressed her nose to his lips. "Except your wife."

"You want me to live here?"

"Yes," she said. "Or we can find another house."

"I love this house," he said.

"Then let's live here."

It was as though there was too much air for the space in his chest. He breathed in her smell, feeling like he might explode with joy. "When are you thinking I would move in?"

"Today seems good." She looked up, arms around his neck. "Can you live with that?"

He pressed his mouth to hers, holding her in his arms and breathing her in. Anna. His Anna. He lifted her off the ground and spun her in a circle. Gently.

She was laughing when he set her down again. "Is that a yes?" she asked.

"Yes," he confirmed.

53

Nine weeks later

When she wasn't at work, Schwartzman yielded to the strange physics of her body. Her hand gravitated to her lower back to support the extra weight on her front. She sat more and put her feet up, allowing the blood an opportunity to drain from her swollen feet. Even at work, she opted for flat, comfortable shoes, ones she hadn't worn regularly since her residency.

Not quite twenty weeks pregnant, Schwartzman already felt huge. She *was* huge, but not nearly as huge as she would be. Halfway through pregnancy, she had gained almost thirty pounds. She'd opted not to do the genetic testing offered in her first trimester, though she'd had a complete blood panel done to be sure her levels were healthy. She took her prenatal vitamins and followed the guidelines for pregnancy nutrition. She found she'd lost her taste—at least temporarily—for coffee and wine and bourbon, which made adhering to the recommendations easy.

At her doctor's appointments, with Hal by her side, they heard the baby's heartbeat, strong and consistent. Despite the encouraging signs, when the time arrived for her midpregnancy ultrasound, she was nervous.

Terrified that the test would reveal some issue with the fetus, she willed her body to support the growing life, to keep it safe. Since returning home from Idaho, she'd been afraid that the pregnancy would terminate. In her mind, each twinge was the start of a spontaneous abortion. She tried to maintain faith in her body's ability to know what was needed, and if something went wrong, she wouldn't blame herself.

If the pregnancy terminated, she would survive. She would go to the hospital and seek professional care. She didn't have a death wish. The opposite, actually. She had a life wish. She felt awash with a renewed sense of purpose, at work and away from it.

Scott Theobold, the medical examiner brought in to cover her while she was gone, maintained a position in the morgue, picking up the slack from her reduced hours. She would not leave her job, but it would not own her either. The most important job she had was going on inside her own body.

Having Hal at the house made daily tasks much easier. He refused to let her lift anything heavier than a saucepan. By the time she'd been home from the hospital for a few weeks, he'd moved in completely. Together, they'd decided what things would be donated. About the recliner that had been his father's, Hal was openly nervous. It wasn't much to look at, but she knew it was important to him. They found a spot for it in the corner of the living room, and she could tell how happy that made him. Even Wiley, Hal's cat, was slowly acclimating to the new space and the fact that she was sharing it with a dog.

As the ultrasound tech set up the machine, Hal gripped her hand.

She could feel his fear through the skin on his palms. "It's going to be okay," she whispered.

"It's going to be perfect," he said.

The tech gave them a knowing smile and squirted cold, clear gel on the mound of her growing belly. She was larger than she had been when she was pregnant before—her first pregnancy had ended much earlier. She was older now—nine years older. Thirty-eight, and with all the increased risks.

She closed her eyes as the ultrasound wand pressed against her, listening to the whooshing as the sound waves echoed through her belly. Hal squeezed her hand, and she opened her eyes to watch the bright pulsing light on the screen.

"Heartbeat looks good," the tech announced.

Hal kissed her face, and she felt a tear slide from her eye. It didn't mean they were in the clear. Though she'd managed to avoid the drugs during the last days of her captivity, her body had been flooded with them in the beginning. The FBI had confirmed the drugs that Butler had used on her were benzodiazepines—not the worst, but they had possible side effects. They wouldn't know the extent of the impact until after the baby was born. Maybe long after.

"You're measuring twenty weeks."

Hal flashed Schwartzman a grin. Few couples knew the exact date of conception, but they did. Their Thanksgiving baby.

"Oh," the tech said, alarm in her tone.

Schwartzman's stomach tightened in a wave of nausea. She studied the screen, searching for what the tech had seen.

Hal was staring, too. "What? What is it?"

"Sorry," the tech said quickly. "Hang on . . ."

"We got pregnant on Thanksgiving," Schwartzman said. "We know that for certain. What are you seeing?"

"The measurements of this little one are perfect," she said. "The amniotic fluid looks good."

"But you saw something," Schwartzman prompted, her panic rising.

The tech nodded, a smile playing on her lips.

"What? The baby's gender?" Schwartzman asked.

"What is it?" Hal asked again, his fingers squeezing her hand tightly.

"We've been through a lot," Schwartzman snapped when the tech didn't answer. "Tell us what you're seeing."

"This," the tech said, shifting the wand across her belly. Schwartzman rose to her elbows and studied the small beating pulse on the screen.

Then the tech swung the wand back to the other side. "And this." The tech was grinning now.

"Oh," Schwartzman said.

The tech laughed out loud.

Schwartzman felt a smile pull on her own lips. After all they'd been through. She felt a wave of nervousness again. "But the measurements are fine?"

"Perfect," the tech agreed.

"What?" Hal said, searching her face. "Anna, what is it?"

Schwartzman laughed, dropping her head onto the pillow and wiping her face with one hand. She waved to the tech. "Show him."

"Show me what?" Hal's voice had an edge, and the fear made her uncomfortable. They'd had enough of that for two lifetimes.

She took his hand and squeezed. "It's okay. Really."

Hal didn't look convinced.

"See that?" the tech said, pointing out the small white pulse on the screen. "That's the baby's heartbeat." Then she navigated the wand around Schwartzman's uterus. "And that's the other one."

Hal looked dumbstruck. "The other heartbeat?"

The two women nodded, watching him. Schwartzman couldn't help but smile at his expression.

"There are two babies," he whispered, his voice full of awe. He looked down at Schwartzman like she was a miracle.

The tech was nodding.

"We're having twins?" he asked.

"It looks that way," the tech said.

Hal raised his hands into the air and hollered, "We're having twins!" His palm struck the ceiling, and he pulled it back, pumping a fist at his hip. "We're having twins, Anna." He started dancing around the tiny room, filling the space and leaving the women laughing.

"He's handling it better than most dads," the tech said.

"I've got to call my mom." He looked up at her, his eyes bright and glistening. "Is that okay?"

"Of course. Call her."

She would call her mother, too. Or maybe she would wait to surprise her when Georgia arrived next week. Her mother's first visit. She tried to imagine her mother's response to the news but couldn't. She could imagine how Georgia Schwartzman would have reacted six months ago—her daughter having left the "ideal" husband and fallen in love with a black man, now unwed and pregnant. With twins.

But her mother wasn't that woman anymore, or that was how it felt. The mother who called her now was talkative and light. She always asked to speak with Hal and was disappointed when he wasn't home. When she got him on the phone, the two chatted for ten, fifteen, sometimes twenty minutes. When Schwartzman came back on the line, her mother was often laughing. "What a sweetie he is," she would say. Or, "Oh, that man makes me laugh."

The tech had stepped off to the side of the exam room, giving her and Hal as much privacy as the space allowed. Schwartzman studied the screen, where an image of the second fetus was frozen, its perfect heart a white mass. Two babies.

"Twins," Hal repeated on the phone to his mother, grinning at Schwartzman. "Yes. They're fine. They're both fine."

A pause. Hal shaking his head, his mother's voice audible over the line. Faith was thrilled, of course.

"No. We don't know the genders." Hal lowered the phone to ask, "Are we going to find out?"

Schwartzman shrugged.

"We haven't decided," he told his mother, his eyes still glued to hers. Still grinning.

When he ended the call, Hal reached out and took her hand, brought it to his lips, and kissed it. She pulled him close and kissed his hand in return.

Hal's phone buzzed. He looked down. "Hailey." He put the phone in his pocket, laughing. "She never thought I'd be a dad."

He was going to be a great dad. The best. Anna thought of her own father and wished he could be there to see Hal. But maybe he was. Maybe he was closer than she thought.

Her father would be thrilled to see her become a mother, even more so that there would be no only child. He'd always wished that she'd had a brother or a sister.

A mother. She would be a mother. Not the mother she would have been nine years ago, under the thumb of a violent and cruel husband. She was going to be a mother with a man who was kind and gentle and supportive.

You earned this. You came through hell for this.

"Here are a couple of photographs," the tech said, handing them two black-and-white printouts. Two little bundles, each cozy in their own amniotic sacs. Two tiny heartbeats, captured on the images like twin stars.

"Fraternal twins," she said.

"How do you know?" Hal asked.

She explained the two amniotic sacs. "It means it could be two girls, two boys, or one of each."

"Really?" Hal said.

From the corner of her eye, Schwartzman noticed the tech looking busy, pretending not to pay attention. Like she knew something. Of course she did. She was trained at this. She knew exactly what kind of babies Schwartzman was carrying.

Schwartzman studied Hal's face. "Do you want to know?" she asked him.

"Do you?"

She nodded, a grin pulling on her lips. "Kind of."

Hal's eyes went wide. "Really? Me, too." He looked back at the screen. "Can we find out?"

"I'll bet we can." Schwartzman stared at the tech until she sensed she was being watched and turned to face them again. "I'll bet someone noticed the gender of the babies," Schwartzman said.

The tech grinned. "We should double-check. I wouldn't want to be wrong." She pulled the ultrasound wand back out of its cradle and added a new layer of gel to the round bump of Schwartzman's belly. "Let's see what we've got here."

The image settled on one of the babies. The *thump-thump-thump* of the tiny heart was like a galloping horse. Schwartzman closed her eyes and thanked whatever force had kept them safe. Her babies. Both babies.

Eyes open, Schwartzman watched as the tech homed in on the baby, pointing the ultrasound camera up between the legs.

"Girl?" Schwartzman asked.

"Girl," the tech confirmed.

Tears streamed down Hal's face. "A baby girl." He made a face. "Oh, dear Lord."

Schwartzman and the tech both laughed. "She'll be perfect," Schwartzman said.

Hal drew a deep breath as the tech shifted the wand and located the second baby. It took no time at all to identify the gender of the second baby. A little penis, clear as day.

"Is that—" Hal asked, pointing to the screen.

"Yes, it is," Schwartzman said. "That is your baby boy."

"A boy and a girl. Instant family," the tech said.

The tech wiped the gel off Schwartzman's belly and then excused herself, leaving Hal and Schwartzman alone. Hal helped her sit up and cupped her belly, palming it as though it were a basketball, though it was larger than that. No wonder she was so big. Twins. Hal's twins. She laid her hands on his.

"Instant family," he said with a chuckle.

They had both come through hell.

And it *had* been hell.

Hal lifted her face to his, kissed her gently on the mouth.

She closed her eyes and focused on the sensation of Hal's skin on hers, imagining the heartbeats inside her—three of them—only her own palpable.

"Should we go home and figure out where all these babies are going to sleep?" Hal asked, helping her down from the table.

"We might need a bigger house," she said.

Hal laughed again. "I wonder what Buster's going to think."

"Buster will be thrilled."

"I wonder what Wiley's going to think," Hal said.

Hal's cat still spent most of her days in the master bedroom to keep out of reach of Buster. They looked at each other a moment and laughed. "Wiley may not be as thrilled," Schwartzman said.

"No, she will not."

There would be challenges ahead.

"I love you, Anna Schwartzman," he whispered, his arm wrapped around her, holding her close.

"I love you, Hal Harris."

He laughed, a big grateful laugh that made her laugh again, too.

Of course there would be challenges.

But not in that moment.

In that moment, everything was perfect.

ACKNOWLEDGMENTS

The first person I would like to thank is you—the reader. Thank you for reading this book, for following Anna's story. Thank you for every book you've ever read. It is the greatest gift you can give someone like me, an author. Without you, there would be no books, and what a terrible world that would be.

Next, my gratitude goes to those who devote their lives to the pursuit of justice. While I always aim for a realistic portrayal of crimes and their management, it is not always possible. Any errors and poetic license are mine entirely.

For research, I am, as always, indebted to the people at the San Francisco Police Department, who have been answering strange questions since book one. Dr. Craig Nelson, associate chief medical examiner, North Carolina Office of the Chief Medical Examiner, has become absolutely invaluable in depicting Schwartzman's profession and the deaths she investigates as accurately as the story will allow. Thank you, Dr. Nelson.

The team at Jane Rotrosen Agency never ceases to amaze. Thank you to all and especially to Meg Ruley, Rebecca Scherer, Michael Conway, and Danielle Sickles. Thank you also to the fabulous Jessica Tribble; to Sarah Shaw and the incredible team at Thomas & Mercer;

to Leslie Lutz for bringing out the best in Schwartzman (and me); to Valerie Kalfrin, Carissa Bluestone, Robin O'Dell, and Stacy Abrams for the thorough edit; and to Kirk DouPonce of DogEared Design for the fabulous cover art.

I am hugely grateful to those who support the process of writing a book and especially to fellow authors Barbara Nickless, Jason Backlund, Randle Bitnar, and Shawnee Spitler, and the eagle-eye proofreaders Whitney, Ronette, Albee, and Dani.

Mom, Nicole, Steve, and Tom, thank you for supporting this crazy dream from the early days. And most of all, my love and gratitude go to the 3/4 that make me whole: Chris, Claire, and Jack. You guys are the moon and the sun and whatever lies beyond. I love you.

If you enjoyed this book, please leave a review to help other readers discover Dr. Schwartzman. Thank you again for spending this time with Annabelle and Hal, and with me.

ABOUT THE AUTHOR

Photo © 2018 Mallory Regan, Forty Watt Photography

Danielle Girard is the author of *Chasing Darkness*, The Rookie Club series, and *Exhume*, *Excise*, and *Expose*, featuring San Francisco medical examiner Dr. Annabelle Schwartzman. Danielle's books have won the Barry Award and the RT Reviewers' Choice Award, and two of her titles have been optioned for movies. A graduate of Cornell University, Danielle received her MFA at Queens University in Charlotte, North Carolina. She, her husband, and their two children split their time between San Francisco and the Northern Rockies. Visit her at www.daniellegirard.com.